QUIV COBRAS

BOOK TWO

THE FRACTURED FAERY

FOR MICKEY AND JAN

Prologue

Friday, 21st September 2018. Pre-amnesia.

If you play a role long enough, sometimes you become that role. I reflected on that unfortunate titbit as I watched the bar from the building opposite. It was a reasonably busy night with all sorts of patrons milling around inside. I wasn't particularly interested in any of them, however; it was the bar's owner who fascinated me.

From time to time, I'd catch a glimpse of Morgan's face through one of the windows, my heart tightening every time. He looked relaxed and happy, which was more than I could say for myself. It wasn't as if I had much choice in the matter, though. I'd been with Rubus for too long to appear that way. Method acting the Madhatter way – act like an evil bitch until you actually become one. The lines between my true self and what I was pretending to be were now so blurred that I was virtually a Robin Thicke song. Most of the time I convinced myself that it was worth it.

I took another drag of my cigarette and blew out smoke, watching it cloud into the air over my head.

'I thought you'd be here,' said a quiet voice at my shoulder.

I half-turned, spotting the familiar features of Charrie, the bogle who ostensibly worked for Rubus too. My mouth twisted in brief acknowledgement before I asked, 'Does Rubus know I come here?'

He snorted. 'What do you think?'

I grimaced ruefully and stubbed out the cigarette.

Yeah, fair enough. If Rubus had any inkling that I popped over here from time to time and quietly stalked his brother, there would be serious consequences.

I shook off the unpleasant thought. 'Were you looking for me?'

Charrie's expression tightened and he raked a hand through his hair, revealing his scalp. He had to be careful not to do that around humans; his skin was always tinged faintly with green but where his hair covered his head the colour was dark jade. 'I am. There is a problem, Madrona. A big one.'

I was used to big problems but something about the look in the bogle's eyes gave me pause. 'Go on.'

'Chen is dead.'

Ice dripped down my spine. 'The dragon?'

He nodded, the gesture taut with the same tension I was suddenly experiencing. 'Rubus sent me to negotiate for the sphere. I had it all planned out – not that we need have worried. There was no way Chen was going to give it up. But when I got to his lair…' His voice drifted off in a cloud of unhappiness.

'Did someone…' I swallowed. 'Did someone kill him?'

Charrie shook his head. 'No. I'm no doctor but it looked like he died of natural causes. He was old. It's not unexpected.'

Gasbudlikins. Unexpected or not, this was the last thing we needed. 'You need to hide his body. Make it seem as if Chen just left the country. We can't let Rubus get his hands on that damned sphere.'

'Rubus already knows that the dragon is dead.'

I hissed, my hands curling into fists. 'How?'

'Amellus was with me.'

For a moment all I could hear was the beating of my heart. It thudded in my ears. Blue lights flickered.

Perhaps this was it, this was the moment my life flashed before my eyes— Then I realised it was a police car zooming off to attend whatever petty crime it had been assigned to.

I exhaled. 'Does Rubus have the sphere?' My voice sounded as if it were coming from a long distance away.

Charrie's fingers twitched, dancing in the air nervously. 'I spotted it and grabbed it before Amellus noticed. But there are Fey swarming all over the old dragon bastard's lair. It won't be long before they realise the sphere is missing. And it won't take a genius to work out I'm the one who's got it.' He raised baleful eyes to mine. 'This is it, Madrona. This is why we've been with Rubus all this time. This is what we're trying to stop. If he gets his hands on the dragon sphere, this demesne is lost. There are seven billion human souls. We can't…' He choked, unable to finish.

I thought quickly. 'Okay. Do you have the sphere now?'

'No. I put it somewhere safe.'

I growled under my breath. 'All Rubus has to do is find you and use one of his damned Truth Spiders. You can't guard against the sort of pain they create. You'll tell him whatever he wants to know.'

'I know that,' Charrie snapped. 'That's why time is of the essence here.'

'Get the sphere and bring it to me. I'll think of a way to hide it. If I keep moving, I might manage to fool the magic. I might be able to keep it safe from Rubus.'

'*Might* being the operative word. There are no guarantees.'

'You think I don't know that?'

Charrie shook his head again. 'It won't work, Madrona. You know that. Deep down, you know it as well as I do. Even if you take it, Rubus will still use the

Spiders against me. Against my family. We had a chance while Chen was alive because the sphere was bound to him as its creator. Now that he's dead, all bets are off.'

I rounded on him, nostrils flaring. 'Do you have a better plan? We can't just roll over and let Rubus take the sphere! I've not stuck to that bastard's side for all these years so that when the manure finally collides with the windmill I step back and let him do whatever he wants! The things I've done to stay in his good books would make a mass murderer flinch. I am not giving up now.'

The bogle's eyes dropped. 'Actually,' he whispered, 'I *do* have a better plan.' With fluttering hands and even more nervous twitches, he outlined his idea.

I stared at him. 'There has to be another way.'

'There's not.'

'Why don't we just take the damned sphere and drop it in the deepest part of the deepest ocean?'

'Because Rubus will catch up to us before we get there! You know this is the only way.'

I pressed my palms against my temples. 'It can't be. If you let me think—'

'Madrona, I have a family. Rubus'll use them against me if he thinks I'm hiding the sphere from him.'

I threw my hands up. 'Exactly! You have a family! Give the sphere to me and we'll switch places. I'll take the fall and then you—'

'No.' Charrie was adamant. 'I was at Chen's lair. Regardless of what happens next, Rubus will know I'm the one who betrayed him. This is the only way it can go.' He sighed. 'There's something else you should know.'

'What?'

'I've got cancer. I'm already dying. This way is less painful. It's better for everyone.'

'Cancer is a *human* disease. You can't…'

‘I belong to this demesne, Madrona. I can get cancer just as easily as any human. Obviously. It’s already spread from my lungs to my stomach.’

Horrified, I gazed at him. ‘I’m so sorry.’ Never had those words sounded so inane.

‘It is what it is.’

‘I still can’t do it,’ I whispered. ‘I won’t.’

The bogle’s answer was simple. ‘You have to.’ He glanced down the street, his spine stiffening. I followed his gaze, inhaling sharply when I saw what he was looking at.

‘The Redcaps. What are they doing here?’

Charrie grabbed my hand, pulling me down so that we were both out of sight. We watched the hulking trio shuffle towards the Metropolitan Bar before pausing about twenty feet away from it. They started to argue.

‘Do you think Rubus sent them here to take care of Morgan? They’re not bound by the truce like you. They’re like me.’ Charrie’s voice wasn’t as bitter as it should have been. ‘They could do it. They could get rid of him once and for all.’

I watched them with narrowed eyes. ‘No,’ I said finally. ‘If that were the case they’d just go in and get the job done. They’re here for another reason.’ I continued to observe the byplay. Despite the public setting, the Redcaps were nearly coming to blows. ‘Maybe,’ I said slowly, ‘they’re planning to switch sides.’

Charrie drew in a breath. ‘Do you really think…?’

I shrugged. ‘Does it matter? Does anything matter right now?’

‘Only preventing Rubus from getting his grubby Fey mitts on that magical sphere.’ Charrie glanced at me. ‘You know that.’

I ran a hand through my hair. Unfortunately I did.

***

An hour later, with my game face on, I stalked into Rubus's latest hideout. He moved around on a regular basis, which I suspected was for no other reason than to annoy everyone who worked for him. Still, at least here of all places I could let my true mood show on my face.

I stomped through the dark corridors. The heavy weight at my back aided my grim march and meant that most of Rubus's minions took one look at me and skedaddled out of the way. Unfortunately my unnatural posture and gait, together with my stony expression, wasn't enough to keep everyone away.

'Mads!' Lunaria called out. 'Hold up!'

I kept moving. Maybe if I pretended not to have heard her, she'd get the message and stay clear.

The tall Fey woman ran up to me. I cursed inwardly and turned to her. 'I'm busy.'

'Have you heard?' Her eyes shone. 'Chen is dead. That arse of a dragon oaf just keeled over, probably from a heart attack. Serves him right. Not that I thought he even had a heart. If he did, he'd have given us his magic sphere long ago.'

For a supposedly intelligent faery, Lunaria could be a total zounderkite. Honestly. Rubus had well and truly hoodwinked her – and everyone else – with dreams of how the dragon's sphere could send us all back home to Mag Mell. What he neglected to dwell on was what would happen to this demesne if that happened.

The sphere was a magically bound object, designed to suck magic from other places. Using it would flood this land with magic – and in the process effectively destroy it. But why should we care? We'd all be back home, hugging our families and exulting in our return after ten long years of exile. I rolled my eyes. As if returning to our hearths was more important than the lives of seven billion people. I quashed the flood of guilt I suddenly experienced.

'Keep your voice down, you towering arsebadger,' I snapped. 'You know anything to do with Chen and his sphere is on a need-to-know basis.'

Lunaria didn't blink at my words or my tone. 'None of that will matter when we get our hands on it. We'll be able to crow from the rooftops that Rubus is going to save us all.'

My hands itched to slap her. 'He's such a hero,' I said flatly.

'Isn't he?' she breathed, not noticing my sarcasm. She beamed at me. 'Anyway, our hero wants to see you.'

My heart sank. The last thing I needed was to be confronted by Rubus when I was on a mission to prevent him from achieving his heart's desire. I tried – and failed – to think of a decent excuse to avoid him. I couldn't do anything that would make him suspicious.

I gritted my teeth and glanced at her. 'Where is he?'

'In the throne room.'

I sighed. Of course he was.

***

Regardless of where Rubus was staying, he always commandeered the largest and best room as his 'throne room'. This place was no different. He'd set it up with his favourite purple velvet chair at one end and a clashing red carpet leading up to it. Frankly, it was a miracle he didn't put a crown on top of his stupid head, something of which I repeatedly reminded him.

'You're not wearing your tiara yet,' I said as I approached.

He was leaning back lazily with one muscled leg

hooked over the left arm of the chair. Early afternoon sun filtered in from one of the high windows, casting a halo around his head as if he were some kind of angelic force. That'd be the day.

'And I've told you, Madrona, that when I find some jewels to decorate a tiara that are as pretty as you, I'll happily wear one.' He displayed sharp, white, even teeth as he smiled. 'When I do, I'll expect you to curtsey.'

My bottom lip curled. I made a point of not kowtowing to anyone, not even Rubus. He knew that – he even expected it. 'I hear Chen has died,' I said in a bored voice. I gestured around the room. 'So where's his little sphere, then?'

Rubus's jaw tightened, the only sign that he was a seething mass of insane fury behind his carefully cultivated mask of handsome blandness. 'We don't have it.'

I evinced surprise. Meryl Streep had nothing on me. 'Really? Did the dragon pass it on to a friend before he passed away?'

'That ornery old bastard had no friends. He was only interested in his treasure. No,' said Rubus coldly, 'I rather think that our little bogle friend has taken it for himself.'

'Charrie?' I scoffed. 'I doubt it. He's too scared of you and what you'll do to his family to step out of line.'

'He abandoned Amellus at Chen's place and hasn't been seen since. There's no other explanation.'

Gasbudlikins. Part of me had hoped I could persuade Rubus that there was another reason the stupid sphere was missing but, even after all this time, he didn't trust me enough to pursue this line of conversation. 'So I presume you want me to locate the bogle?' I asked.

'I think it's better if you don't get involved. No,' he said thoughtfully. 'What I need you to do is ramp up the sales of pixie dust. We need as many Fey with us as possible when I use the sphere. I can't have my brother getting wind of what I'm up to and trying to stop me before I save us all. It would be just like him to steal the sphere from me because he wants to steal my thunder. He'll want to get all the adulation for re-opening the border. Drop the dust prices and bring as many Fey as you can into our fold. I'll create an army of addicts before I let Morgan take my glory from me.'

I was sure part of Rubus realised that Morgan would take the sphere from him because he wanted to save the humans from the chaos which flooding this demesne with magic would cause, not because he wanted to be worshipped as the supposed Fey saviour. But there was no point in mentioning this – and at least being sent out on a pixie-dust mission would grant me enough leeway to disappear for a while without raising suspicion.

I didn't want Rubus to think I was too eager to leave the dragon sphere and Charrie alone, though. 'I'm good enough to locate the bogle. And I'm strong enough to take the sphere from him.'

'That's probably true,' Rubus answered. 'But do you really think I'd trust someone who hates me with such an important task?' He laughed at my expression. 'I'm not as stupid as you think, Madrona. I know how you feel about me. You might follow my every command but I still feel your hatred every time you look at me.'

I sniffed. 'I don't hate you, I'm just not necessarily excited by your existence.'

Rubus laughed and clapped his hands in delight. 'You're still pissed off that I forced you to leave Morgan. You know he despises you now, even more than you despise me. And don't forget that the reason we're all stuck here is your fault.'

My whole body went still. 'As if I could,' I muttered. As if Rubus would let me.

Rubus unhooked his leg from the chair, stood up and walked towards me. He reached out and brushed a tendril of hair from my face. I was getting good at not flinching when he touched me but I still had to suppress an internal shudder.

'You're too nasty for my brother, Madrona,' he said. 'Spend time with him and he'll realise what a bitch you've become. You think he hates you now? Wait till he meets the real you, the new improved version of you. He'll drop you faster than he'll drop his trousers to get into your pants. You'll only disappoint him.' Rubus smiled. 'You and I are alike. You and I are the ones who should be together. You're mine, Madrona,' he said softly. 'Not Morgan's. Don't forget it. You know what I'm capable of ... and vice-versa.'

I curved my lips and smiled back at him. 'You *are* impressive,' I breathed. I'd resort to whatever was necessary to get Rubus off my back. Today of all days, I needed the freedom to move around the city unhindered. 'And you don't have to worry about me. I'm here, Rubus. I'm on your side. I want to get home as much as you do.'

His eyes danced. 'One of these days, I'll trust you fully,' he said. 'But not today. There are still plenty of Fey in Manchester who've sworn off dust or who haven't tried it. By the end of this week, I want every damn one of them to be desperate for another hit.'

'Then your wish is my command.'

Rubus licked his lips. 'Oh Madrona,' he said huskily, 'if only that were true.' He reached out again, his fingertips brushing against my breast. 'One day.'

I forced another smile. 'I'll just nip to the apothecary and get more dust,' I said. 'Then I'll be on my way.'

'Does my touch repel you so much that you have to sprint off like that?'

I opened my mouth to answer but he pressed his

finger against my lips. 'Don't protest. Neither of us will enjoy it if you lie to me. Run off, then. You'll come round when I have the dragon sphere.' He stepped back and turned away, heading back to his chair.

I watched him, wishing for the umpteenth time that the truce wasn't in place and I could slide a dagger between his ribs and be done with all this. The truce was immutable, though; no Fey could harm another, regardless of how much they might want to. I sighed inwardly then I turned on my heel and left.

Pushing away my not inconsiderable antipathy to Rubus, I flew to the apothecary's laboratory. Carduus was a creature of habit and I knew he'd be having his afternoon tea at this time. I only had a small window of opportunity to grab what I needed without him knowing.

I banged open the lab door and darted inside. Fortunately his shelves were well stocked and he was unlikely to miss any magic potions for a few days, if at all. Without wasting any time, I went over to the far wall.

It took scant seconds to locate both the vials of liquid rowan and the white baneberry. Part of me was tempted to leave the latter behind and tell Charrie that I'd not been able to find it, but he'd only find another way to get it. Besides, I'd promised him that I'd do my best. Right now he was my only real ally and I couldn't let him down, regardless of the consequences.

Double-checking that the coast was clear, I shrugged off my coat. I carefully slid Charrie's sword from its hiding place at my back, untying the ribbons that held it tightly in place, then I grabbed the rowan and coated the blade. I rubbed it down and made sure no edge remained untainted. I shoved the glistening blade back, secured it and adjusted my coat so that there was no sign of the weapon. That would have to do.

I twisted left, searching the rest of the shelves until

my gaze snagged on a dusty, red-hued bottle. I stared at it as if it were one of Rubus's damned Truth Spiders. A moment later I grabbed it. Considering how much depended on its damned contents working, it felt lighter and smaller than it should have done.

With tense shoulders, I reached for a small empty vial and hastily decanted half of the bottle's contents into it then I refilled the bottle to the brim with water so it appeared untouched. I even took the time to grab a handful of household dust and blow it gently onto the red bottle after I'd returned it to its place on the shelf. No one would ever know I'd gone near it.

With that perilous deed completed, I swallowed and carried on, picking up as many vials of pixie dust as I could. I needed to take as much as I could carry so it appeared that I was following my orders. I crammed a bag full of the vials. I'd dump them somewhere safe as soon as I could. Once I was out of Rubus's den, the pixie dust would only slow me down.

***

We needed plausible deniability at every step of the way. Charrie and I had already synchronised our watches, something that would have made me smile if our situation hadn't been so serious.

At precisely 5.23pm, Charrie strolled out of the east exit of Stretfort Mall and headed down the street, just as I wandered past ostensibly on the way to sell some pixie dust to the Fey who worked in the nearby opticians. In case someone was watching me, I jerked my head as if I were surprised to see the bogle. Then I took off after him, maintaining a decent distance between us.

Although I knew where he was heading, I made a show of keeping well back. By the time I reached the fringes of the forest surrounding the golf course, dusk was falling. As I started moving uphill, the sword at my back chafed at my skin. Unwilling to risk scratching and poisoning myself with rowan, and convinced that no one was following me, I unfastened the ribbons so I could hold the sword instead. Then I continued upwards, weaving in and out of the trees.

It took longer than I'd anticipated to get to the rendezvous point. Charrie was already waiting next to the eighteenth hole, hopping from toe to toe as his nervousness gave him away.

I raised a hand to him in greeting and walked forward.

'Is it coated?' he asked, jerking his head towards the sword.

I nodded. 'Yes.'

He exhaled. 'Good. That'll put you in the clear if a Fey comes across it. The only reason I'd scrub it with rowan would be to kill a faery.'

'I've been thinking,' I said. 'If you take the memory-loss potion instead of me, then you'll be able to escape the Truth Spider. You won't need to go through with this dreadful plan.'

Charrie scowled at me. 'We've been through this. Rubus will still take his revenge on my family. My *children*, Madrona. We're bogles, we're not protected by the truce,' he reminded me for the umpteenth time. 'The only way my kids will survive into adulthood is if Rubus has nothing to gain by hurting them. If I'm not around to be upset by their pain, he won't bother to hurt them.'

'Your children need their father.'

'It's my life versus seven billion humans, Madrona. And I'm already dying.'

'But…'

'Just give me the white baneberry.'

I stood my ground. 'No. There has to be another way.'

'You got it, right? You got the baneberry?'

I clenched my jaw. 'Yes.'

'You brought it with you because you know there is no other way. We have to keep the sphere away from Rubus. Once I'm dead, cut off my head, wipe off your fingerprints and drink the memory-loss potion.'

'What if it doesn't work? What if I don't call the police when I come round?'

'You will. You won't remember anything about being a faery. Calling the police will be your only option. There's an old phone box in front of the clubhouse. It's part of the reason why I chose this location. The police will take my body and put it in the morgue. They'll also put everything I'm carrying into an evidence locker where it will stay. Rubus won't know the police have the sphere and, even if he finds out, he won't be able to get to it.'

'What if they release your belongings to your family?'

'They won't. They won't believe you could have killed me so it'll remain an open murder investigation. All the evidence will be kept until my murder is solved – which will never happen. They won't find the white baneberry in my system either.'

'It still feels like a lot could go wrong, Charrie. If we put our heads together, we can find a better way. We can still run.'

He sighed. 'No, we can't.' His eyes met mine. 'You gave up your life and your love because of Rubus.'

I gave a short, humourless laugh. 'He didn't give me much choice.'

'There was a choice. You knew that by siding with him, you'd have a better chance of keeping an eye on him and stopping him doing something like this. You became a drug dealer. You effectively killed yourself, Madrona, metaphorically anyway. And you would kill yourself for real if you believed it would keep the sphere safe.' He paused. 'Wouldn't you?'

I could hardly lie to him. 'Yes.'

'And the same is true for me. Give me the baneberry, Maddy.' I sighed. Charrie offered me a sad smile. 'This will work. I promise you.'

'Except,' I pointed out, 'I won't remember enough to know that it's worked.'

'That's the way it's got to be.'

I squeezed my eyes shut and dug out the small vial containing the white baneberry. 'Charrie…'

'Hush,' he said. 'I know.' He took it from me and, without another word or a moment's hesitation, he unscrewed the top and downed the contents.

'Remember,' he said, wiping his mouth, 'it'll work quickly. As soon as I'm dead, drink the memory-loss potion. You'll have about five minutes to get rid of both bottles so there's no trace of magic. Any potential reveal spell will have to be fooled. Then cut off my head with the sword before getting rid of your own prints. Once that's done, as far as the old Madrona is concerned all this will be over. You might be arrested for a short while but, without your memory and without any evidence, the police can't charge you.'

Even if they did, I'd probably deserve it. I nodded anyway.

'If Rubus questions you, you won't remember what happened. The fact that the sword is coated with rowan will suggest that I tried to kill you or that maybe I was planning to kill him. I'll be blamed, not you. He'll run round in circles trying to work out what happened. He'll think someone else, someone nastier, killed me and took the sphere for themselves. Not a Fey. Maybe another dragon.' Charrie shrugged. 'Who knows? Either way, Rubus won't blame you and he won't blame my family. And, most importantly, he won't have Chen's sphere.'

'You'll still be dead,' I pointed out. I watched him. He was already turning pale. The baneberry worked fast.

'I already was anyway.'

'You're saving everyone,' I said. 'You're a hero and no one will ever know. Not even me.'

'You don't need to be recognised to be a hero,' he told me.

Then his knees gave way.

Chapter One

Ten days later. Post amnesia.

I peered down. We had to be at least ten storeys up. I had no idea what Rubus was planning but I suspected that I wasn't going to like it one little bit.

'This entire city is mine, Madrona,' Rubus said, sweeping out an arm. 'Those humans down there might not know it but I am their lord and master. I give them protection.'

I scratched my head. 'But you're looking for this dragon-sphere magic-sucker thingumabob that belonged to some dude. Chen? Chin? Whatever. If you find it and use it, won't all these people be killed?'

His handsome face darkened with fury. 'There's no if. I *will* find it. That fucking bogle, Charrie, took it and he has to be somewhere. He can't just have vanished into thin air. Besides, over-population is a serious problem. The humans could do with a bit of culling. Magic never did any of us any harm. I suspect it will be the making of the entire race.' He leaned towards me. 'One day they'll thank me for it.'

'Only if any of them are still alive after you've flooded their world with magic that doesn't belong there,' I said.

He glowered at me, his green eyes spitting venom. 'I'm rather tired of this attitude. It was very tiring moulding you into the Madrona I needed last time. I'm not sure I have the energy to do it all over again.'

I shrugged. 'Then let me go.'

'I can't do that. I won't let Morganus have you.'

Like I was a thing to be passed around between the pair of them. I sighed and rolled my eyes. 'Then kill me.' I waved a dismissive hand in the air. 'Push me off this building and be done with it.'

'I thought this had been explained to you,' he snapped. 'The truce prevents me from hurting you in any way. It cannot be broken.' He scowled. 'Believe me, I've tried to break it.'

I arched an eyebrow. 'Really?' I asked, genuinely curious. 'What did you do?'

'Do you really, truly, want to know?'

I licked my lips. I didn't know who I was before all this happened; I didn't remember. What I did know for sure was that I had to get Rubus to trust me. And to do that I had to be Miss Evil Incarnate. Shamefully, I didn't think it was going to be all that hard; I already had the evil inside me. 'I do,' I breathed. 'Tell me. What did you want to do?'

Rubus eyed me for a moment, suspicion clouding his gaze. 'I wanted to punish Morgan,' he challenged. 'I wanted him to suffer for suggesting we bide our time and wait for the border to re-open. For telling me that we should keep our heads down and not draw any attention our way. For ordering me to let the humans remain in charge.' He sniffed. 'So I tried to grab him. I was going to teach him a lesson and use a red-hot poker to blind him in both eyes. It would have been poetic justice – he kept telling me I wasn't seeing things clearly. Ha! If I'd taken his eyes, it wouldn't have been me with the vision problem!'

'A spoon,' I said, my own eyes wide. 'You should have scooped them out with a spoon, one by one. You could have fed the first one to a dog while Morgan watched with his other eye.' I bared my teeth into a grimace of a smile. 'Then you could have injected him with rowan. That shit hurts like buggery.'

He raised an eyebrow at me. 'What do you know about rowan?'

'I inadvertently poisoned myself with some,' I said, suddenly realising that my big mouth might get me into trouble here. The last thing I wanted was to tell him that I'd cut myself on a rowan-edged sword that was laying underneath Charrie the Bogle's body. The very bogle that Rubus was so desperate to locate. 'It's a long story.'

Seeking a way to avoid telling him how I'd poisoned myself, I tried to draw attention from the *how* towards the *what*. 'Do you know that when you've got rowan in your system, your faery skills change? I glamoured myself without realising it and then I couldn't change back to my normal gorgeous self until I'd taken nux. It was quite disturbing.'

Rubus looked me up and down for a long moment.

'You're trying to imagine me as a hairy man right this second, aren't you?'

'No.' He tapped his foot impatiently. 'Maybe.'

'I had very itchy balls,' I informed him.

Even the blank-faced minions standing behind us looked horrified at that particular titbit. 'Where did you get the nux from?' Rubus asked, through gritted teeth.

'Morgan, of course.' There were some things I couldn't lie about.

'If you'd been with me, I'd have helped. I have more nux than he does.'

This sounded like a case of comparing dick sizes. 'I'm sure you would have helped,' I told him. 'But I wasn't with you so I had to take help where I could get it. Rowan is freaky stuff.' I shrugged. 'Using it would work wonders if you wanted to hurt someone. Like your darling brother.'

Rubus stared at me. 'You really expect me to believe

that you'd be happy if I poisoned Morganus? You've forgotten that I'm much, much smarter than you are, Madrona.'

'I've forgotten everything,' I told him in return. 'But I can already tell that you're a man after my own heart. Morgan is a stickler for the rules. And for being good. You're … different. I like that.'

Rubus folded his arms; he didn't believe me for a second. That was okay; I had plenty of time to work on him. It wasn't like I had to be anywhere else. Maybe I should change tactics slightly, though.

'Tell me what happened near the Travotel,' Rubus asked. 'Who were those humans I took care of for you? What did they want?'

I wondered whether I should point out that technically Rubus hadn't done a damned thing to 'take care' of the humans – he'd sent his minions to do the job for him. But the last thing any of us needed was for Rubus to look too closely into the matter. The truth was that they were vampire hunters out to capture Julie because, in their narrow-minded view, she was an unnatural creature. Yes, she was a vampire but she had no special abilities beyond life-enhancing longevity. Regardless of that – and the binding magical non-disclosure agreement I'd signed to keep that part of her secret – Rubus couldn't be allowed to discover the truth.

'They were stalking a friend of mine.'

Rubus raised an eyebrow. 'You have friends?'

'You have brains?' At the answering spark of anger in his eyes, I sighed. 'She's a new friend. Obviously. I met her not long after the amnesia started. She's a soap star.' I didn't want to have to give away Julie's name unless I had to.

'A soap star?' He frowned. 'Wait. There's only one soap filmed in Manchester. Do you mean *St Thomas*

Close?'

How in gasbudlikins had Rubus heard of it? 'Yeah,' I said, heavy reluctance colouring my answer.

For a brief moment, giddy boyish delight filled his expression. 'I love that programme!' he exclaimed. 'Who is it? Who's the star you know? Maybe you can introduce us!'

Uh-oh. 'Actually,' I said, 'I signed an NDA because I promised to do some work for her. Help her out with those stalkers. I can't tell you anything about who she is.' I met his eyes. 'My word is my bond, Rubus. I'm sure you know that.'

He wasn't listening. 'You will arrange an introduction at the earliest opportunity. Whoever she is, she will want to meet me.' He splayed out in his hands in a dramatic flourish. 'I am Rubus, after all.'

'She's not a faery,' I said. 'She's not going to know who you are.'

'She will,' he answered confidently. 'Make it happen, Madrona.'

I supposed it would at least give me an excuse to find out how she was. The surly Redcap Finn had obviously managed to escape with her in tow and no doubt was already aware that Rubus had executed his brother. I'd have to make sure Finn was alright – and it would give me a chance to find out about Morgan.

My heart tightened at the thought. I prayed he was alive; it had been difficult to tell after our fight with the vampire hunters. Rubus had whisked me away before I'd had chance to check on him. To all intents and purposes, Morgan had appeared to be unconscious. I could only hope that he was okay. I didn't know what I'd do otherwise.

Rubus clasped his hands to his heart, his green Fey eyes dreamy. He let out a happy hiccup and then shook himself. 'Anyway,' he said. 'We need to get down to business. This really is most tiresome and I'm a very busy person.' He said this last part with the air of a harried martyr. Rubus was, of course, nothing like that. He was an evil arsebadger who I'd shove off this rooftop if I could.

'Well,' I told him earnestly, 'I'll do my best to hurry things along so you can get on with your other plans. I want your day to be just as wonderfully pleasant as you are.'

Rubus flicked me a look but I smiled back innocently. Apparently deciding that complaining about my acid tongue was a waste of time, he pointed down to the street below. 'As the truce prevents me from harming you directly, and I don't want my best pixie-dust seller to become addicted to the stuff herself and lose her ability to attract new clients, I've had to come up with a different method to persuade you to my side. This worked very well last time.'

He held out his palm and a lanky Fey jumped forward and gave him a brick. 'All I need you to do, Madrona, is to drop this little beauty. It's bound to hit someone on the head.' His expression gleamed. 'There will be a lot of blood. There always is.'

I clapped my hands. 'I love blood!'

I reached over, snatched the brick from him and dropped it over the parapet. Rubus's jaw dropped open and both of us leaned over to watch its descent. It narrowly avoided hitting three young women, crashing just to the left of them instead and cracking the pavement. Several pedestrians' heads swivelled up to see where it had come from. Both Rubus and I pulled back out of sight to avoid being spotted.

I pouted. 'I missed.'

Rubus watched me, his expression inscrutable. I

couldn't even begin to guess what he was thinking. 'So you did,' he murmured.

'Morgan told me I was an evil bitch,' I confided. 'I thought I'd try and live up to his expectations. It didn't take long to realise how much fun it is being bad to the bone.' I dropped my voice into a conspiratorial whisper. 'I think I might be a bit of a psychopath.'

'A *bit* of a psychopath?'

'I have discovered,' I said airily, 'that I'm also known as the Madhatter. I believe it rather fits.' I added a maniacal grin for extra effect.

Rubus didn't appear particularly impressed. 'Morganus gave you that nickname. You keep forgetting that I know you were with him when I found you.' His left eyelid twitched almost imperceptibly. 'It looked to me as if you were very concerned about his welfare.'

'Dude!' I thumped his arm. 'Of course I was concerned! He was all upset that I'd left him for you. I made a bet with myself that I could still get him to unzip his tight jeans for me. He's a sexy arsebadger.' I gave Rubus a critical look. 'You look quite alike, you know.'

Rubus was astonishingly put out. Honestly, he was like a child. 'You like him more than you like me.'

'Well,' I said, 'he might have called me an evil bitch but he was also quite nice to me and helped with those stalkers and with the nux. You all but abducted me.'

Rubus glared. 'I helped stop those stalkers more than he did. And I can be very nice too.' He leaned forward. 'If you'll let me. I'm working hard to get all us faeries back home to Mag Mell. Morganus is doing nothing more than pulling a few pints and walking around the city pouting.'

I smirked. 'He probably likes his steak well-done too.' I waggled my finger at Rubus. 'But it doesn't change the fact that I have no reason to be impressed by you, despite all your fine words. You put a damned giant spider on me!'

'It was a Truth Spider. I had to learn the truth from you. I had to know I could trust you,' he growled. His eyelid was twitching even more furiously.

'But,' I said softly, 'how am I supposed to know whether *I* can trust *you*?'

Rubus didn't answer. His eyes remained fixed on mine until suddenly he turned round and addressed the waiting group of patient minions. 'We are leaving,' he said. 'You lot go search for the bogle. The others can prepare for Plan B.'

Plan B? Wariness ran through me. I opened my mouth to ask Rubus about it but he jerked his thumb at his patiently waiting minions and indicated the time for chat was over. 'Bring her.'

I exhaled. Despite what else might be going on, I thought I'd done rather a neat job of flipping the conversation. I might not remember anything specific about Rubus but I had no doubt that he was both dangerous and crazy. If I could keep him focused on what he had to do for me, rather than the other way around, then I might just find a way out of this mess.

I didn't want to have to throw any more bricks at the soft skulls of human beings. It had been remarkably difficult to time the toss to avoid hitting anyone directly. Even then I'd been nervous that I'd got the trajectory wrong. It was just as well it wasn't a breezy day. Gasbudlikins. Maybe I *was* evil. I had no desire to be indiscriminately evil, though; that would be a complete waste of energy.

***

We took the lift down to the lobby. I was flanked by

two Fey arsebadgers all the way down. Maybe they were expecting me to fling myself upon Rubus and attack him, or make a run for it while in the tiny enclosed space by throwing myself at the doors and shrieking. Considering how nasty Rubus's aftershave was, that was quite a tempting move. It really was unpleasantly overpowering.

When we finally reached the bottom and exited the lift – and I was able breathe through my nose again – I spotted a woman wearing a T-shirt and jeans heading towards the ladies' toilets. A cartoon picture of a snail was emblazoned across her chest and her eyes, which she quickly cast to the ground when I glanced at her, were bright green.

'I need to pee,' I announced loudly.

'Cross your legs,' growled the nearest Fey.

I did as he suggested, bowing slightly at my waist and hobbling forward. 'It's not helping,' I complained. 'Do you have a bottle or something? Maybe I can squat here in front of you. Will that suit you?'

Rubus sighed. 'Bring the car round to the front. I'll wait for her there. You two stay with her till she's done.'

I beamed. 'Thank you. I don't want to leave a smelly wet patch on your car's upholstery.'

Rubus walked out of the front building while I – and my two minders – dashed to the toilet. I banged open the door, assuming they were following, and darted into the nearest cubicle.

'You'd think,' I called out, as I settled onto the loo seat, 'that the amnesia I'm suffering from wouldn't affect my bodily functions. After all, it's a problem with my mind, not my body. But I have to pee so much! And clearly my stomach is disturbed because I've got constipation too. It's hard work straining your bowels all the time. I don't suppose you've got any laxatives on you? I could do with releasing some of that stinky brown stuff so—'

'We're going to wait outside,' one of the Fey snapped, interrupting me in mid-flow. 'Don't be long.' A moment later I heard the door open and close behind them.

I breathed out, jumped to my feet and cocked my head. One of the many things I'd discovered about myself was that I possessed incredible hearing. Having already latched onto both Fey's heartbeats, I could tell that they'd positioned themselves directly outside the restroom door. Of course, they also had the same excellent hearing. I would have be careful.

I unlatched the cubicle door at the same time as the snail woman did. She flashed me a crooked grin and walked to the basins, turning on every tap. I reached for the automatic hand dryer, set it off and kept my hand in place so that its sound also filled the room. When I glanced back, the woman had gone. In her place was a heart-breakingly familiar face.

'I wasn't sure you'd get the reference,' Morgan murmured. 'But I had to be subtle enough to avoid detection.'

As if I'd forget that he was Snail Boy. He was named after a sea snail and I'd thoroughly enjoyed laughing at him for it. I grabbed him, yanking him towards me so I could hug him. It was awkward with one hand out of action under the dryer but I pressed him tightly against me.

His hands wrapped round my back and his lips found my ear. 'We still have to be careful. I couldn't hold the glamour for much longer and if we're overheard before…'

'I know,' I whispered. 'I'm just glad you're okay.' I pulled back slightly and looked into his eyes. 'I didn't want to go with Rubus. There wasn't any choice though. I promise. I—'

'Shhh,' he said. 'I know. I was drifting in and out of consciousness when he showed up and took you but I heard enough of what he said.' He paused. 'And did. I've had people out looking for him. When you were spotted coming into this building, I got here as quickly as I could.'

'I'm really glad you did.' Unexpected tears pricked at my eyelids. Well, that was a surprise. I pulled back so I could look at Morgan's face. 'Jinn?' I asked, even though I already knew the answer.

Morgan's expression shuttered and he shook his head grimly. 'Julie and Finn are fine, though. They were far enough away to avoid detection. I don't think Rubus ever knew they were there.'

'And the sphere?' I asked in a low, urgent voice.

'It's safe. Rubus won't find it. Not now.'

I passed a hand over my face in relief. At least that was something.

Morgan's eyes searched mine. 'Are you okay?' he asked gruffly. 'Has he hurt you?'

'No. Lots of bluster and threats but I'm fine.' I gazed at him. 'More to the point, how are you? You could have died back there.'

'It'll take more than a few vampire-crazy humans to finish me. You should know that by now. I have a sore head and my insides feel like a bullet has bounced around them – probably because it did. I'll live, thanks to what you did to bring down that sniper.'

He squeezed my arm and the gesture squeezed at my heart. I reckoned the pair of us needed a good shag before I melted into a puddle by his feet. It felt damned amazing to be thought of as Morgan's saviour; surely I deserved some decent sex in return.

Unfortunately, he had other plans. 'Now, listen. I've

rounded up the troops. There are a dozen Fey loyal to me outside. As soon as we leave here, those two hefting lumps will see me and make a move. They can't actually hurt either of us although I'll be expecting a lot of noise. We can cope with that. You'll be back at the Metropolitan Bar within the hour, Maddy.'

Suddenly I took a step back. 'I can't do that. I have to stay with Rubus.'

Morgan stilled. 'Why?' His voice was completely flat and the warmth in his eyes vanished immediately.

I twisted my hands. 'Because he's dangerous! You told me what he was like morally but you failed to mention that he's completely crazy as well. He's desperate to get his hands on the sphere. Goodness knows what will happen when he fails. He said something about a Plan B. We need to know what that is. We need someone on the inside. I think that's what I was doing all along when I was drug dealing for him. It's not that I'm a superhero or a supervillain.' I grinned at Morgan. 'I'm a super spy.'

He raised his eyes briefly to the heavens. 'And you think that Rubus is crazy,' he muttered. His expression remained cool. 'You want him.'

Good grief. He was as daft as his brother. 'Sometimes I wonder who ties your shoes for you in the morning, Morgan. I don't want Rubus. I want to stop Rubus.'

Morgan folded his arms across his broad chest. 'He has been stopped. The sphere has been taken care of. There's nothing to worry about any longer.'

'He's been stopped *temporarily*,' I argued. 'He's not going to give up. He's determined to save all the Fey and return us to Mag Mell, regardless of the consequences. Remember what Artemesia, your apothecary friend said? Forces unseen will lead me to places and people who are related to my memory loss. I was led to Rubus so I have to stay with him now.'

'He found you,' he snapped. 'Not the other way around.'

'Does it matter? He won't stop at anything to become our glorious saviour. If he can't locate the dragon sphere, he'll find another way. He was prepared to flood this entire demesne with magic and effectively destroy it to achieve his goal. What if he finds another way that's equally destructive? I would much rather toddle off without a backward glance in his direction but we can't let him continue with whatever else he's planning! If I stay with him, I can get him to trust me again. I know I can. With me on the inside, we'll know his every move.'

'And what,' Morgan enquired, 'will you do to get him to trust you?'

'Whatever I can!' I said, the words out of my mouth before I thought about them. When Morgan's gaze shuttered, I realised what he thought I was referring to. 'I don't mean sex! I'm not going to open my legs for him.'

'What if he demands it?'

I glowered. 'I can look after myself.'

'Apparently so.'

Our argument had been conducted in annoyed whispers but we obviously weren't doing a good enough job, even with the noise from the running taps and the hand dryer masking us. There was a sudden thump on the door. 'What's going on?' one of the Fey arsebadgers called.

I shoved Morgan into the nearest cubicle just in time. The Fey opened the door and looked inside. 'Who were you talking to?' he demanded.

'Myself,' I answered back. At his narrow-eyed look, I shrugged. 'I'm the Madhatter.'

'You're Madrona. We're not allowed to call you the

Madhatter.'

I twirled round, flapping my arms. I needed the Fey to be distracted enough to focus on me – and not listen closely enough to realise there was another heartbeat only a metre away. 'Madhatter!' I sang out. 'I'm the Maaaaaadhattter!'

'Get out of there,' he snapped. 'Rubus is waiting.'

'I love how you state the obvious with such a sense of discovery,' I told him. The Fey growled at me. I patted him on the back and followed him out. 'Were we friends before I got amnesia?' I enquired.

'No.'

'Were we lovers?'

'No.'

'Nothing more than work colleagues?' I asked. 'That's a bit dull.'

He glared at me but at least his partner snickered. Then they took their positions at either side of me and escorted me out to the waiting car.

I resisted the urge to look back. It was just as well killing glances weren't a faery skill or I reckoned the skin would have been stripped off my back by now. Morgan was not a happy Fey bunny. And despite my relief that he was still up and breathing, I had to admit that neither was I.

Chapter Two

Once Rubus's driver had set off, I buckled up my seatbelt and sniffed my fingers. Rubus glanced at me. 'I was just checking,' I said. 'I can't remember if I washed my hands or not.'

He grimaced in disgust. 'You were gone for long enough to manage that.' He reached into the door pocket and passed me a hand sanitizer. 'Please.'

I shrugged and took some. 'You're not a fan of germs?' I enquired.

Rubus didn't bother to answer. Maybe, I thought hopefully, I could introduce salmonella. Or legionnaire's disease. If I did it accidentally on purpose, surely that wouldn't break the truce? I pursed my lips. Hmmmm.

'What?'

I frowned at him. 'Eh?'

Rubus rolled his eyes. 'You've obviously thought of something. What is it?'

'I was wondering about the truce,' I said. 'And how it works.'

'It's magic,' he answered tersely.

'Well, I got that part. Duh.'

Rubus growled. I shrugged then I raised a hand and attempted to strike him. My hand froze in mid-air and a flash of pain overtook me. 'Ouchy!' I yelled.

For the first time, Rubus bestowed me with a genuine smile. 'That's how it works.'

I stared at my hand. Straining, I tried to fling it forward in another bid to punch him. More pain coursed through my system and my damned hand wouldn't budge. Beads of sweat popped out on my forehead with the effort. Eventually, I dropped my hand and gave up. 'Damn,' I whispered.

'The truce has its uses,' Rubus said, obviously still amused.

'Explain it to me.'

He raised an eyebrow. 'Is that an order?'

I dismissed his curt enquiry. 'A request.'

He ran a hand through his hair, in a gesture that was achingly familiar of Morgan. 'When we realised the border to Mag Mell was closed, there was a meeting,' he said. 'All the Fey in this demesne were present. Even you.'

I sniffed. 'Well, I'm Fey, aren't I?'

He ignored me. 'It was decided that there was considerable danger to other life forms if things continued as they were. We Fey don't always … see eye to eye. Not that it should be a problem for anyone if there's the odd argument. We're obviously superior to humans – we're the top of the food chain. Who cares if any of them get hurt?'

'Indeed,' I murmured. 'Do we cook them before we eat them?'

Rubus recoiled. 'Eat humans? Are you insane?'

'You said we're at the top of the food chain.'

'I mean figuratively speaking. Good grief, Madrona. We're not monsters.'

I begged to differ but I nodded wisely. 'Morgan said something similar. About the truce – not the eating people part. We all signed it so there'd be no fighting between us.'

Rubus's lip curled. 'It was a stupid idea from the start. I had no choice but to agree. A strand of magic was taken from each of us and they were woven together to form the truce. It means we're all bound by it.'

'And it can't be broken?'

He raised his shoulders in a heavy shrug. 'Perhaps if we could see the magic that ties us all, we could find a way to break it. But you can't break that which is invisible to sight, sound or touch. It is what it is.'

Even without his tales of trying to poke out his brother's eyes, I'd have recognised that Rubus had already put considerable effort into finding ways to destroy the truce so he could work his wicked ways around the world. Rather than dwell on his failures, which I doubted would improve his mood, I took a different tack. 'Why weren't Redcaps and dragons and bogles included in the terms of the truce?'

Rubus laughed humourlessly. 'We didn't know about the dragons until recently. And the others weren't considered important enough – or powerful enough – to bother about. That's why they're so useful to me now, despite their lack of powerful magic.' His expression darkened. 'They're useful when they're loyal. Both the Redcaps and the bogle have betrayed me and I can't help thinking that you are involved with both. It can't be a coincidence that Charrie, the bogle who worked for me, disappeared at the same time as you lost your memory.'

'Honestly,' I said, 'you could well be right. But I can't remember either way. All I have to go on is what other people tell me.'

Rubus smiled again. 'That's why we're going to bring back your memory. I need to know what's inside that pretty little head of yours.'

A complicated mixture of both dread and joy snaked through me. 'You know how to get rid of my amnesia?'

'Not yet,' he answered. 'But I know someone who might.'

***

The remainder of our journey was conducted in silence. I debated asking about the mysterious Plan B but decided I'd already put too much effort into playing the role of loyal minion. I didn't want to unravel all the goodwill that I'd established with Rubus. I was a super spy; I'd just have to spy to find out more. That way I could keep him sweet and save the world all at the same time. Go me.

Unfortunately, when we finally arrived back at Rubus's latest hideout, I was escorted to my small nondescript room without any opportunity for either sneaking or spying. It was hard to believe that I'd stayed here before on a regular basis. Not only was the room tiny but it had all the charm of a wart-covered bullfrog. Before I could protest, I was unceremoniously locked inside. Nope, Rubus definitely didn't trust me yet.

I lay down on the narrow bed and locked my hands beneath my head. Whatever my old self was really up to, it was clear she'd been playing the long game. Spying antics aside, I wasn't sure I could be arsed with that; the long game could take decades. Sure, I'd been selfless and come here of my own volition when I could have escaped with Morgan but I had my limits. I'd been here for three days already and it was testing my patience. There had to be a way to stop Rubus in his tracks for good but he had to trust me first.

I was drifting off to sleep, because every good villain needs a nap from time to time, when there was a faint knocking at the small window. Frowning, I opened my eyes and peered up. Several sycamore seeds had plastered themselves against the glass. I closed my eyes again. A moment later, I sprang upwards and opened the window so I could scoop them in.

It wasn't autumn yet.

As soon as the seeds touched my skin, the tiny pods began to unfurl. I should have realised. I knew that Morgan had the power to command nature to his bidding; after all, he'd used dandelion seeds to track me when I'd been with Julie. This had to be something along the same lines. He'd obviously seen the error of his ways and was sending me a grovelling apology. I grinned when tiny pieces of paper appeared, each one in a tightly curled roll inside the pod. I unfolded each one eagerly and laid them out on the bedspread.

The writing was miniscule. With only one word written on each piece of paper, I had to squint to read and it took some time to arrange the messages into an order that made sense. I'd been hoping that it would also tell me that the whole message would self-destruct in sixty seconds; alas, it simply stated that I should dispose of the paper before anyone noticed it. The rest of the message was equally disappointing.

You are in danger. Rubus will test your loyalty. Be careful. A friend.

I stared. Was this supposed to be news to me? I knew I was in danger; it didn't take a genius of my level to realise that Rubus would go all out to make sure I was on his side and not Morgan's and that I should take every care. What a bloody waste of time. I wasn't even convinced that it was Morgan who'd sent the message. After all, he hadn't apologised and hadn't left any scribbled kisses for me to sigh over. And, thinking about it, he probably wouldn't know which hideout Rubus was currently using or which window belonged to me.

No, this was the work of a different Fey. The trouble was that I had no idea who. I tapped my mouth thoughtfully. I was going to gamble that it was someone in Rubus's employ, someone who was a super spy like me and flying under the radar to stop Rubus's nefarious plans. I'd have to keep my eyes peeled for anything suspicious.

There was a sudden sharp knock at the door. I hastily scooped up the scraps and shoved them into my mouth, swallowing them down. The door swung open and one of my Fey buddies from the rooftop appeared. 'He wants you,' he said gruffly. 'In the laboratory. He'll meet you there shortly.'

I stood up, brushing the wrinkles out of my clothes and smiling disarmingly. 'I assume you're going to escort me,' I said. 'I don't know where the laboratory is. Does it contain a mad faery scientist? I certainly hope so.'

The Fey didn't blink but simply waited stoically. Honestly, these guys were no fun at all. I sighed melodramatically and gestured at him to lead the way. Without so much as a flicker of acknowledgment, he turned. Like any good little captive, I followed.

***

I wasn't sure what I'd been expecting of somewhere ominously titled 'the laboratory'. Steaming potions and a few cauldrons, perhaps. The reality was disappointingly mundane. There were a lot of shelves with a lot of vials and bottles and pretty colours. I recognised the pixie dust almost immediately but there was nothing else I could confidently name and none of the vials had identifying labels.

I thought about what Artemesia, the apothecary Morgan had introduced me to, had suggested about her uncle's over-reliance on his own knowledge. This had to be his place and, at least by its appearance, he seemed to know what he was doing.

There were some herbs on a rack, tied up by their stems so they could dry out. There was even a workbench. It was spick and span and without a single speck of dust. There weren't even any grinning skulls lying around.

The Fey who'd escorted me left me at the door. In the absence of anyone else, I was free to wander around and inspect everything. I opened a few bottles and sniffed surreptitiously. Some of them smelled even worse than Rubus's aftershave. There was no paper to be seen; neither were there any books.

The fact that I'd been left here alone couldn't be an accident. Perhaps this was the scenario my mysterious sycamore friend had been trying to warn me about but I couldn't see why. Nothing in here was recognisable and, after my bout of rowan poisoning, I had a healthy suspicion of any strange potions or lotions. I hopped onto the nearest table and started swinging my legs.

It was almost fifteen minutes before anyone joined me. When the door finally opened, I was so bored that I could have happily chewed off my fingers just to pass the time.

I swung a head lazily in the direction of the incomer. A small bespectacled Fey, whose green eyes were magnified by his bottle-top lenses, edged in. He looked rather young to be Artemesia's apothecary uncle. All the same, I played along. 'Are you the mad scientist?' I asked. 'You're wearing glasses, so I assume you're intelligent.' I glanced over him critically. 'Your hair looks a bit too neat and tidy though.'

I jumped off the table and wandered over to him then I reached up and mussed his brown fringe. The fact that he allowed me to do so was telling in itself.

'N–no,' he stammered, once I stepped back, satisfied with my hairdressing attempt. 'I'm Galanthus. We've met. Many times.'

'I have amnesia,' I informed him. 'I don't remember

anyone.'

He lowered his voice and swung his eyes from side to side, as if double-checking that we were alone. I watched him carefully. Unless I was mistaken – which was unlikely – he was over-acting. 'We're friends,' he said. 'Good friends.'

I beamed and opened my arms expansively. 'Then we should hug!' I reached forward, drawing him into a massive bear hug. He didn't resist – but he did have the faintest lingering scent of Rubus's aftershave clinging to him, like a dissipating cloud. Ha! I was right. This guy was a plant – and I didn't just mean because of his daft faery name.

I released him from my hold. 'It's so difficult to know who's an ally and who's not around here. I wish I could remember more.' I trilled a laugh. 'I wish I could remember *any*thing.'

He swallowed, his Adam's apple bobbing in his throat. 'There's not much time,' he told me. 'I don't want Rubus or anyone else to see me here. I had to take this opportunity to talk to you, though. We've been working together to bring him down. Even if you don't remember, you'll understand how dangerous he is. I really work for Morganus.' His eyes widened. 'But don't tell anyone.'

'You work for Morgan?' I repeated breathlessly.

He nodded vigorously. 'There's a meeting tonight. It's only a few streets away. If you can get out, you should come along.'

I did my best to look disappointed. 'I don't think I can. They keep locking me in my room and I can't remember how to use magic to open locks.'

He pointed to one of the bottles nearby. 'That's dreadwort,' he whispered. 'It's been imbued with magic. Take three sips and you'll have the temporary ability to unlock any door. It'll help you escape.'

I raised my eyebrows and walked over to the green bottle. I had no way of knowing what it really contained so I simply nodded wisely. 'Excellent! This is just what I need. How long does it last?'

'At least a day. If you take some now, it'll still be working tonight. We're meeting Morganus on the corner of Prue Street and Leith Road. At midnight exactly.' He gave me a final meaningful look and shuffled out again.

I snorted. If this was the sort of test that Rubus was going to come up with, I reckoned I'd be back in his inner circle within hours rather than days.

I wondered whether the green bottle contained a lethal poison and this was Rubus's way of killing me while avoiding the strictures of the truce. I uncorked it and sniffed. It was completely odourless. Maybe it wasn't poison at all; maybe it was nothing more dangerous than water. Either way, hell would freeze over and I'd ice skate a dance with the devil before I'd let any of it touch my lips.

It wasn't much longer before Rubus himself appeared. An older man hobbled behind him. No doubt this was Artemesia's uncle in person – maybe he would have a way to cure my amnesia. As nervous as I was by the thought of what revelations might ensue, right now I decided I'd happily snog his thin chapped lips if he could. Amnesia could get rather tiresome after a while.

'Ah,' Rubus said. 'Madrona. You're here.'

'You say that like you're surprised to see me,' I commented. 'You did order me here. I was frogmarched all the way on your instructions.'

He waved a dismissive hand. 'One never knows what might happen. Not every command I issue is followed immediately.'

There was no way that could be true. The arsebadger ran an extraordinarily tight ship. 'Indeed,' I said. 'Or when you might have traitors who pop in and encourage me to flee this place at midnight for secret assignations with your brother. Honestly, between you and Morgan you're supposed to be the better bet but if you can't trust your own people then I'm not sure what I'm doing here. I want a general who keeps his troops in order.'

Fury lit Rubus's face before he quickly shuttered his expression. Hopefully my gibe would at least stop him from using his own people again to try and weasel betrayal out of me. 'I don't know what you're talking about.'

I shrugged. 'Some Fey came in here, told me to drink that potion,' I pointed out the offending bottle. 'He said that I'd be able to walk through locked doors and sneak out to meet Morgan at midnight tonight.' I gestured at myself. 'Look at me! I need my beauty sleep! I'm not going anywhere at midnight.'

Rubus looked me up and down. 'Yes, you certainly need some sort of makeover. Have you put on weight?'

'I don't know,' I said. 'I can't—'

'—remember,' he finished for me. 'Yes, yes.' He looked at me with malice. 'What was the name of this supposed traitor?'

'Galanthus,' I said, without missing a beat. And then, because I was on a roll and needed to gain Rubus's full trust, I glanced at the man behind him. 'I suppose you're Artemesia's uncle. She really doesn't like you very much.'

This time there was real, not faked, surprise in both their expressions. 'You've met her? Recently?'

'Obviously it was recently,' I drawled. 'Morgan took me to her.'

Artemesia's uncle leaned forward. 'Where is she?'

'She seemed rather concerned about keeping her whereabouts secret from you,' I told him.

His face scrunched up. 'Morgan has been filling her ear with evil whispers. She's my family. She should be by my side.'

'Because you want to protect her? Because you miss your niece and your family gatherings?'

'No,' he snapped. 'Because she stole from me. She has several books of mine that I'd like back. Not to mention that I could do with a proper lab assistant. She has no right to set up in direct competition against me.'

Well, I thought, at least he was being honest. I shrugged. Fair enough.

I reckoned I was taking a calculated risk. It would speed me towards my goal of getting Rubus to trust me again, plus I was convinced that Artemesia would already have moved on. She'd been nervous enough that I'd blab about her location so she wouldn't trust me to stay quiet, especially now that I was back in the villainous bosom of Rubus himself.

'She has a shed,' I said. 'Or at least it looks like a shed from the outside. Inside it's quite remarkable. It's by the river.' I outlined how Morgan and I had got there. 'She's probably gone by now though,' I added. 'She wasn't very happy when I showed up and she made it quite clear that she'd have to up sticks to keep herself safe.'

Rubus tutted. 'Children these days.' He looked at me assessingly. 'That's very helpful though, Madrona. Thank you.'

I curtsied. Artemesia's uncle turned to leave. 'I'll go now.'

Rubus caught his arm. 'I'll send someone else, Carduus. If Artemesia is still there, she'll run a mile if she sees you. Besides,' he pointed at me, 'Madrona needs help.'

Never was a truer statement made. 'I'll need to take

samples from her. Until I know what caused her amnesia, I'm unable to cure it.' Carduus glared at me as if all this was my fault. 'It wasn't as a result of anything I gave her. I even checked my own supplies and potions. Nothing is missing.'

That was something at least. I stretched out my arms. 'Sample away.'

'I'll leave you to it,' Rubus said. 'Once you're finished, Madrona, I'd appreciate it if you would fetch your soap-star friend for me.' It was clear that he wasn't making a request.

I shrugged. 'I'll do my best.'

'You'll do better than that. I want to meet her.' He placed his palms together and held them up to his lips as if in prayer. 'I do hope it's Stacey,' he murmured to himself. 'She's my favourite.'

Gasbudlikins. No wonder my career as Julie's bodyguard hadn't lasted more than two days. Her character was indeed Stacey. Instead of keeping her safe, I was virtually being asked to deposit her in the lap of an evil faery with delusions of grandeur.

'Are you going off to punish Galanthus now?' I enquired.

Rubus appeared momentarily surprised. He'd forgotten all about the supposed traitor, proving once and for all that it had all been a set-up. 'Yeah,' he murmured unconvincingly. 'He's going to pay for what he's done.' He was halfway to the door before he turned and glanced at me. 'By the way,' he added, 'before you got amnesia, you took a large quantity of pixie dust with you to sell. I'd like it back.'

'I don't have it now. I don't know where it is.'

Rubus shrugged. 'I don't care. Just find it.'

He didn't add 'or else' at the end of his sentence. Somehow he didn't need to.

Chapter Three

After being prodded and poked by Carduus, along with being stuck by various needles and swabbed in some unmentionable places that I'd rather not think about again, I left the laboratory and made my way towards the main entrance. I was expecting at least one – if not more – Fey goons to fall into place alongside me. When my journey was uninterrupted and I was left alone, however, I allowed myself an imaginary high five.

Rubus didn't have any evidence that I was involved with his missing sphere or the lost bogle. He didn't even have any evidence that I trusted Morgan rather than him. It looked like I had been granted enough freedom to move around the city unhindered. I was still on a leash but it was one of those extendable ones rather than a choke collar. All to the good.

I skipped along, pausing every so often to check my reflection in shop windows and car side-mirrors. As far as I could tell, I wasn't being followed but that didn't mean that Rubus hadn't planted a darned dandelion-seed tracker on me. I shook out my hair and brushed down my clothes as best as I could but I couldn't be sure that I was clean, no matter how much I wiggled around.

It would be far safer to avoid going anywhere near Julie's home. Anyway, at this time of day she was at work. With that thought in mind, I headed for the nearest taxi rank, slid into the front seat of the first cab and buckled up.

'Where to?' asked the driver. He was a friendly looking fellow with a shock of pure-white hair and a lot of laughter lines around his eyes.

I gave him the name of the television studios. He bobbed his head and set off.

Fortunately the traffic was light at that time of day and it took less than an hour to reach the studio gates. Along the way, the taxi driver and I exchanged the sort of typical inanities that passed for small talk.

'Weather's been good lately.'

'Yep. It's nice to have some sunshine for a change. Have you been busy?'

'Ticking along. There are a lot of tourists at this time of year so I've not done too badly, especially with ferrying people to and from the airport.'

'That's good.'

'Certainly is. Especially with all the doom-and-gloom news about tax rates rising.'

'It's all doom and gloom these days.'

'Terrible, ain't it? Did you see the bit about the Chinese place that went up in flames? I've driven the bloke who owned it. Nice bloke. Chen Lee, I think he was called.'

I'd only been murmuring my responses and half paying attention until that point. Suddenly I sat upright. This had to be that freaky amnesia thing working again – the magic was trying to reassert natural order by leading me to where I needed to go.

'There was a fire?' I questioned.

Sensing my shift from detached politeness to agog interest, the driver smiled. 'A huge one.' He tutted. 'I went past there the other day. The whole building is little more than a shell now.'

'Where?' I asked. 'Where is it?'

'The east end of Belmont Street,' he said. 'You can't miss it.'

Making a quick decision, I checked how much cash I

had on me. It was probably enough. 'Can you wait for me at the studio?' I asked. 'Then take me to Belmont Street afterwards?'

'You really are interested, ain't ya?'

I shrugged. 'I'm morbid that way,' I said cheerfully.

He sent me a sidelong glance and shuffled away from me slightly, as if my morbidity were contagious. 'Sure,' he said. 'I can do that.'

I guessed the lure of a fare back to the city centre was tempting despite the fact that I was a weirdo. Excellent.

***

The driver dropped me at the main studio gates before circling round to find an appropriate, law-abiding parking spot. I strode up to the security guards. From my previous visit here with Julie, I knew that they took their jobs seriously. That was good for Julie but right now it was bad for me.

'I'm here to see Julie Chivers,' I announced.

The two guards exchanged glances. 'We don't know anything about this,' one said.

'Yeah,' the other agreed. 'We can't let anyone in without prior arrangement.'

'I've been here before. I'm her bodyguard.'

They both stared at me. It took a full second before they burst out laughing.

I put my hands on my hips and glared. 'I'm not lying.'

Cheeks suffused with red, and stifling more laughter, the first guard held up his hand. 'Wait here.' He ambled into the small office to his left. Through the window I saw him picking up the phone.

'You don't really expect us to believe that a girly like you is Ms Chivers bodyguard?'

I sniffed loudly. 'You shouldn't judge people by appearances.'

'Do you have a gun?'

'No.'

'Can you do karate? Or kung fu?'

'No.' I could pull a nasty face though, so I did just that. Unfortunately, the security guard wasn't in the slightest bit impressed.

The other guard in the office popped his head out of the door. 'Someone here says that Ms Chivers' bodyguard is already with her.'

Finn. It had to be Finn. I breathed out a sigh of relief. That was something; he was so vicious he'd guard her with his life. But it didn't particularly help me.

'Just tell her that Madrona is here!' I called back.

'What kind of name is Madrona? You Spanish or something?'

'Or something,' I muttered.

The guard picked up the receiver again, his lips moving as he spoke. There was a momentary pause then a flicker of surprise crossed his face. 'She's on her way out to meet you,' he said. He gave me a closer look. 'Does it pay well? Being a bodyguard, I mean?'

His buddy snorted. 'No way is she a bodyguard. She's not even wearing an earpiece. And even I could bring her down within seconds.' He patted his rotund belly for effect.

I was tempted to provide a demonstration; it would be easy enough to warp time just enough to get in front of this arsebadger and knee him in the groin before he realised what had happened. But given what Morgan had told me about the dangerous effects of using that kind of magic – such as bringing about the end of the world – it probably wasn't worth it. Probably.

Fortunately I didn't have to wait very long.

Automatic doors swished open in the building opposite the guardhouse and both Finn and Julie walked out. She was in full make-up and, as a result, looked rather different to normal. Finn caught sight of me and looked psychotic. That was pretty normal for him.

Without paying the guards any attention, Finn strode ahead and walked up to me. His fists clenched and his jaw was tight. 'You,' he spat.

From behind him, Julie smiled her relief. 'Darling! How are you?'

'Alive,' I grunted, looking her over. Despite the overdone make-up, which I assumed was part of her soap character Stacey, she seemed alright. 'You?'

Before Julie could answer, Finn butted in. 'Alive is more than can be said for my brother.'

I swallowed. 'I'm truly sorry about Jinn. I tried to stop Rubus from killing him but…' My voice trailed off.

'You didn't try hard enough.'

I couldn't argue. 'No,' I said softly. 'I didn't.'

Finn wasn't mollified and I didn't blame him. 'Morgan said he forced you to go with him. Have you escaped or did he let you leave?' he demanded.

'Neither, really. I'm working for him again.'

His mouth twisted into a snarl. 'You're what?'

'I'm doing what you did. I'm undercover.'

'It didn't work for us. What makes you think it'll work for you?'

I sighed and pushed back my hair. 'It did work for you. You, Jinn and Winn helped stop him getting his hands on the sphere.'

'They're dead.'

'And Rubus is sphere-less. Would your brothers have thought it was worth it?'

Finn muttered to himself and looked away. Julie patted his arm. 'I'm assuming you're here for a reason,

Mads.'

I supposed I might as well get to the point. 'He wants to meet you.'

Finn's head snapped back. 'You told Rubus about her?' His voice dripped with derision.

'Not in so many words. He knows I'm friends with an actor from *St Thomas Close*. It turns out he's a fan. He doesn't know which actor, nor does he know about…' I shuffled '…your, er, ethnicity.'

'Are we supposed to be grateful that you kept your mouth shut about that?' From the look on Finn's face, he was about ready to swipe my head off my shoulders. Pointing out that Julie's magical blood-enhanced NDA meant I couldn't say anything about her vampirism even if I wanted to probably wouldn't help.

'I wasn't thinking.'

'Well, there's a surprise. Even on a good day, you're as bright as a fucking black hole.'

Okay, enough now. I'd been prepared to grant him some leeway with his guttural snarls because he was grieving but this was too much. 'And you're twice as dense,' I hissed back. 'Obviously, I'm not going to bring Julie to Rubus. I was actually thinking that she could give me someone else's name. Another actor.' I looked at her. 'Maybe someone you dislike.'

Her eyebrows flew up, startled. 'You want me to give you the name of an enemy so you can take them to your evil faery boss in my place? Darling, you're even more Machiavellian than I realised.'

I shrugged helplessly. 'Is it such a stupid idea? You've got Finn inside the studio with you. When I was your bodyguard, you didn't want me hanging around while you were working. You're obviously still worried about any remaining vampire hunters. We can get Rubus to keep a look out for them. It'll tie up some of his minions, keep them busy for ages and kill two birds with one stone. Truthfully, I couldn't avoid telling Rubus about you. He was always going to ask questions about what was going on at the Travotel when he killed Jinn. If there'd been another way out, I'd have taken it. This mollifies Rubus and keeps you safe from him.'

'And potentially kills a co-worker.'

'They won't be killed.' Maybe. 'And you're an actor. Surely there's a lot of rivalry. There must be other actors around here who you wouldn't mind putting in harm's way. Not,' I added hastily, reacting to the disturbed expressions on both Finn and Julie's faces, 'that they'd be hurt. Rubus just wants to say hello. I'll make sure they're safe.'

The plan I'd come up with had seemed brilliant when I'd mulled it over in my head. Now I was voicing it aloud, it occurred to me that perhaps it had a few flaws.

'I might work in a soap opera but I don't live in one.' Julie shrugged. 'I don't hate anyone that much. Neither do I believe that you're mean enough to put an innocent person at risk like that.'

'She's the Madhatter,' Finn spat. 'She's more than capable of it. She's evil.'

'Maybe you have to become evil to stop evil,' I retorted.

Julie put her hands up in a vague protest. 'Darlings,' she murmured, 'enough. I'll do it myself. I'd quite like to meet this Rubus and see what he's really like.'

Finn immediately started to complain. 'You can't do that! I can't protect you against him!'

I heaved in a breath. 'Obviously, you can't go with her. The thing is,' I shuffled my feet, 'as dodgy and dangerous as all this is, it might help. I need Rubus to feel relaxed and happy. Right now, without the sphere he was so desperately searching for, he's liable to blow up half the city on a mere whim. He's told me he's got another plan up his sleeve. We can't let him succeed. Anything that can be done to massage his ego and calm him down can only be a good thing. He's putting on a good show of being amenable and happy but under the surface, he's seething. He likes your soap opera. He'll feel good about meeting one of its stars and it might just give all of us enough of a break to find out what else he's planning. It really doesn't have to be you, Julie. Any *St Thomas Close* actor will do. I can pay them for their time.'

Julie shook her head adamantly. 'No,' she said. 'I'll do it.' When Finn opened his mouth to protest again, she turned to him. 'You did this,' she said. 'You and your brothers worked for him in order to stop him. What I'm doing is pathetic in comparison. It's just one meeting.'

Finn glared. 'Fine,' he spat. 'But the meeting takes place somewhere public. It doesn't last longer than an hour. And you,' he jabbed his finger at me, 'will guarantee her safety.'

I bobbed my head. 'Done.'

The Redcap was still unhappy. 'I'll believe it when I see it,' he growled.

Chapter Four

I was aware that I was treading a very fine line. I could be a good person who was prepared to do terrible things in order to achieve a greater goal, or I could easily slip into being a terrible person who was kidding herself that she was better than she was.

Magical sphere or no magical sphere, the cold, casual, callous way in which Rubus had ended Jinn's life convinced me that I had to find a way to stop him in his tracks. I wasn't entirely sure how far I was prepared to go to achieve that goal but I hadn't reached my limit yet. The only real truth I'd discovered was that I clearly wasn't cut out to be a superhero. It was probably just as well; virtually no one looked good in a leotard. Even me.

After arranging a date and time for Rubus to meet Julie, my friendly taxi driver dropped me off at Chen's building. He was right about one thing, I thought as I gazed at the hollowed-out, scorched building. The whole place was little more than a shell. Coming here was probably a waste of time.

Unwilling to give up on this new lead, however, I walked past the warning signs to stay away and headed through the tumbledown doorway. Fallen bricks and blackened debris were lying everywhere. If I'd breathed too hard, I wouldn't have been surprised if the entire structure had fallen down on top of my head. I could only assume that Rubus had ordered the place to be torched in case there were clues leading back to him, or other material that could be scavenged and used against him. Whoever and whatever Chen had been, he was obviously a canny bastard to have got hold of the sphere in the first place.

I took my time, edging carefully from one burnt-out room to another. The devastation was almost total. Charred paintings hung lopsidedly on charred walls. The furniture, which had probably been rather grand, was now little more than a collection of four-legged skeletons. I toed various scraps of paper but any writing that had been scrawled on them was now illegible.

I craned my neck upwards, tempted to try and gain access to the first and second floors. There was little left of the staircase but, if I took my time, I could probably manage it. I was planning the safest route when there was the crunch of a footstep behind me. I whirled round, relaxing slightly when I saw it was Morgan.

I waggled my eyebrows at him. 'At last. I wondered how long it would take you to find me.'

Morgan didn't blink. 'I wasn't looking for you.'

I smiled. Yeah, yeah. 'I'll accept your apology if you go down on bended knee. You don't have to grovel much. Just a little will be acceptable.'

His mouth twitched slightly. 'Why would I apologise?'

'You're funny. Go on. Let's get it over and done with and then we can move on.'

'I really have no idea what you're talking about.'

'You're here to apologise for being so gruff earlier. My idea about staying with Rubus so I can keep an eye on him and stop him from harming anyone else is an excellent one. You have to bow down to my greater wisdom, not to mention my sacrifice.'

He crossed his arms. 'That's not why I'm here. I have nothing to say sorry for, Maddy.'

I peered at him. Ah. He appeared to be telling the truth. He did indeed believe that he was still in the right and I should have abandoned Rubus at the first opportunity. I pursed my lips. 'Oh. Well, it's good that you still care enough to check up on me and make sure I'm alright.'

I saw the faintest hint of amusement zip across his face. 'I didn't know you were here.'

'You put another of those dandelion tracker things on me, right?'

'Nope.'

'It's okay, Morgan. You can tell the truth. No one else is around.'

He raised his emerald-green eyes heavenward. 'I'm not lying, Maddy. It didn't occur to me that you'd be here.' A note of bitterness entered his voice. 'To be honest I assumed you'd be with Rubus, doing whatever he wants you to do. *I'm* here because I heard the building had burnt down and I wanted to see it for myself. All this crap started with Chen and his sphere. The fire makes me wonder what else might have been going on.'

I frowned, vaguely hurt. 'You could have *pretended* to be here for me.'

His mouth twitched. 'I thought you preferred it when we were honest with each other.'

'I prefer it when *I'm* honest with *you*. The reverse isn't necessarily true.'

This time he was definitely suppressing a smile. 'That's hardly fair.'

I gestured down at myself. 'How do I look?'

He looked me over with a critical eye. 'Awful. You don't look like you've slept properly for days. There are bags under your eyes. Your hair isn't as glossy as normal and you're far too pale.'

It was my turn to fold my arms. 'Good grief. There's honesty and there's far too much information. This is one of those situations when a lie would be perfectly welcome.'

'Indeed,' he murmured. He folded his arms across his broad chest. 'How do *I* look to you?'

Gasbudlikins. What I should have said was that he looked like a grotesque troll. With a terrible, flesh-eating disease. But his dark hair was just the right side of mussed-up and the shadow of stubble around his strong jaw gave him an irritatingly debonair appearance. His T-shirt stretched against his chest, hinting at his hard body underneath. He was also wearing spicy aftershave but, unlike Rubus, Morgan's scent was neither distastefully overpowering nor nausea-inducing. His smell made me want to rub myself against him like a cat.

I sighed. 'You look devastatingly, stomach-squirmingly gorgeous.'

Morgan's mouth curved into a proper smile and he stepped towards me. 'Go on.'

I sniffed. 'Aren't there more important things to do than talk about how good you look?'

He reached down and tucked a stray curl behind my ear. Unfortunately, the gesture was identical to what Rubus had done to me not that long ago. With my guard down, I couldn't stop myself from wincing. Morgan's face immediately shuttered and he stepped back.

'Sorry,' I muttered. 'It's just that your brother did the same thing earlier. It's hard having to act a role around him all the time. I don't want to have to do the same around you.'

His expression softened. 'That might be the nicest thing you've ever said to me.'

'Give me a chance and I might say more. Just remember that I've only known you for ten days. You've known me for a lifetime.'

Morgan grimaced. 'Artemesia is still working on that. She's not yet come up with anything to cure your amnesia.'

'Rubus has set her uncle onto it as well,' I told him. 'And speaking of him, I might have mentioned where Artemesia's hideout is. I trust she's already moved on. She suggested that she'd have to do so because I couldn't be trusted.' I shrugged. 'She was right.'

'She was packing up five minutes after you left.'

I breathed out; at least that was something. There were only so many disasters I could be responsible for. Artemesia reuniting with her evil apothecary uncle didn't have to be one of them. 'Good,' I said. 'That's good.'

Morgan watched me. 'Is it?'

'I'm still on your side.'

A muscle ticked in his jaw. 'It's not about sides. It's about doing what's right.'

'It's always about sides, Morgan.' Before we could descend into an existential argument, I pointed upstairs. 'I was about to head up there and see what I could find. Down here is just a burnt-out mess.' I paused. 'Are you coming?'

He smiled again. 'Lead the way.'

Taking our time, we stepped gingerly upwards. Along the way, I filled him in on everything that had occurred, from my plans with Julie to Rubus's attempts to test me. None of it made Morgan happy. 'You have to be careful, Maddy. Rubus isn't an idiot. Far from it.'

I snorted. 'He's dangerous – and he makes me look like the very definition of sanity – but I've not seen much evidence of intelligence. He doesn't completely trust me, not yet, but he's proving quite easy to manipulate.'

Morgan sucked in a breath. 'You have to take care. Believe me, I've tried to thwart him on numerous occasions. He sees several moves ahead and always ends up with the upper hand.'

'You give him too much credit because he's your brother,' I scoffed. 'He doesn't achieve as much as he thinks he does.'

'He managed to get you.'

A flicker of pain ran through me. 'That was the old me.'

'Was it?' he asked softly.

I sighed. The truth was that I didn't really know.

We stepped onto the scarred first-floor landing. Although the damage here was extensive, there were a few odd corners that appeared untouched by the flames. There was an oriental rug, which still had patches of its original red wool visible beneath the layer of ash. A cabinet stood at the end of the hallway. It was open and obviously empty and its door hung off one hinge but it appeared salvageable.

Morgan nodded. 'There might be enough here to make this work.'

I gazed at him blankly. 'Huh?'

He chuckled. 'You still don't know everything that you're capable of. Faeries can do more than affect time and lust after home.'

'I shot a magical beam at the sniper who was firing at us at the Travotel,' I said importantly. 'Alas, it was with my hand rather than my eyes. It would have been cool to shoot laser beams from my pupils.' I stared at him. 'Unless we do have laser vision?' I crossed my fingers.

'No.'

Darn it.

'Most of our skills have little to do with fighting. We're Fey, Maddy. Our role is to enhance the earth and the environment, not to destroy.'

'Tell that to Rubus.'

Morgan's expression was rueful. 'That's the trouble. He believes that he is enhancing life and, in a way, he is. He's seeking to return us to Mag Mell, which is why he has so many followers. That and numerous pixie-dust addicts.'

'Have you tried yourself?' I asked. 'To re-open the borders, I mean?'

'Again and again and again.' His mouth turned down. 'Whatever occurred to slam the borders shut in the first place, I can't see a peaceful way to return them to their former state.'

'So now you advocate patience?'

He nodded. 'You can see why Rubus's call to action is more desirable.'

Yeah, I supposed I could. 'And maybe,' I said, 'you can see why it's a good idea for me to stay by his side.'

Morgan rolled his eyes but I could tell he agreed with me.

He dug into his pocket, pulled out a small white object and passed it to me. I held it up and examined it. 'A shell? Is this a memento of you, Snail Boy? Are you trying to ensure that I don't forget you?' As if that was likely to happen, I snorted to myself.

'It's a communication device,' he said shortly.

I stared at it. 'I'm pretty sure it's a shell.'

Morgan sighed. 'It's a communication shell.' He pulled out an identical one. 'I have its pair. You speak into it and I'll hear you. It's completely secure and easy to conceal.'

I burst out laughing. 'So what you're really saying is that this is a shell phone.'

'Why is that so funny?' he enquired.

'You know. Shell. Cell.' At his expression, I gave up. 'If I have to explain it, it doesn't work.' I eyed the thing. It would come in handy. Another thought occurred to me. 'Hang on a gasbudlikin minute,' I said. 'You're carrying this around so you *were* expecting to see me. You were planning to give it to me all along,' I crowed.

Morgan shrugged. 'So?'

'You really did come here to look for me.'

'I really didn't.'

I pointed to the shell. 'This proves otherwise.'

Irritated, he ran a hand through his hair. 'Let's just say that I had the feeling I'd bump into you again before too long. I didn't come here with any expectation of finding you.'

'Yeah, yeah. You keep telling yourself that.'

He tutted.

I smiled. 'For what it's worth,' I murmured, 'I'm glad you're here. And I'm grateful for the shell.'

For the first time Morgan seemed unable to meet my eyes. 'You're welcome.'

'Now I can booty call you whenever I want,' I beamed.

Morgan's gaze flashed to mine. 'That's not why I've given it to you.'

'Methinks the gentleman doth protest too much,' I whispered. I breathed in his heady masculine scent. Mmmm. As if agreeing with me, the building around us creaked. I shook myself; we were here for a reason and it wasn't to have mind-blowing, no-holds-barred sex. Unfortunately.

'Anyway,' I prodded, getting back to our earlier conversation, 'what did you mean? What might work?'

Morgan took a moment to answer. Apparently I wasn't the only one who'd been using their imagination for things other than arson investigations. He licked his lips. 'Along with slowing down time, we can also make use of magic to reveal what used to be.' At my look, he explained hastily, 'I can't bring back your memory or reveal who you used to be inside.' He tapped his temple. 'The sort of magic I'm talking about affects only surface appearances. The complexity of the mind is a completely different thing. Affecting the biology of living things, rather than just their appearance, is far too complex for even the most adept faery.' He waved a hand around. 'But as far as this place is concerned, I can hinge onto the undamaged spots and use them to create an image – a reality-based glamour, if you will – of what once was.'

'That's all as clear as mud,' I said cheerfully. 'This faery shit is complicated.'

Morgan laughed. 'Yes, I suppose it is.' He shot me a look and jerked his thumb at my head. 'Either that or your wheel is still spinning even though the hamster is dead.'

I gasped. 'I'm really jealous of people who don't know you, Morgan.'

His grin broadened and he blew me a kiss. I stuck my tongue out at him but my insides were doing a happy cha-cha-cha. If we could hang around here for the rest of the year and do nothing more than throw insults at each other, my life would be perfect. Would that it could be so.

Morgan fixed his eyes on the cabinet in the corner, his pupils narrowing into pinpricks as he focused. 'Watch,' he murmured.

He extended his arms, his thumbs lightly touching his middle fingers. It seemed as if he were drawing power from the very air around him. I could almost hear the buzz.

Our surroundings started to flicker and blur. I blinked to clear my vision and, a moment later, not only had the cabinet repaired itself but the walls shimmered with green-and-gold wallpaper. What had been bare scorched floorboards beneath my feet were now strips of burnished mahogany, complete with a carpet runner in rich red.

I gazed around, my mouth hanging open. 'This is amazing.' I stepped forward to touch an oil painting and marvel at its texture but, as I did so, my foot went straight through the floor. There was a tremendous sound of splintering wood.

Morgan leapt forward, grabbing my arm and hauling me upwards. 'Careful,' he warned. 'It's only an image of what was. This entire building is still unsafe.'

I could feel his heartbeat thrum next to mine. For the briefest of seconds, I enjoyed the sensation of being pressed against him then I pulled away. 'Let's see what there is to see.'

Taking more care, I tiptoed gingerly into the nearest room. It appeared to be some kind of study area. There was an antique desk and numerous books. The far wall remained untouched by Morgan's magic so, aping his moves, I spread out my arms and connected my thumbs to my fingers just as he had. Disappointingly, nothing happened although I did feel a brief tug of magic. Discarding his actions I tried my own, flicking both middle fingers up at the wall and grimacing. Just as Morgan had managed it out in the hallway, I managed it here. The burnt wall repaired itself, re-forming back into its former glory. I beamed. Go the Madhatter.

'I did it!' I crowed.

'Well done,' Morgan murmured. He cocked his head and frowned. 'That's not right.'

I put my hands on my hips. 'My magic is just as good as your magic.'

'I'm not denigrating your skills, Maddy. I mean that something's not right about the wall.' He glanced at me. 'Remove the spell for a minute.'

He was just jealous, I decided, but I did as he asked and flicked my fingers back at the wall. The glamour vanished, leaving the depressing black flakes of plaster and charred timber frame instead.

'There,' Morgan murmured. He pointed. 'You see this?'

I squinted. 'It's a hole. Half this building is a hole.' I

looked harder. Hang on a minute. Without waiting for Morgan to give the word, I turned the spell back on again. A painting, a square painting, had covered the hole. I edged up and poked my finger at it before removing the glamour again. Huh. Snail Boy had sharp eyes.

'Something was here,' I said. 'Built into the wall itself.'

Morgan nodded grimly. 'What better way to hide a theft than to burn the building to the ground? It was probably a safe of some sort. Whoever destroyed Chen's home took the time to remove his safe first. Maybe they even used the fire to dislodge the safe from the wall. Either way, this is important. I'd have said the sphere would have been kept here, except the building didn't burn down until two nights ago. Where was Rubus then?'

I shrugged helplessly. 'I don't know. Until today, I've been locked up in a room.'

Anger sparked in Morgan's eyes. 'Rubus is afraid of you and what you're capable of.'

'Or he just doesn't trust me.' That was more likely. Another thought struck me. 'Or he needed me out of the way because he had things to do – like come here and burn the place to the ground.'

'And steal Chen the Dragon's safe,' Morgan agreed. 'You need to get back to Rubus. And you need to find out if he has the safe and what's inside it. We've saved the sphere, Maddy, but what if there are more objects like it?'

My mouth was dry. Gasbudlikins. This could be very, very bad. I still glanced at Morgan, though, and murmured, '*Now* you're glad that I didn't run away from Rubus, aren't you?'

He tutted but didn't otherwise respond.

'Score one to the Madhatter!'

'You're a bad winner,' he told me.

'And you're a sore loser.'

We stared at each other for a moment. Morgan's eyes dropped to my lips and I couldn't stop my tongue from darting out to wet them.

There was a loud crash from somewhere over our heads and we both jumped.

'We should get out of here before the building collapses,' he whispered.

I nodded in agreement and turned to walk away. I knew without glancing back that Morgan was watching my arse. As he should.

Chapter Five

Evil Madrona, I told myself, as I strode back into Rubus's rabbit warren of a place. Evil Madrona, not Superhero Madrona.

'Hey, Madrona,' Lunaria called out.

'Evil Madrona,' I snapped back, without thinking.

She blinked. 'Uh…'

Gasbudlikins. 'I'm trying out new nicknames,' I said. 'To be honest, I like the Madhatter but I'm not sure that Rubus is a fan.'

'No,' she agreed. 'And it's important to keep him happy.' She said this last part with a completely straight face, as if she wholeheartedly believed it. I did too – but I suspected that was for entirely different reasons.

'Where is our self-styled king?' I enquired.

'In his room,' she told me. 'Down the corridor, last door on the left.'

'Thanks.' I suddenly remembered who I was supposed to be and gave her a critical look up and down. 'Are you wearing *that*?'

Lunaria blinked, her skin paling. 'What's wrong with it?'

I shrugged. 'Nothing. Don't mind me.' I smiled prettily. 'It's perfectly … nice.'

Lunaria's fingers twitched at the fabric of her rose-sprigged dress. She looked utterly crestfallen. Unfortunately, my bid to be mean and nasty also filled me with an irritating wave of guilt. 'We should go shopping,' I told her. 'The clothes I've been given, and which I presume my old self rather liked, are nothing more than "nice" too. We work for Rubus. We should dress like we do.'

Lunaria's eyes suddenly shone. 'That'd be brilliant.'

'I wouldn't go that far,' I said. 'Let me talk to Rubus first then I'll come find you. Okay?'

She nodded vigorously. 'Okay, yes. Thank you, Mads! You're amazing.'

I wrinkled my nose as I walked away. While it was a good idea to keep Fey like Lunaria on my side so that I could hear the gossip, I wasn't sure that becoming bosom buddies with his minions would encourage Rubus to trust me. But Lunaria had looked so hurt…

'Evil Madrona,' I muttered again under my breath. If I couldn't convince myself that I was evil, I wasn't sure I'd convince anyone else. I'd have to try harder. I considered punching the wall next to me for no other reason than because I was the Madhatter but decided I liked the skin on my knuckles where it was.

Hmmm.

A stocky-looking Fey who I vaguely recognised was standing outside Rubus's bedroom. His expression didn't change when I approached but I noticed that his chest expanded slightly, puffing out as if he were trying to make himself look larger and more imposing than he really was. I paid him no attention and moved towards the door handle. I'd barely touched it when he placed his hand on my arm.

'Boss in't be disturbed.'

In't? What kind of word was that supposed to be? 'The boss is not to be disturbed, you mean.'

He gazed at me unblinkingly. 'Thass what I said.'

I didn't have the time, the patience or the vaguest inclination to continue this conversation. As I shook off his hand and sniffed, the Fey wasted no time in thrusting out his arm to bar my approach. This was one of those occasions when I could wholeheartedly agree with Rubus that the truce was a pain in the proverbial arse. If it didn't exist, I could have beat this arsebadger to the ground or maybe even killed him with my thumbs if I felt like it. Then he'd be sorry. Unfortunately the truce prevented violence of any sort, so the only thing I could do was resort to my other wiles.

I darted out my tongue and slowly licked my lips then I widened my eyes slightly. I did everything apart from grab my breasts and plump them up in front of the Fey's face. 'I'm sure he'd like to see me,' I purred.

He didn't even react. 'No dice.'

I threw up my hands. 'Oh, come on!'

He shook his head. 'Nope.'

'It's important.'

'Don' care.'

I gritted my teeth. Why was this so difficult? 'Rubus!' I bellowed. 'I need to see you!'

Crickets, I cursed to myself. 'I saw my soap-star friend! She's agreed to meet with you!' I called.

I waited a beat. Still nothing. Gasbudlikins. I had no choice but to resort to the truth. What a shambles. 'I have information about Chen too!'

There was still no sound and Rubus's door remained tightly closed. A glimmer of a smile played around the Fey bouncer's lips. I pushed myself onto my tiptoes so that my eyes were level with his. 'You have no idea who you're dealing with,' I hissed.

'I heard you got umnesia. You don' know who you're dealing with either. You don' even know who you are.'

Touché. 'It's amnesia, you tool.'

He shrugged. 'Whatever.'

I reached into my pocket. 'Do you know what I have in here?'

'No.'

'Pixie dust,' I told him. 'Delicious, homesickness-reducing pixie dust. Have you ever had any?'

For the first time he looked uncomfortable. 'No.'

'It's fabulous.' I gently brushed my fingertips against the centre of his chest. 'It takes away the ache, the one that's always there. It'll make you feel better.'

He stiffened. 'I like the ache. It reminds me that what Rubus is doing is helping us all. He'll take us back to Mag Mell. He'll lead the way.' His lip curled. 'Your dust shit is just temporary.'

There was a feverish light in his eyes. Yeah, okay. I was beginning to understand why so many Fey were around here, hanging off Rubus. It wasn't just about pixie dust; the blasted man was like a cult leader who was promising guaranteed entry to heaven.

That didn't mean I was going to give up. From what Morgan had suggested, I'd been an outstandingly effective drug dealer. I wasn't going to let all that slip away. 'So you don't want a free sample?'

'No.'

I nodded. 'Okay. That just means there's more for the others. I'm impressed that you're resisting, especially when I know that Rubus likes pixie dust because it makes his trusted people like you feel just that tiny bit better. He knows it's only a temporary solution but he's doing his best to help us out. If you'd rather not do as he suggests, however…' My voice trailed off.

There was a flicker of doubt in the Fey's expression. It was faint but it was definitely there. I was finally getting somewhere. Trying not to let my triumph show on my face, I smiled softly at him. Then the door opened.

'You can come in,' Rubus said.

'Just a minute,' I told him. 'I'm getting better acquainted with your bodyguard here.'

Rubus rolled his eyes, reached out and pulled me in,

closing the door behind him.

'Hey!' I protested. 'I was just about to make a sale!'

'Do you have any dust on you?'

I frowned. 'No, but—'

'Do you realise that Amellus is already loyal? I don't need my trusted soldiers to become drug addicts, Madrona.'

'Yeah, but…'

Rubus smiled. 'You're still in there,' he said quietly. 'You might not remember but you're still my Madrona. You were quite prepared to forget why you'd come here because you wanted to sell Amellus some dust. We're so similar, you and I.' His eyes gleamed. 'Win at all costs. Right?'

Oh. It occurred to me that he had a point. I twitched uncomfortably. 'It's not like that,' I said in stubborn denial. 'I was just trying to find my place here, that's all. I know who I used to be – sort of – and I'm trying to get that back.'

Rubus raised a questioning eyebrow. Perhaps I was protesting too much.

'Well,' I said, 'it's not like I belong with Morgan, is it? He's all angelic and good and self-righteous. And I don't want to be on my own. It's boring. And,' I brushed my own fingers against my heart, 'it hurts.' I sniffed loudly. 'So this must be where I'm supposed to be. But you don't trust me and I don't seem to have any friends. I just want to find something I'm good at. Is that so bad?'

'I wasn't criticising you, far from it. In fact, you have no idea how happy this makes me.' He glanced behind, his eyes drifting towards his unmade bed. Uh-oh.

I looked away hastily before I was forced to register the open invitation on his face. 'Anyway,' I said, in my best brisk and business-like tone and without even pausing for breath, 'I do need to talk to you. First of all,

I've been contact with my soap-star friend. She will meet you for dinner tomorrow night. I told her that you're a perfect gentleman and that she shouldn't worry about being with you. I even told her she could leave her bodyguard at home.'

'You're still not prepared to tell me who she is?' he enquired, stepping back. I started to relax again.

'I signed an NDA. I told you.'

'That's a human thing,' he dismissed. 'Who really cares about some daft piece of paper?'

'She does. If you want to meet her, we need to do things her way,' I said. 'I can't control her. Besides,' I added, raising my shoulders, 'it'll be a fun surprise.'

'Much as I know you like to shock, I'm not a fan of surprises,' Rubus told me.

I snorted. 'Try being me. I've been nothing but surprised since I woke up last week.'

'Poor, poor Madrona.'

I couldn't tell whether he was being sardonic. 'It's really hard.'

'It must be.' He gazed at me assessingly for a moment. 'You shouted something about Chen too.'

So I did. I tilted up my chin and kept my eyes focused on Rubus's face. I needed to absorb every twitch and every tell. This was important. Sticking to the truth as closely as I could, I outlined what the taxi driver had told me before moving onto the really juicy stuff. 'So I got him to drop me off at Chen's place. He was right, the whole building has been pretty much destroyed. None of the surrounding structures were damaged. I'm no arson expert but it looked deliberate to me.'

For a long moment Rubus didn't say anything; he simply stared at me, his green Fey eyes as hard as sea glass. I watched him, praying for a reaction to give me a clue about might have happened to Chen's safe or where

Rubus might have taken it.

When he did finally speak, he didn't try to hide anything. His lips pulled back over his teeth in an animalistic snarl and his muscles quivered with barely repressed tension. 'What are you doing investigating the dragon? Haven't I given you enough to do? What about my dust that you lost? I still need it back, Madrona. This amnesia business only takes you so far, you know. You're still under orders. *My* orders.'

I blinked, taken aback by his sudden, livid fury. 'I … er … I…' I had been expecting another of Rubus's inscrutable masks, not this no-holds-barred emotion. Given that a moment ago, I was sure he was ready to invite me to fall on his duvet and spread my legs, this volte-face was more than a little disturbing. And people called *me* the Madhatter. At least I was fairly consistent.

'I was taking the initiative,' I said. 'The information about Chen fell into my lap. It was no trouble to swing by there and see his place for myself.'

'Don't take the initiative. Don't think. Just do what the hell I tell you to do.' He glared at me. 'Stay away from anything to do with Chen or Charrie's disappearance or my fucking sphere.' He jabbed his finger at me. 'Those are my concern, not yours. Understood?'

'Well, yes, but—'

'Good,' he growled. 'Now get out.'

I was tempted to stand my ground and argue but this wasn't Morgan. The anger ripping through Rubus's body, and which I could swear was making him shake, was genuinely scary. He couldn't hurt me – the truce saw to that – but that didn't mean he wasn't uber-intimidating.

My delay in reacting only served to increase his anger. 'If you think this is one of those times when you can snap out a silly insult, Madrona, you are severely underestimating the situation.'

'I wasn't—'

'Get the fuck out!' he roared.

I was smart enough to do as he asked. Wheeling round, I skedaddled out of his room. As soon as the door closed behind me, there was a screeching roar and the sound of breaking glass. Rubus was very, very annoyed.

That answered one question then. He didn't know about the fire – and he didn't know about Chen's missing safe, either.

***

It was tempting to hang around and see what happened next. Which minion did Rubus trust enough to talk to? Where would he go now? But loitering outside his room, especially with the annoyingly stoic Fey guard outside, would only draw further attention to myself. If I skipped off with Lunaria for the shopping expedition I'd promised, I'd appear more trustworthy. Sneaky Madrona understood not to over-cook her goose. A good spy might lurk and listen; a great spy would appear blithely unconcerned, stay under the radar and look for clues only when it was absolutely safe to do so. And anyway, I really needed some better clothes.

I caught up with Lunaria out towards the front. She was deep in conversation with another Fey. As I approached, she passed him a memory stick. He grunted his thanks and strode away before I could reach the pair of them.

'Hey,' I said. 'Sharing your illegally downloaded porn collection with another person isn't a great idea, you know. At least when it's a guy. Your memory stick will come back all sticky.'

Rather than smile, Lunaria looked flustered. She

smoothed down her hair with one hand. 'That? That wasn't porn. It was just some…' she hesitated, as if trying to think of the most plausible lie ' …photos,' she finished with an awkward grimace.

'Sexy photos?'

She shook her head, alarmed. 'No!'

'Kinky photos?'

'Madrona, stop it!'

I opened my eyes wide in mock horror. 'It's not water sports, is it? And I'm not talking about surfing. I mean the sort of water sports where your partner—'

'Madrona! Enough!'

I held up my hands. 'Okay.' I grinned wickedly. 'I submit.'

Lunaria rolled her eyes. 'You're incorrigible.'

My grin widened. 'I know.' I looked her up and down. The flowery dress I'd insulted earlier had been replaced with a boring jeans and T-shirt uniform. It was depressingly identical to my own outfit. 'Come on,' I said. 'Rubus is in a foul mood and I don't feel like I've had any fun for ages.' I pursed my lips. 'I can't ever remember having *real* fun. Isn't that depressing? I definitely need some retail therapy.'

She clapped her hands. 'Great! I was thinking we could hit the big department store out on the high street near the library. There are all sorts of designer labels there.'

'Mmmhmm.' I took her arm. 'Let's walk. Maybe we'll find a few boutiques along the way.'

'I literally can't wait.'

My smile vanished. 'You literally *can* wait. You literally have to wait.'

Lunaria stared at me. 'It's just a figure of speech.'

I bit back my retort. Evil Madrona did not have to mean Pedantic Grammar Bitch Madrona. Maybe I'd indulge that side of myself later, though.

Chapter Six

We tottered happily down the pavement together. Lunaria was a good foot taller than me so it was easy to block her constant stream of inane chatter by keeping my head angled down. I amused myself by stoutly refusing to alter my path for other pedestrians. It was rather fun playing chicken with everyone else. At one point I almost collided with some metrosexual guy with a man bun. He scowled at me when he was forced to sidestep to avoid smacking into me. I beamed. *My* pavement.

We'd just reached the first bank of shops when Lunaria delved into her pocket and drew out a packet of cigarettes. She offered me one, looking surprised when I declined. 'It's so terribly passé for villains to smoke these days,' I said, pretending I knew what in gasbudlikin hell I was talking about. 'I've quit.'

'Good for you,' she told me. 'But we're not villains. We're the good guys. We're working to bring everyone home – or at least we're working to help Rubus bring everyone home.'

I resisted the urge to reach up and throttle her. She was too tall for my hands to reach anyway. 'Aw,' I said instead, pointing across the street at a woman holding a toddler's hand. 'Isn't that kid cute?'

She followed my gaze. 'Yeah,' she said unconvincingly.

'You agree with me?' I gave her a surprised look. 'It's barely knee height and it's probably already a terror. Snot is dripping from its nose. I can smell its nappy from here!'

'The kid's mother wouldn't thank you for calling her

child "it",' Lunaria murmured.

'At least when Rubus brings us all home to Mag Mell, there won't be any more kids like that. That woman will finally be free of all her obligations and responsibilities.' I gave them both a critical eye. 'If she survives.'

Lunaria frowned. 'What are you talking about?'

'You know.' I pointed towards them. 'When Rubus gets back the sphere and uses it to force open the borders to Mag Mell so we can get home, this entire demesne will be flooded with magic. I've had it all explained to me. Most humans won't survive. This place isn't meant for magic.' I leaned in towards her. 'If they're not good enough for the magic, then they're not good enough to live. Just like that brat over there.'

Her brow furrowed slightly. 'Sure,' she said. 'You're right.' She sounded unconvinced and I allowed myself a tiny smile. If I couldn't bulldoze my villainous way into making faeries like Lunaria see that what Rubus was doing was wrong, I'd have be more subtle. Judging by the expression on Lunaria's face, it was already working.

'Look!'

Lunaria jumped, seemingly reluctant to see what had caught my eye this time. 'What?'

'That's the shop we need!' I burbled. I took off across the street, ignoring the car bearing down on me and the screeching of a horn as I crossed. I didn't check to see if the Fey was following me. I knew she would be.

The shop in question had covered windows with nothing on display. I smiled cheerily and entered. The dim interior was exactly as I'd hoped – pink and red lights, tacky plastic sex toys and a range of interesting whips.

'Madrona,' Lunaria whispered at my back. 'This isn't a clothes shop.'

'I know. Isn't it great?' I ignored the greasy-haired man with a twinkle in his eye at the counter and headed for the clothes rail in the corner. 'This,' I declared, alighting upon a black leather corset and pulling it out. 'This is what I want.' I glanced at the shop assistant. 'Do you have any matching trousers?' I asked.

'Crotchless?'

I tapped my mouth as if considering. 'Hmm. Probably not a good idea.'

He pointed to another rail. Lunaria stood in the middle of the shop, as if afraid to touch anything. I smirked. 'Come on, Loony,' I murmured. 'I reckon there's plenty in here that'll fit you. And that Rubus will appreciate.'

That last part did the trick. While I ambled into the pungent dressing room to try on my outfit, Lunaria started searching for something. Some shiny red PVC would do wonders for her complexion.

***

We spent far longer in the sex shop than should have been necessary. That wasn't because we were perusing all that was on offer with keen buyers' eyes but because it took so long to get into the clothes. I tried not to think about how many other people had tried on this same pair of tight leather trousers and decided that, now I was wearing them, I was going to stick with them. The corset was particularly pleasing. If I were a breast man, I'd definitely be appreciative of the plumped flesh I was currently displaying. I wondered which anatomical part Morgan favoured.

Lunaria, whose outfit was very similar to mine, walked out of the shop with a bow-legged gait like she'd just spent three weeks riding a horse across a dusty,

American state. She plucked at the leather that stretched tautly across her thighs and grimaced. 'It's quite itchy, isn't it?'

'I rather like the feel of it against my skin,' I said, enjoying the gaping mouths of the pedestrians, both male and female, who passed us. I was hoping for some irritating human male who took the outfit as an invitation to wolf whistle – or worse. I had a lot of pent-up aggression after dealing with Rubus and I could do with dragging someone into an alley and beating them up.

I frowned down at my arms. I possessed weak muscles and hadn't had time to pump some iron in a gym or learn a swanky martial art. Perhaps I could glamour myself some fabulous new biceps – though I'd have to be careful not to overdo it. I didn't want to ruin my new dominatrix look.

'What are you doing, Madrona?' Lunaria asked, glancing at my screwed-up face.

'Trying to glamour myself some muscles,' I said. I flexed. 'Do these look bigger to you?'

She laughed. 'You're funny.'

Was I? I frowned at her. She just smirked back.

I was about to ask her to explain when something odd caught my peripheral vision. I half turned, my gaze catching on a flutter of purple fabric that disappeared behind one of the rooftops opposite. That was … interesting. It wasn't windy enough for it to be a kite or a piece of loose rubbish caught by a breeze. I maintained my pace and kept my head pointed forward but I was fully alert for further signs.

'Do you really think Rubus will like my outfit?' Lunaria asked, oblivious.

'He'll love it.' I had no idea why she believed I had insights into Rubus's mind. I did have amnesia, after all. Even if my old self had been close enough to him to know what his penchants were, for all I knew now he had a kink for frilly waitress uniforms. If I were to take a guess, I reckoned that he probably couldn't give a shit what anyone else wore. The man was far too self-obsessed.

There was another flicker of movement over the rooftop and this time it wasn't a piece of flapping fabric; I could have sworn it was actually a face, peering round a chimney at us. We were being followed but by what – or by whom – I had no idea. Maybe this was someone related to Morgan. Either way, I had to ditch Lunaria and find out.

'You know what?' I said. 'You should go ahead. If we stroll into the hideout together, the attention will be on me because I look so hot in this outfit. You want Rubus to notice *you*. If you go in first, and I give you a bit of time to find him, he'll focus all his interest on you.'

Her eyes shone. 'Do you really think he'll be interested?'

I pointed at her. 'Look at you! If he's not, then the man's a fool!' I gave her a little nudge. 'Go on. I'll wait here for about twenty minutes then head in. You can tell the others that I stopped to buy some shoes or something.' I shrugged. 'Or whatever.'

Lunaria leaned over and kissed my cheek. 'You are the best friend ever.'

'You can thank me later,' I said drily. 'Go on.'

Wreathed in smiles, she darted ahead. I watched her go, waiting until she was out of sight before I swung round. Alrighty, Mr Tail. Where are you now? I held my breath. A moment later there was a loud squawk and several birds flew up into the air. I couldn't see any sign of a person but I now knew where they were hiding. With my shoulders pulled back, I marched across the street.

I gazed upwards. From this angle, I couldn't see a

damned thing. In an alternate universe maybe I could have managed to shimmy up the drainpipe then sprint catlike across the rooftops to catch the fellow – but it seemed highly unlikely in this outfit. I decided that improvisation was the only way to go.

Glancing around, I spotted a litter bin nearby. I reached inside, hoping for something like a dog-poo bag filled to the brim. The first thing my fingers grabbed was a fizzy-drink can. Well, at least it would be aerodynamic.

Rather than launching it directly at the spot where I assumed my tracker was cowering, I aimed slightly for the left; after all, this could be a friend rather than a foe. I released my makeshift missile, sending it upwards. Unfortunately, despite my best efforts, my aim was off. Instead of smacking into the tiles next to the chimney, the can bounced off a dirty satellite dish and rolled back down, landing next to me and spraying sticky juice all over my new leather trousers.

I cursed to myself as I bent over to wipe them down. As I did so, I heard a muffled yelp followed by a thud. By the sounds of things, Mr Tail had fallen off the roof of his own accord. Abandoning cleaning my trousers, I straightened up and glanced round. He must have landed on the other side of the buildings.

I couldn't waste any more time. I sprinted down the pavement, rounding the first bend so I could go round the back of the terraced row of shops. This street was quieter and I couldn't see anyone. I ran as fast as I could – and almost missed him. It was the clatter of a dustbin lid that eventually gave him away. Whoever he was, he was a clumsy arsebadger.

I wheeled round, my eyes scanning the area. There, crouching down with the offending bin lid held in front of his body as if it were a glorious shield, was a small man of about seventy years old.

I stalked over until I was standing in front of him. I put my hands on my hips. 'Well, well, well,' I drawled. 'What do we have here?'

He pulled the dustbin lid up a bit higher, concealing his face.

'You know,' I said, 'just because you can't see me doesn't mean I can't see you.'

He let out a petrified squeak. A moment later, he threw the lid on the ground and darted off in the opposite direction.

For an old guy, he was a speedy bugger. Mouth open, I watched him for a second before launching myself after him. My delay meant that he almost managed to disappear after he turned right at the end of the road. I pumped my arms and legs; no way was I going to let an arsebadger of a pensioner beat me in a race.

He veered in and out of the wandering pedestrians. At first I thought he was running randomly, panic making him head any which way. When I caught sight of the bus stop ahead – and the waiting bus – I realised he was cannier than I'd expected and he had a plan. He was going to jump on the bus to get away from me. Well, I was wise to him. Nobody escaped the Madhatter.

I put on an extra spurt of speed. He was almost at the bus – but so was I. Even if he managed to clamber aboard, he wouldn't have the time to explain to the driver that a crazed, leather-bound, S&M-inclined woman was after him before I joined him and yanked him off again.

Twenty metres. Nineteen. Eighteen. A woman with a pram appeared out of nowhere and I screamed at her to get out of my way. She froze. Cursing, I leapt round her. Mr Tail was at the bus. Gasbudlikins.

I threw myself forward, realising too late that he'd not been aiming for the double decker after all. Right in front of it – and concealed by its large shape – was a taxi rank. As I ran past the front of the bus, the old man slammed the door of the nearest taxi and it took off.

Yelling in frustration, I jumped into the next taxi. 'Follow that cab!'

The taxi driver slowly put down his newspaper with its half-finished crossword. 'Pardon?' Then he turned and looked at me, tired eyes taking in my outfit. 'Nice clothes!'

'Follow that fucking taxi!' I screeched.

The driver's amusement at my clothing vanished. 'You're not James Bond. We're in Manchester, not Monaco. Get out.'

Belatedly it occurred to me that screaming an order might be my best move. The taxi driver pointed at the door. I looked over his shoulder and out of the front window. The old man had already disappeared.

I ground my teeth. The only good thing about any of this was that no one had been around to witness my humiliation. It wasn't worth arguing with the driver, not any longer, so I did as he asked and stumbled out.

That was when I caught sight of Artemesia, standing on the other side of the busy road, laughing.

Chapter Seven

We sat down at a table towards the back of the coffee shop, well away from the windows in case any Fey loyal to Rubus might pass by. I ordered a black coffee, figuring that it was a beverage that would match my dark, twisted soul. However, as soon as Artemesia's hot chocolate with marshmallows, cream and sprinkles arrived, I immediately regretted my choice. The moment she got up to use the loo, I swapped the drinks around. I managed three gulps of cocoa goodness before she came back. She gave me enough of a glare to compel me to swap them back. Ho-hum.

'I've not found anything to restore your memory,' she told me. 'I have a few ideas but nothing definite. You're welcome to experiment with what I've come up with so far but I should warn you that there will be side-effects.'

She said this last part so casually that I could only assume the side-effects were horrific. 'Such as?' I asked, wanting to be sure.

'Definitely paralysis. Possibly loss of hearing.' She smirked. 'And perhaps the added bonus of extra facial hair.'

Lovely. 'I'll pass, thanks.'

She shrugged. 'Your choice.'

I toyed with my teaspoon. 'I met Carduus, your uncle.'

Artemesia went very still.

'He ran some tests on me. I also told him and Rubus where your shed was.'

She didn't blink. 'I expected as much.'

'I only told them because I knew you didn't trust me and that you'd already have moved on,' I said, earnestly.

'So what you're saying is that you betrayed my trust because I didn't trust you?'

I wrinkled my nose. 'Uh, sort of. It was a calculated risk.'

Artemesia's gaze was steady. 'A calculated risk is fine when you're the one taking that risk. You were risking my life, not your own.'

On that point, I wasn't going to back down. 'If I can get Rubus to trust me, it'll be worth it.'

She shook her head. 'He's never going to trust you fully. He never trusted the old you fully. He's certainly not going to trust the "new" you.'

I took a sip of my coffee. It seemed that no one fully trusted me. To be honest, I didn't fully trust myself. But this was now – what about back then?

I squinted. I needed more information. 'What do you mean he never trusted the old me? He called me "my Madrona". Well, *his* Madrona.' I scrunched up my face. 'You know what I mean.'

She sighed. 'He wants to own you. He probably *believes* he owns you. A lion keeper in a zoo probably thinks the same about his lion. But that doesn't mean the keeper would fully trust a wild animal.'

I preferred the straightforward lion analogy to the wild animal one. 'I certainly feel like I'm caged up,' I admitted. 'Even if Rubus is no longer locking me in my room.'

Artemesia grimaced. 'Locking you up?'

I smirked. 'I'm the Queen of the Jungle. He's scared of me.'

'Except he's the emperor,' she pointed out grimly. 'Don't mistake fear for wariness. Or cunning. Look, this is only the second time I've met you so I'm going on hearsay rather than solid fact.'

I nodded and waved a hand at her. 'Idle gossip goes further than most people realise. I understand its usefulness. Go on.'

'Everyone was surprised when you ran to Rubus. We all knew about his rivalry with Morgan. Most Fey put it down to typical sibling rivalry – that kind of behaviour is hardly unique. We also all knew that Rubus had been angling after you for years. You were known for being quite vocal in your refusals.'

I clasped my chest with both hands. 'Me? Vocal? I can't believe it.'

Artemesia smiled. 'Anyway, one minute you were all googly-eyed with Morgan and there was talk of a wedding.'

I blinked. 'Really?'

'It was a big deal. Everyone wanted to know who was special enough to get an invitation. It's not easy for us being here, you know. Anything that can take our minds off Mag Mell and home is a good thing.'

'Like pixie dust,' I agreed.

She tutted. '*Not* like pixie dust. That's different. It's an addictive drug that you use to get people to do whatever you want. A wedding is happy and fun.'

'Drugs are happy and fun.' I paused. 'Until they're soul-destroying and family-wrecking and mind-eating and body-killing. Then again, I've heard that about marriage too.'

'Indeed.' Artemesia raised her eyebrows and watched me for a moment without speaking. No wonder she was an apothecary-scientist type of faery; I felt like a bug under a microscope every time she looked at me. 'Word is that you popped the question. You got down on one knee and Morgan agreed.'

My mouth felt suddenly dry. 'Oh.'

'The next minute you'd abandoned him and were shacking up with Rubus.' She narrowed her eyes. 'It all happened very quickly.'

I couldn't fathom it. In certain lights, it could be argued that Rubus was the better looking of the two. Plus, while Morgan was no timid mouse, Rubus did appear more self-assured. Ostensibly, he also had greater power because more Fey seemed to trail round after him – and not all of them were dust addicts. But Morgan was kind. He had a way of looking at you as if you were the only person in the world. Every faery had green eyes but Morgan's contained flecks of warmth. He would risk his life for a stranger for no other reason than because it was right thing to do. He would kiss me in a hard and possessive way, thrusting my body up against a wall, one hand in my hair while the other slid down my body, ripping off my clothes, cupping my breasts, his skin hot against mine, his cock pressing…

'You're turning red,' Artemesia commented.

I coughed. 'Everything you've said suggests to me that Rubus would be *more* inclined to trust me. If I abandoned his brother for him, surely I'd deserve to be in the inner circle.'

She shrugged. 'All I'm saying is what I heard. Rubus apparently kept you on a very short leash. He frequently had people checking up on you. You were his best pixie-dust dealer but he still shut you out of meetings and still turned up at odd moments to make sure you were doing what you were supposed to be doing.'

I scratched my head. Hmmm. 'This has to be because I was a spy infiltrating Rubus's ranks for the well-being of the world and he already had suspicions about my true nature.'

'So what's different now?'

I grinned at her. 'Now I'm a *super* spy.'

Artemesia rolled her eyes. 'Whatever. It didn't look like you were doing a great job of spying when I saw you out on the street. You were flapping your arms and running after an old man.'

'An old man with unbelievable sprinting prowess who'd been crawling around the Manchester rooftops in order to follow me.'

'See? He's probably another one of Rubus's lot.'

'No.' I shook my head. 'Something about this guy was different.'

'Green eyes?'

'I didn't get close enough to see.' I gnawed my bottom lip. 'Keep looking for that amnesia cure,' I told her. 'I'll keep working on Rubus. He's planning something, I can tell.'

'I'm not your servant.'

I stood up and looked at her assessingly. 'Come on, Arty,' I purred. 'This is fun, isn't it? Every good spy has a team of crackheads behind her.'

She frowned. 'Do you mean crackpots?'

I grinned. 'If the shoe fits…'

'The only crackpot around here is you,' Artemesia muttered. 'And I'm not on your team. I wouldn't trust you if you were the last faery in this demesne. I certainly wouldn't work for you.'

I supposed I couldn't blame her for that. She'd come around, though. I curtsied in her direction and left. After all, I still had a lot of super-spy work to do.

***

Rubus's lair was eerily deserted when I returned. I'd half expected him to be stomping around the corridors and bellowing but there were only a few harried Fey wandering around, each apparently with their own jobs and tasks to complete.

Rubus had instructed me to locate the pixie dust I'd apparently lost and I supposed I could venture out again and at least pretend to look for it. Maybe I'd dumped it near the golf course where I'd woken up; it wouldn't hurt to head back there to look for the darned stuff. I didn't actually want to find it, though. Once I had it back in my possession, Rubus would make me go out and sell it not to make money but to create an even larger army of thralled faeries. I'd delay doing that for as long as I possibly could.

Taking advantage of the lack of people, I ambled around and poked into corners. I was fairly circumspect; I didn't try to break into Rubus's bedroom or throne room. I avoided the laboratory and anywhere that might appear important. It was possible that this quiet time had been engineered as another test to catch me out so all I did was wander from room to room and get a good idea of my surroundings so I could map out the place in my head. In any case, the Fey hangers-on who stayed here were remarkably thrifty and possessed very few belongings. You'd think this was a priests' hangout rather than a villains'. It was all terribly dull.

In one of the larger rooms there were a few squashed sofas and a battered television. I sat down and tried to find the remote control so I could watch the local news and see if there was more information about the fire at Chen's place.

I was just getting comfortable when there was a scratching at the door. I glanced over just as a note was pushed underneath it. I sprang up, grabbed the note and pulled open the door. There wasn't a soul to be seen.

Puzzled, I unfolded the paper. In the same handwriting as the sycamore papers was a single sentence. *L is looking for video evidence.* Well, that made zero sense. Video evidence of what?

The only L I could think of was Lunaria. I stared at the piece of paper before remembering the memory stick I'd seen her with earlier in the day. I hadn't been all that interested at the time, despite my jokes about porn, but perhaps I should have paid more attention.

The joy of skulduggery aside, I had the feeling that I'd done enough today to encourage my friendship with her and invite her confidence. Who wouldn't want to be pals with me? I'd given her fashion advice; I'd even stepped back to give her the chance to impress Rubus all on her own. I was virtually a selfless martyr and she was lucky to know me. Hadn't she said 'best friends forever' when we said goodbye? Something nauseatingly ridiculous like that. I reckoned I could prevail upon her to spill the beans. With that thought in mind, I ripped the note into tiny pieces and discarded them before heading off in search of her beanpole figure.

Given how quiet it was, I wasn't sure she was here but I found her without too much trouble. She was in the kitchen with a gigantic tub of ice cream on her lap and a morose expression on her face. 'Looney Tunes!' I beamed.

Lunaria barely even glanced up. She huffed, then delved into the tub again for another heaped spoonful. Ah. 'Did Rubus not like your new look?'

She shoved the spoon into her mouth and sniffed. 'Said he was busy. Didn't even remark on it.' She gestured down at herself. 'I'm wearing red leather and he couldn't even be bothered to comment.'

I almost clapped my hands in delight. The scorned woman – what a perfect bonding opportunity. 'What an arsebadgering bastard,' I said.

'He's not a bastard, he's wonderful. It's me who's the problem.' She sniffed. 'If I looked like you, he'd notice me. If Morgan wanted me too, then Rubus'd notice me.'

My heart leapt. 'Morgan wants me? How do you know?'

Lunaria's brow furrowed. Oh yes. This conversation wasn't supposed to be about me. 'I mean,' I said, 'fuck off.'

'Wh – what?'

I threw my hands up into the air. 'You heard me. Fuck. Off. You can't say that about yourself. First of all, you're gorgeous. Second of all, this has nothing to do with me and nothing to do with appearances. It's what's inside that's important.'

Lunaria stared at me. 'You sound like a Hallmark card.'

'I know. It's disgusting. I just vomited in my mouth. But it's also true. Screw Rubus. If he's not going to see you for the wonderful person you are, he's not worth it.'

'This is my only chance, Madrona. Once he's saved us all and we're back in Mag Mell, he'll be a hero. He'll have women throwing themselves at him. If I don't get him now, I'll have no chance later.'

Gods save me. I raised my hand to slap her hard on the cheek but unfortunately the damned truce kicked in. The sharp pain that should have brought her to her senses flashed through me.

Lunaria looked aghast. 'You were going to hit me!'

'Not hard,' I lied. 'And only because you needed it.' I pointed at her. 'You'll have to hit yourself.'

'Huh?'

'Go on.' I mimicked the action for her. 'Slap your cheek.'

'You're crazy.'

'We all know that already. Go on,' I said sternly. 'Do it.'

Unbelievably, she did as I commanded. Her hand left a faint red imprint on her cheek. 'Ouch,' she complained.

'Do you feel better?'

'No, I just feel sore.'

'Then do it again.'

She did. This was fun. I wondered idly whether I had the power to encourage Rubus to stab himself. Probably not, but it might be fun trying.

'I'm not sure this is helping, Madrona.'

'You'd be surprised. Now, repeat after me: "I am a strong Fey woman who does not need someone like Rubus to affirm my existence".'

'I am a strong Fey woman,' she burbled, 'who does not need Rubus to affirm my existence.'

'Perfect.' I gave her a hard look. 'He doesn't appreciate you, you know. I'm sure he's got you running around all over town to do his bidding.'

'Yeah,' she said. 'He does.'

When she didn't elaborate, I prodded further. 'The things he's got you doing are probably a waste of your time. You're too intelligent to be just an errand girl.'

'Well,' she demurred, 'actually he's got me investigating…' She stopped in mid-sentence and stared at me.

'Go on.'

'No one. I'm not investigating anyone. I…' Her head swung from side to side. 'I should go. I promised Carduus I'd help him with a few bits and bobs in his laboratory.' Before I could think of a way to stop her, she fled.

Gasbudlikins. That hadn't been helpful other than to highlight the fact that she was tasked with something that I wasn't supposed to know about. I gnawed the inside of my cheek. I'd have to resort to other methods.

I headed out of the kitchen, double-checking that

Lunaria had dashed off in the opposite direction, then I made my way back upstairs to the bedroom area. I wasn't sure which room was hers but it didn't take long to work it out. I could immediately rule out the small rooms with clothes littering the floor – she was too proud and keen to please to leave her sleeping area in a mess. I hesitated in one room, wondering if the stuffed teddy bear on the narrow bed could be hers, but the perfume lingering in the air didn't register.

When I popped my head around the next door along, I knew I'd hit the jackpot. Her room could only be this one – it was the only one with a photo of Rubus beaming down from the wall. There was a faint lipsticked mark on it. I eyed it with some distaste. The shade matched Lunaria's. She really did have it bad.

Sneaking inside and closing the door behind me, I began to rummage. There had to be a clue here somewhere. I lifted up the mattress and checked the drawers in the bedside cabinet. When nothing jumped out at me, I flipped open the lid of the slim, silver laptop on the dressing table. Rubus continued to gaze down at me from the photo. I stuck my tongue out at him and opened the laptop lid.

The screen asked for a password. I inputted Rubus's name and gained access to the machine's contents on my very first attempt. Yes, I was a pure genius; either that or Lunaria was entirely too predictable. I didn't waste too much time congratulating myself; instead I opened her recent documents. Something had to be here.

The last three files that Lunaria had opened up were videos. Maybe she really was just looking at porn. I clicked on the first one, more out of prurient curiosity than anything else, but when I saw what was there I frowned.

It appeared to be CCTV footage. I glanced at the date

in the corner. September 21st. That wasn't all that long ago. An uneasy feeling drifted into my stomach.

The footage was taken at night and, as far as I could tell, it was from some sort of park. Then the angle changed and I was watching a small flag fluttering in the night breeze. With a sick feeling in my stomach, I opened up the next file. This video was of somewhere similar. I peered, noting the tall bag with the golf clubs sticking out of it that was propped against a nearby wall. I quickly opened the third one. There was no doubt now: Lunaria was retrieving footage from various golf clubs around the city – footage from the night when I'd woken up with amnesia.

I'd told Rubus that I'd found myself on a golf course but I hadn't told him which one. He was sending Lunaria out to get evidence about what I'd really been up to. Except even *I* didn't know what I'd really been up to. This didn't bode well for me.

I checked the names of each golf course. None of them were the one I'd been at but if Lunaria was visiting every course in the city and its surroundings, it was only a matter of time before she found the right one.

I cursed. If there was indeed a video of my pre-amnesia self wandering around the eighteenth hole, it was vital that I got my mitts on it before Rubus did. Because whatever else I'd been doing, and whether I'd killed Charrie or not, I'd definitely taken Chen's magical little sphere from the bogle's body. If Rubus discovered that I'd had it in my possession, even briefly, then all hell would break loose.

Chapter Eight

My first inclination was to speed out of the building and run for the hills, or at least the proverbial hills where the real golf course and scene of the crime were located. But that wouldn't be smart. I calmed my beating heart and tried to think. I had to get hold of the CCTV before Lunaria did – and I had do it without raising any suspicion.

I returned the laptop to its original position and swept a quick glance around Lunaria's room to make sure I'd left nothing out of place. Then I pressed my ear up against the door and listened. There was no sound of anyone in the corridor outside. Stepping out and shaking myself down, I hastily exited and made a beeline for my own room.

There were no handy sycamore messages, nor any sign that someone had been rummaging through my things, let alone sneaking a peek into my room to spy on me. All the same, my anonymous friend had warned to be careful and, after his second more specific message concerning Lunaria, I was more likely to trust him. Or her. But without an identity for my friendly would-be saviour, I'd have to rely solely on myself. And perhaps a couple of minions of my own.

I delved into my pocket and pulled out Morgan's shell. I could work alone or I could take advantage of my dire situation and spend more time with his green-eyed gorgeousness. There was no choice to make. I flipped the shell over in my hands, not entirely sure how the thing was supposed to work. Then I lifted it up to my mouth and shrugged.

'Ring ring!' I sang. 'Ring-ring! Ring-ring!'

Morgan's disembodied voice appeared. 'Madrona?' he asked, sounding concerned. 'What's the problem?'

'Ring-ring! Ring-ring!'

Even across the shell sound waves, I heard him sigh. 'I've picked up. What's going on? I wasn't expecting to hear from you this quickly. If this is just you playing around…'

I sobered up. As much fun as it would be to mess around with the shell, there wasn't time. I quickly outlined my unpleasant discovery – and what I planned to do about it. At least Morgan did me the favour of listening.

'How do you know Rubus hasn't already discovered the golf course in question?' he asked.

'There were only three files on Lunaria's computer and none of them was from my place. We have to strike quickly though,' I said. 'We can't afford for Rubus to realise that you have the sphere.' I paused. 'Unless you've managed to destroy it?' In that scenario, all that would happen was that my secret identity would be unmasked. I'd suffer – which of course would majorly suck arse – but at least the world would be safe. And I could breathe a sigh of relief because that was the kind of fabulously selfless person I was.

'No,' he said. He sounded pissed off. 'I've tried and Artemesia has tried but the damn thing was created by a dragon. It's been forged with magic and techniques that are unknown to us. If we knew another dragon, we could quiz them about how to get rid of the fucking thing once and for all. But we don't know any dragons.'

'We could travel to Mount Doom and throw it in,' I suggested.

Morgan's response was swift. 'We don't have a Gollum to help us.'

I beamed. Clearly we were on the same wavelength. It was fate, I decided; we were obviously meant to be together.

'The best we can do,' he continued, 'is hide it – and hide it well. For now, I've put it in—'

'Shut up!' I screeched, then clamped my hand over my mouth as it occurred to me that half the damned hideout had probably heard me. 'What I mean,' I hissed, 'is that you can't tell me where it is. You can't even *hint* at its location. I'm still with Rubus. If he pulls out one of his freaking Truth Spider things and asks the right questions, we're all screwed.' I shuddered. Frankly, Rubus wouldn't need to wait until one of the Truth Spiders bit me and I gave him everything I knew because of the pain. Just the sight of hairy spider legs would give me the wobbles enough to spill all my secrets.

'You're right.'

Of course I was right. I was always right. Almost always right, anyway. Over fifty percent of the time, which was almost always in my book. 'Will you be able to get enough Fey to help out?' I asked.

'Please,' Morgan scoffed. 'I don't even need to ram pixie dust into their veins to do it either.'

I winced slightly. 'Great. Finn won't want to leave Julie alone, you know.'

'Stop worrying. I'll leave a few people in his place. Anyway, there's been no sign of any more vampire hunters. I think Rubus has killed them all.'

I supposed the slimy Fey bastard had to be good for something. 'Excellent.' I rubbed my palms together. 'I'm going to hang up now.'

'Okay.'

I waited for a few seconds. 'Are you going to hang up?'

'I'm already putting the shell away.'

'Bye, then.'

'Goodbye.'

Silence filled the air. 'You're still there, aren't you?' I enquired, crossing my fingers and hoping that he was.

'Yes.'

'You hang up first,' I said.

'Technically, it's a shell. It can't be hung up.'

I pursed my lips. 'You know what I mean.'

'I do. I'm putting it away now.'

I nodded. I could still hear him breathing. I squeezed my eyes shut and cupped my hands over the delicate shell. 'I'm sorry,' I whispered. 'I'm sorry I asked you to marry me and then dumped you. I don't know what I could have been thinking.' With my heart in my mouth, I unfurled my fingers. 'Morgan?'

There was no answer; this time he'd definitely gone. I sighed and shoved the shell into the pocket of my jeans. It was probably for the best.

***

Morgan mustered his troops faster than I'd have thought possible. I was just settling into a curry-flavour Pot Noodle when a breathless Fey appeared in the doorway to the kitchen.

'Have you seen Rubus?' he gasped.

I forked a mouthful of salty goodness into my mouth and chewed thoughtfully. He blurted out the question again, tripping over his words in his haste. I held up my finger to indicate he should wait then took my time finishing my mouthful. When I eventually swallowed, I tilted my head and looked at him. 'Actually,' I said and paused for a moment, 'no.'

He hissed out an angry breath and spun round, ready to depart.

'Can I help with anything?' I asked.

'There are faeries all over Chen's place!'

I raised an eyebrow. 'Isn't that where everyone went this afternoon? I told Rubus about the fire so I'm assuming he sent a bunch of us to go and investigate.'

He wrung his hands. 'Not *our* faeries. Morgan's faeries! They've pitched up with shovels and metal detectors. They're demanding that we get out of the way and allow them access to the site.' His eyeballs writhed from side to side in a comical fashion. 'There are more of them than there are of us!'

'Oh no,' I murmured. 'Disaster.'

From out in the corridor there was the sound of a door opening, followed by Rubus's unmistakable gruff tones. The Fey in front of me sped out. Reluctantly abandoning my Pot Noodle for now, I ambled after him.

'Sir! Rubus! There are at least twenty of Morganus's faeries over at Chen's place. They're demanding access and causing a real scene!' The Fey's bottom lip quivered – I hoped he wasn't about to cry. We could all do without that embarrassment.

Rubus looked unimpressed. 'So? Tell the lot of them to get lost. We were there first.'

'They've got some kind of council-sanctioned piece of paper. They're saying they'll get the police involved if we don't vacate the site.'

That was interesting. Morgan clearly had friends in high places who were prepared to jump to his every whim. It paid to be a barman with access to good alcohol, I decided. I squared my shoulders and stepped up, moving past several concerned Fey and planting my feet directly in front of Rubus.

'I'll go and sort this out,' I drawled. 'I have a history with Morgan. He'll listen to me.' I smoothed my hands down over my corset and sashayed my hips for effect.

Rubus's face suffused with dark anger. 'He's my brother. I'll deal with this.'

I saluted. 'Lead the way then. I shall follow and back you up to the hilt.' I allowed the faintest dreamy expression to cross my face. 'Morgan will—'

'Morgan will listen to me. You will stay here,' he snapped.

I did a good job of looking crestfallen. 'Oh come on, Ruby baby. I can't just sit around here and twiddle my thumbs. I have a new outfit to show off.'

He glared at me. 'Then go out and find my fucking pixie dust that you lost! You're not going anywhere near Morganus. The rest of us will stop him. He has no right to go rooting through Chen's place. I don't know what my brother thinks he's playing at by involving the humans. The man's a fool.' He flapped his arms at the cluster of faeries round him. 'He'll do anything to stop us getting back home to Mag Mell,' he spat.

The whole group murmured in shocked agreement. Sheep.

I widened my eyes. 'Do you think he's looking for something specific? Is it that magical sphere thingy? Do you think it's there?'

Rubus muttered something inaudible under his breath. He turned round and started marching out again. I watched him go while the Fey who'd brought the supposedly terrible news looked anxiously at me. 'I don't think Morgan is there,' he confided in a worried whisper. 'I didn't see him.'

I shrugged. 'He might be on his way,' I said. Or he might be planning to meet me beside a certain golf course now that Rubus was suitably occupied for the next couple of hours. 'I wish I could be there,' I said. 'But I guess I'll have to go out and scour the city for a cache of missing pixie dust instead.'

The Fey grimaced. 'Rather you than me.'

I offered up a melodramatic sigh. 'Life's a bitch.' Unless you are one already.

***

Night had fallen by the time I made it to the rendezvous point. Both Morgan and Finn were waiting there, stamping their feet to keep out the cold. Finn appeared particularly unhappy. The antsy expression on his face immediately worried me.

'Is Julie alright?' I asked, as I emerged out of the tree cover to join them.

'She's fine,' he said shortly.

I glanced askance at Morgan. He raked a hand through his hair. 'There's a website,' he said. 'Her name is being touted about.'

'She's a famous soap star. Surely her name is going to be bandied around. You said there had been no sign of any more vampire hunters.'

'No physical sign,' he answered heavily. 'But in the last couple of hours there have been suggestions on a few online forums that she's not all she seems. So far the gossip has been limited to a discussion about how she manages to look so young when there's no evidence that she's been to a plastic surgeon. The internet is a rabbit warren of conspiracy theories. All it takes is one enterprising hacker to go looking for information on her, though.'

'Google is hardly going to tell the world that she's a vampire,' I scoffed.

'No,' he replied. 'But it might tell the world that her birth certificate is fake. Plus, there's a photo.'

'It's her,' Finn grumped. 'In 1903. Right now it's a joke: Julie Chivers has a lookalike who's long dead.

Except…'

'It's not a lookalike. It's her,' I finished.

He nodded grimly. 'We haven't been able to tell whether these are more vampire hunters who are on her trail and have decided that they'll just expose her if they can't capture her. Or whether it's just shitty luck and it's entirely innocuous.'

'What can I do?' I asked.

'You've got your hands full with Rubus. Focus on him,' Morgan said.

'I'm capable of multi-tasking. I can chew gum and walk all at the same time.'

'I'm dealing with it,' Finn said. From the way he was bunching and unbunching his fists, he wasn't dealing with it very well. Still, I reflected, at least looking after Julie's wellbeing would take his mind off his dead brothers – although part of me was waiting for the Redcap to snap and try to take off my head for being involved in both their deaths.

He gave me a derisive sniff. 'You stick to running around and panting after Rubus.' He threw a scornful glance at my clothes. 'Clearly you're more suited to being a honey trap than helping people. Stay on your knees and keep that mad faery occupied.' He raised his hand and gestured a crude mimicry of a blowjob.

I didn't need to look at Morgan to know he was furious. 'Gee,' I drawled to Finn, 'I didn't realise you were such an expert on my life and how I should live it. Please continue with your wonderful insights. I'll take notes.' I paused. 'Arsebadger.'

A rumble sounded in Finn's throat and a moment later he sprang at me. I saw Morgan lunge to pull him back. I frowned at him and shook my head in warning just before Finn's fist connected with the side of my head.

I staggered slightly. That hurt. 'Is that the best you've got?' I taunted.

Finn flung himself at me again, knocking me to the ground. His fists flew. I dodged a few of the punches by jerking my head from side to side but he still landed several. Feeling woozy, I writhed underneath him then rolled to extricate myself. As soon as I was clear, I jumped back to my feet. Finn kicked out, his boot slamming into my stomach. Winded, I doubled over.

'They're dead!' he screamed at me. 'They're both dead!'

I squinted, raising my eyes to look at him. His expression crumpled almost as if I'd hit him and his knees seemed to give away. He collapsed to the ground, his shoulders shaking with heartfelt sobs.

I spat out a thin stream of blood, wiped my mouth and hobbled over. I thought about touching him but decided it would be wise to leave him be. I limped over to Morgan, who was watching us both with a stony expression. He lifted one hand to my stomach, pressing it against the bruise that was already forming. The pain eased almost instantly and I groaned with relief. He moved his hand up to my face but I shook my head. The visible bruises would come in handy later.

After what seemed like an eternity, Finn's crying subsided. He hiccupped and straightened up, shooting me one more viciously angry glare. Then he ignored me completely and addressed Morgan. 'We're here for a reason.' His voice was thick with unspent tears. 'We should get a move on.' He turned and headed up the hill, his heavy footsteps trudging towards the clubhouse less than half a mile away.

I grimaced slightly, wincing at the throbbing pain in my jaw and my left cheek. As I turned to follow him, Morgan grabbed my elbow and stopped me. 'You did that deliberately,' he said quietly. 'Finn's insult about being a honey trap didn't bother you but you still goaded him into becoming even angrier.'

'I'm not sleeping with Rubus,' I told him. 'He wouldn't turn me down if I offered and he's come close to inviting me into his bed, but I don't think he's really that interested in me. He'd only do it to piss you off. I get the impression he thinks he's too pure for such base instincts.'

'I know,' Morgan answered, surprising me. 'If you were having sex with Rubus, Finn's comment would have angered you.'

'Score one for the amateur psychologist,' I said tiredly.

'I'm not the only one.' He kept his eyes on mine. 'You wanted Finn to get angry because you knew he needed to let off steam and you didn't mind being a convenient punch bag. You didn't once try to hit him back.'

'You're reading too much into it,' I dismissed. 'How was I to know that moronic Redcap would attack me? Pah.' I rolled my eyes. 'You ought to keep him on a tighter leash.'

Morgan watched me for a long moment, his expression shadowed by the darkness around us. 'You're not fooling anyone, least of all me.'

'I'm an evil bitch, Morgan. My motives are very simple.'

'If you're an evil bitch, why are going to such lengths to stop Rubus?' he asked.

I shrugged. 'What can I tell you? I thought that if I helped you prevent an apocalypse, you'd let me have wild, abandoned sex with you. You know, for old times' sake.'

'Sure,' he said quietly. 'Whatever you say.'

'I'm just being honest,' I told him. 'We did decide that was the best policy, after all.' I couldn't quite meet his eyes. Silence stretched out between us. Gasbudlikins, this was awkward.

Morgan heaved in a deep breath. 'Well, Madrona,' he said finally, 'in the interests of honesty, you look hot as hell in that outfit.' He smiled at me.

My stomach did a little flip-flop. I ran my hands over the leather corset. 'I know.' I grinned back, suddenly feeling I was on surer ground. Then, because it seemed like the perfect opportunity and I didn't want any further questions about my true motivation, I reached for him and drew him close, wrapping my arms round his neck. 'Go on,' I said. 'This is your chance to push me away.'

His emerald eyes held mine. 'No can do.' A heartbeat later, his mouth was on mine.

I groaned, initially out of surprise and then because of a sudden flash of deep-seated lust that started at my toes and rose upwards like a flame. The dull ache that had settled deep in my chest seemed to vanish. Everything seemed to vanish. I could feel Morgan's heart beating through his ribcage. He tasted of spice and wine, and the heat of his body pressing against mine was almost searing.

'Maddy,' he whispered, his breath hot against my cheek.

I closed my eyes. His stubble scraped my skin but it only inflamed me further. His hands reached for my hips, curving tightly at my waist as if he couldn't bear to let me go. His teeth nipped gently at my bottom lip – then he pulled back, breathing hard.

'Don't go back to Rubus tonight,' he said. 'Come home with me.'

This time, I couldn't argue. I gave a brief nod and smoothed my hands down my body as if to readjust my clothing. My fingers were shaking.

'We should catch up with Finn,' I said, reluctant to move.

'Yeah,' Morgan said. 'We should.' He bent his head down and pressed one more brief, hard kiss onto my lips. Then he gave me a dazzling smile.

I swallowed, not sure if my legs were still strong enough to carry me up the hill to the golf course and the clubhouse. We had to go now, however; if we didn't, I'd be tempted to tie him to the nearest tree so I could continue this at my own pleasure and in my own time.

With my heart still hammering, I turned. I reached for Morgan's hand and held it until the very edge of the treeline.

***

I wondered if returning to the original scene of the crime was going to dislodge some memories. Alas, my forgetfulness remained as strong as Finn was stupid. I stared round at the area in the front of the clubhouse. I could remember leaving but I couldn't remember arriving.

'Look!' I chirped to the Redcap, who was waiting sullenly as if he knew exactly why Morgan and I had taken so long to catch up to him. 'Finn, that's the phone box you destroyed with a bullet. If I'd not moved back at the right time, my head would have been blasted to smithereens.' I sighed. 'Good times.'

Morgan's green eyes flashed and he stalked over to inspect it. 'They've not wasted any time in repairing it.'

'We did that,' Finn said sourly. 'Or Winn did anyway. He repaired it. Stayed up half the night to do it, as well. We couldn't afford to have the golf-course management inform the police about vandalism. We could dispose of Charrie the Bogle's body but we're not miracle workers. We couldn't get rid of every trace of DNA and we couldn't risk raising human suspicion. Redcaps don't usually get much credit but we prepare for every eventuality in order to achieve success. It's why we managed to fly under the radar with Rubus for so long.'

'You didn't coat the bullets with rowan,' I pointed out.

He glared. 'There wasn't time for that. It was either follow you or prepare the weapons.'

I nodded as if taking him seriously. 'You didn't prepare for me beating you all and escaping with your cash either.'

Finn's jaw clenched.

'You didn't prepare for the possibility of CCTV cameras filming our every move.'

Before he could attack me again, Morgan interrupted. 'Enough, children! We're here for one reason and one reason only and that's to get hold of the CCTV footage from the night in question before Rubus does. There's no point squabbling over its existence – it's there and we have to get hold of it. We might not get another chance, so stop fannying around.'

Finn and I glanced at each other. 'Fannying?' I enquired. 'I'm not fannying.'

'I'm not fannying either,' Finn agreed. 'If the Madhatter isn't fannying and I'm not fannying then the only fanny remaining is … you.'

I stifled a giggle. Okay. Finn wasn't all bad.

Morgan sighed. 'Gods preserve me,' he said. He allowed himself one heated glance in my direction, which promised even more than I dared imagine, then shook himself and pointed at the main door to the clubhouse. 'Come on, you two.'

We walked up to the dark, silent and closed doors. I

scanned round, checking the exterior walls. I couldn't see any cameras. Maybe, I thought hopefully, this golf course didn't possess any CCTV cameras. It was high time some luck landed in our direction.

Morgan beckoned me forward. 'I take it you don't remember how to deal with locked doors?'

'Kick them in?' I suggested.

'I rather think,' he said drily, 'that it would be a good idea if no one discovered our intrusion. There are other ways of gaining access.' He smiled. 'Faery ways.'

I rubbed my palms together. Excellent. I still wasn't sure what powers I possessed so I was more than willing to let Morgan play the role of professor. Come to think of it, he'd actually look rather sexy in tweed… Whatever he wore, I'd still tie him to a tree so I could have my wicked way with him.

'Raise both your hands,' he instructed. 'And focus on the lock. You need to visualise the mechanism inside. We don't want to damage it because we don't want anyone to know that we were here. You just need to see the lock turning in your mind's eye and…'

There was a click. I let out a crow of delight. 'And we will gain access.' My eyes gleamed. 'We should do this more often. There's a bank not too far from Rubus's current place. I can sneak inside. I'm sure there will be loads of cash lying around, just there for the taking.'

'We're not bank robbers, Madrona.'

I pouted. 'You're no fun.'

Finn, apparently bored by this exchange, muscled past us. He turned the door knob and entered the silent building. I shrugged at Morgan and followed him in.

The darkened reception area of the clubhouse greeted us. There was a solid wooden desk with nothing on top other than a blank computer screen and a glass bowl of boiled sweets. Photographs of golfing prowess adorned the walls, along with a large board proclaiming the winners of the local tournament for the last seventy-odd years.

I reached over, grabbed a sweet and unwrapped it. The sound of the wrapper filled the small space and Finn and Morgan glared. 'What?' I asked. 'It's not like anyone is here to hear us.' I popped the sweet into my mouth then immediately spat it out again. Yuck. Aniseed flavour.

'Pick that up,' Finn hissed.

'I'm not surprised this place is always deserted if this is the quality of their freebies,' I said, bending down to scoop up the offending sweet and drop it in the bin.

'It's a bit hard to play golf in the middle of the night,' Finn pointed out.

I considered this. 'I don't feel that the possibilities for that have been fully explored. You could have LED golf balls and glow-in-the-dark flags. Maybe some rave music to add to the ambience.' I beamed.

'Let's just get a move on, shall we?'

'You're just jealous that you didn't think of the idea first.'

Finn sighed. Obviously deciding that talking to me further would only highlight his own creative inefficiencies, he turned away and stomped behind the reception desk. He opened the door marked Staff Only and walked inside.

Morgan strode ahead, his head swinging from left to right. I grabbed another sweet. Maybe they weren't all aniseed. Nope. I spat it out again. It hit the marbled floor and rolled. I shrugged. Maybe I'd leave it there just to confuse whoever was here in the morning.

It didn't take long for my two boys to find the room we were looking for. Finn was about to leave the reception area when Morgan called out in a hushed voice and beckoned us over. Behind an ugly rubber plant was a door with the word 'Security' emblazoned on it. We went inside.

Whoever owned the golf course didn't give much consideration to their security guards. The room was little more than a cupboard. Yellow high-vis jackets hung on the coat rack along one wall. There were various blinking red lights and a computer on a desk on the other.

Finn sat down and turned on the computer screen. Almost immediately, several grainy black-and-white images flickered into view. I leaned down to get a closer look, drawing in a sharp breath when I saw some of the live images.

'That's the eighteenth hole,' I said grimly. 'That's where I woke up.'

Finn tapped a couple of keys on the keyboard. 'There are bloody cameras everywhere.'

Morgan pointed to an old newspaper article pinned to a board on our right. 'There's been a lot of vandalism to the green,' he said. 'They must have installed the cameras after the last incident.'

'Arsebadgers,' I muttered.

'The vandals?' he enquired. 'Or the golf-course managers?'

'Both.' I sniffed. 'Can you access the old footage, Finn?'

'Hang on.' He tapped a few more keys. It figured that he was an IT whizz; he had that pale look of someone who never saw the sun, coupled with the sort of deep-held angst that only comes from spending your masturbatory hours with a computer screen.

A list of files appeared on the left-hand side of the screen, each one labelled with a date. The dates were in descending order. 'The whole system is automated,' Finn said. 'Unless a problem's reported, there would be no reason for anyone to search for any footage. That makes us very lucky. No matter what is on those videos, the Madhatter will get away with murder because no one will have bothered to watch them.'

'Hey!' I protested. 'No one has proved that I killed that bogle! The evidence is purely circumstantial.'

'Until now,' Finn said. He clicked on the file marked twenty-first of September. 'We're about to discover what really happened that night.'

I held my breath. I really didn't want to discover that I was a cold-blooded murderer. All the same, I couldn't rip my eyes away from the screen. 'Eighteen,' I whispered, scanning the named videos. 'Play Eighteen.' Almost without realising, I reached out and took Morgan's hand. He squeezed reassuringly.

'We'll deal with whatever's there, alright?' he murmured. 'Let's not jump to conclusions.'

I licked my lips nervously. 'Sure, yeah. Right.'

Finn grinned. 'Hang on to your checked trousers, boys and girls.' He clicked.

The video started. I stared. So did Morgan and Finn. Our odd trio leaned forward, watching the flickering screen.

Finn punched the keyboard. 'It's corrupted,' he said. 'The damned file is corrupted.' He was right. There was nothing to see but fuzz.

'Try a different file,' Morgan said, tension tracing every word.

Finn did as instructed, opening up the video entitled 'Car Park'.

'It's corrupted too,' he said. He tried another and another. 'Every damn video from that night is worthless. There's nothing to be seen.'

I clapped my hands. 'That's fantastic! I was worrying about nothing. This was a long way to come to put our minds at rest but now there's nothing to worry about. Even if Rubus finds this place, he won't find any evidence of me or the sphere. All's well that ends well.'

Neither Morgan nor Finn reacted. 'Try another date,' Morgan said.

Finn opened up the files for the day after. Every single video was fine. We watched for a few moments then he located another file. Still fine. The only corrupted videos were the ones that would incriminate me.

'Maybe it's just a coincidence,' I hedged.

'Yeah.' Finn didn't appear convinced.

'It could happen.'

'Mmm-hmm.' He scratched his head for a moment then tapped again on the keyboard.

'What is it?' Morgan asked, leaning forward.

Finn's shoulders sagged. 'What I was afraid of.' He pointed at the screen. 'Three hours ago, someone downloaded the files we were looking for. No doubt they then added a bug to corrupt the originals. We're too late. Someone got here before us.'

Gasbudlikins. 'Rubus,' I whispered. 'That arsebadger. That fucking tosser. That…'

Morgan squeezed my hand tighter. 'You need to leave him for good now,' he said. 'Not just for the night but forever. It's too dangerous for you to return to him.'

I desperately wanted to argue. We needed a route into the inner workings of Rubus's mind so that we could stop him from doing evil. Real evil, not just Madrona evil. If I walked away now, we'd be handing him the opportunity to do whatever the hell he wanted. I was still no closer to learning more about what Plan B was. What if it was even more dastardly and evil than Plan A? And there were twenty-four more letters in the alphabet to go. There was a lot of thwarting to do if we were to win the day.

'Much as I hate to admit it,' Finn said, 'Morganus is

right. We don't know exactly what's on those videos but we do know that you took the sphere from Charrie. Once Rubus has proof of that, all bets are off.'

I flattened my mouth into a grim line. I wasn't prepared to give up, not yet. 'What about the CCTV from tonight?' I asked. 'Whoever waltzed in here and messed with those files must have been captured on camera three hours ago.'

'Does it matter?' Finn questioned. 'It'll be one of Rubus's dust slaves, no doubt. He's probably already handed them over. There's no way Rubus is still at Chen's place.'

I held my ground. 'It's still worth checking.'

He shrugged, returning to the first screen and rewinding the video. We watched it anxiously. 'There!' I jabbed my finger at the screen.

'It's just a shadow.'

'A shadow of a person.'

'But not the actual person. He or she knew where the cameras were and avoided them. Clever.' Finn fast-forwarded. 'See? There's no sign of anyone until we come into view.' Footage of us arriving out the front appeared, Finn looking morose, me looking nervous – and Morgan looking at me.

Morgan sighed. 'Can you delete us?'

The Redcap nodded. 'Piece of cake. It'll only take a moment. You two should—'

He was interrupted by a loud thud followed by a pained yelp from outside our little room. All three of us froze. We weren't alone after all.

Chapter Nine

I sprang for the door. I didn't have any particular goal in mind, other than getting hold of whoever was out there. It had to be the same arsebadger who'd already messed with the CCTV footage. I'd wrest the footage from them and stop them handing it over to Rubus. Somehow.

Morgan pulled me back. 'You can't just leap out there, all guns blazing,' he whispered. 'It could be anyone.'

I scowled and shook him off. All the same, I slowed down and opened the door carefully, pulling it ajar just enough to see who had made that godawful noise. It took a moment for my eyes to adjust but, when they did, I realised with some satisfaction that the night prowler must have skidded on the sweet I'd spat out. That was why he'd fallen. There was something to be said for aniseed foulness after all then.

I watched as the lump on the floor straightened up. A glimmer of moonlight landed on his face as he turned and illuminated his features. I immediately recognised him. Well, well, well. It was the old bugger who'd been tracking me across the rooftops earlier. He wasn't going to escape my villainous clutches a second time.

I motioned to Morgan to remain where he was. If the elderly arsebadger thought I was alone, I might be able to gain the upper hand. I'd lull him into a false sense of security. Even if he were a faery, which seemed unlikely because his superior hearing would have alerted him to our presence, we had Finn with us. Finn was not bound by the truce and he'd be more than capable of hurting the sneaky, white-haired bastard. I squared my shoulders and stepped out as quietly as I could.

I managed three paces before he noticed me. Baleful, shadowed eyes lifted in my direction then widened in horror. Without missing a beat, he spun round toward the door, skidding on the marble floor in his haste to get away. Not this time, buddy.

I darted after him.

He had his hands on the door handle and was scrabbling to open it when I reached him. Feeling my breath on the back of his neck, he dropped his arms and slowly turned.

Now we were face to face, I was rather unimpressed. He didn't look like much at all. He might have the ability to sprint away at unnatural speeds, as well as rooftop-crawling skills to match Spiderman's, but he was as weedy as me.

I checked his irises. Coal-black. This was no faery.

'Hand over the video,' I ordered.

'I … I … don't know what you're talking about.' His voice was high-pitched and squeaky, as if he'd never quite made it past puberty.

All it took was one threatening step towards him before he deflated, right in front of my eyes. 'I don't have it with me.'

'Bullshit.'

'I'm telling the truth!'

The sound of footsteps alerted me to Finn and Morgan's approach. 'You know this guy, Maddy?' Morgan asked.

'He's the old bloke who was following me earlier today. Watch it,' I advised. 'He's a lot more spry than he looks.'

Finn snarled and pushed past me. 'I don't recognise him,' he hissed. He grabbed hold of the old man's purple shirt. 'Who are you? You must work for Rubus but I've never seen you before.'

'I don't work for that prick!' The man shook his head vehemently, making his jowls jiggle and his hair flap.

'Then what are you doing here?'

'Investigating.'

'Look, buster,' I growled. 'If you're going to insist on giving us one word answers, I'm going to insist on beating the information out of you. Be more specific. What are you doing here?'

He glowered at all three of us but there was no mistaking the defeat in his expression. Even so, I remained on guard. He'd already escaped me once today; I wasn't about to be embarrassed again. 'You're faeries.' He jerked his head at Finn. 'You're a Redcap.'

'Yeah? And?'

'I'm Mendax.' When none of us reacted, he sighed heavily. 'You must have heard of me. I'm the most famous of my kind.' At our expressions, he exhaled loudly in exasperation. 'I'm a dragon.'

Finn was so surprised that he let go of the man's shirt. I was equally dubious. There was very little about this arsebadger that suggested fire or power or magic. 'Prove it.'

He rolled his eyes. 'How? Because if you're suspecting forked tongues, long tails and scales, then you flappy faeries are even more stupid than I thought. Why Chen ever spoke to you in the first place, I'll never know.'

All three of us stiffened at that. 'What do you know about Chen?'

'He was my friend,' Mendax said accusingly. 'My best friend. I won't have you lot stamping all over his grave.' His chin jutted out. 'I won't allow it!'

'That still doesn't explain why you were following me, or why you're here.'

Mendax raised a bony finger and pointed at me. 'You're with Rubus. Rubus stole from my friend. I'm simply trying to get his property back. You're not the rightful owners.'

We had to tread very carefully here. Fortunately, Morgan seemed to realise this. Maintaining a low, controlled voice, he asked, 'What property are you talking about?'

Mendax's eyebrow twitched. Mendax. Honestly. Why didn't I meet anyone who was called John or Sam or Charlie? Even a Dick would have been welcome.

'Oh, I think you know exactly what property I'm talking about,' he squeaked. 'A small metal object,' he held up his hand to indicate size, 'about this large. It has the potential to solve all the Fey's problems. And to initiate the apocalypse for everyone else.'

'What do you know about it?' Morgan asked, his voice dangerously low.

'I told you!' Mendax said. 'I was Chen's friend. He told me all about it. He told me how much you stupid faeries wanted the thing. He bequeathed it to me and I'm going to find it. Chen would be devastated if he thought that it had fallen into your hands.'

'We're not with Rubus.' Morgan folded his arms. 'We don't want him to get hold of the sphere any more than you do.'

The old man brightened. 'Then you know where it is?'

There was a moment's silence. 'No,' Morgan said eventually.

I nodded at the lie. I didn't trust this squeaky old dragon either.

'What's with the voice?' I enquired. 'Have you been sucking helium?'

His black eyes narrowed. 'You got a problem with

the way I talk?'

I shrugged. 'You say you're an all-powerful dragon but you talk like Mickey Mouse.'

'I *am* an all-powerful dragon!' he snapped. 'I'm very rich.'

Finn rolled his eyes. 'Bloody dragons,' he muttered. 'All they care about is gold. This guy is a waste of time.'

I fixed my best evil glare on Mendax. 'Tell us where the video is. The one you downloaded from here.'

'I told you. I don't have it with me.' The whine in his voice was quite extraordinary. What was the point in being a dragon if you weren't going to stomp around and breathe fire? All this supernatural business seemed like over-blown hype to me.

It wouldn't take much to intimidate this bloke into giving us the file. I smiled nastily and raised my fists. 'Yeah, yeah. If you won't hand it over, we'll just have to take it from you.'

'That's enough, Maddy,' Morgan said, moving towards Mendax as if to protect him from my vicious stare. I was about to argue when it occurred to me that this was a strategy. I shrugged. If Morgan wanted to play good cop then I'd happily play bad cop. It was a stretch, sure, but I'd cope. I snarled, like any real dragon should, but let him to take the lead.

'Why don't we sit down,' Morgan suggested, pointing to a small lounge area opposite the reception desk, 'and talk this out?'

'No.' Surprisingly, Mendax seemed determined to hold his ground.

'There are three of us and there's only one of you,' Finn said. 'Maybe you should do as the man suggests.'

'I won't let you beat me! I won't! I'm not weak like Chen!'

I couldn't remember a darned thing about Chen but if

he'd been even half as shaky and weak as this guy, it was a wonder that he'd hung onto his sphere for so long.

'I promise that we won't touch you,' Morgan murmured. 'Not while we're inside this building. I take my promises very seriously.' His expression was earnest and open. 'It appears that we're on the same side here. The enemy of my enemy is my friend.'

Mendax swung his black-eyed gaze from me to Morgan to Finn. I was almost certain he was going to spin round and try to high-tail it out of here. I was hoping he would because that would give me the excuse I needed to knock out several of his teeth.

Unfortunately, Morgan appeared to have reassured him just enough. 'Fine,' he said. He turned and stomped over to the nearest chair, settling himself into it and crossing his legs.

Morgan, Finn and I exchanged looks then we walked over to join him. I would have settled myself on the arm of Mendax's chair so that I could loom over him appropriately but Morgan steered me to the sofa opposite. With the three of us seated in a row, facing the blinking dragon in the middle of a silent, darkened golf clubhouse, it suddenly felt like the world's most bizarre job interview.

'So,' I said in a deep voice, 'tell us about your strengths and weaknesses.'

Everyone looked at me strangely. It was just me that thought this set-up was like a job panel, then.

'As if I'm going to do that,' Mendax sniffed. 'Would you tell me yours?'

I considered. I didn't see why not. I leaned back in the chair and mirrored his body language, technique one of putting the arsebadger at ease. Technique two was not pulling out his toenails one by one. 'Well,' I said, ticking off on my fingers, 'I'm highly intelligent.'

Finn snorted loudly. I pointedly ignored him.

'I'm obviously incredibly attractive, not just because I possess beauty but because I have a cultured *je ne sais quoi* which I know is ridiculously alluring.'

This time Morgan turned astonished eyes towards me.

'I also have fabulous faery magical powers, which I'm able to utilise with both restraint and abandon when the situation calls for it. As for weaknesses, I have an unhealthy penchant for junk food and I enjoy seeing arsebadgers like you get hurt more than I should.' I bared my teeth in a smile.

'You're mad,' Mendax whispered.

My smile widened. 'I'm the Madhatter,' I corrected.

Morgan rolled his eyes. 'This isn't getting us anywhere.' He relaxed his shoulders and focused on Mendax. 'You ask us a question, we'll ask you a question. *Quid pro quo*. You can go first.'

Mendax frowned, obviously still wary, but willing to play along for now. He thought for a moment. 'Did you take the sphere from Chen?' he asked finally.

I breathed out. That was a fairly easy question.

'No,' Morgan said. 'We believe it was a bogle called Charrie who did that. We also believe he was under orders from Rubus.' He linked his fingers and leaned forward. 'Why were you following Madrona earlier today?'

'I've been keeping an eye on Rubus and his organisation,' Mendax admitted. 'She vanished for several days and now she's acting strangely. Given that her disappearance coincided with both Chen's death and the loss of his sphere, I thought I'd follow her. I figured that she must have stolen it and I was hoping she would lead me to it.'

So far, so head-bangingly boring. Morgan pointed his

index finger at Mendax and indicated it was his turn to ask another question. Mendax's mouth tightened and he looked directly at me. 'That bogle is dead,' he said. 'Why did you kill him?'

I drew in a sharp breath. Finn threw me a sidelong look. 'I knew it,' he muttered.

'I have amnesia,' I said. 'I don't know if I did kill the bogle. I don't remember anything.'

'Oh, you killed him alright.' Mendax glared at me with a mixture of disgust and fear. 'I have the video evidence to prove it. You cut off his head with a sword.'

I stared at him then at my hands. They didn't look capable of such a violent action. 'I couldn't have,' I said. I pointed to my biceps. 'I barely have the strength to pull myself up a wall. I certainly couldn't swing a sword with enough lethal force to slice off a head.'

The image of Charrie's decapitated body lying by the eighteenth hole not too far away from here flashed into my mind. It couldn't be true, I decided. The dragon was lying.

Mendax wrinkled his nose derisively. 'If you're not going to be honest, this conversation is completely pointless.'

'I'm being as honest as I can be!' I protested. 'As I've already told you, I've got amnesia. I can't remember what happened but I really don't think I could have killed anyone.'

Mendax shot a look at Morgan. 'Am I honestly supposed to believe that she can't remember anything? How stupid do you lot think I am?'

'Well, so far,' I drawled, 'your intelligence matches that of a free condom machine in a nunnery.'

The dragon got to his feet. 'I don't have to put up with this. I'm leaving.'

Morgan put a warning hand on my arm. 'She'll stay

quiet from now on.' He squeezed my arm. 'Won't you, Madrona?'

'No,' I snapped. Then I looked at the pale determination on Mendax's thin face. 'Fine, I'll keep my mouth closed. It's not my fault that he's afraid of strong women, though,' I muttered.

Mendax lifted his chin. 'I'm not afraid of strong women but I *am* afraid of anyone who can cold-bloodedly kill another living being.'

I kept my mouth resolutely shut but only because I'd promised to do so, not because I didn't have a come back. I folded my arms and leaned back. Mendax took his seat again.

'I wasn't lying before,' he said. 'I don't have the video file with me. I came here and took it and it's now in a safe place, far away from here. I only came back to keep an eye out because I had an inkling that you might return.' He reached into the inside pocket of his coat and drew out a smartphone. 'But I do have proof of what she's done.' He raised an eyebrow at Morgan. 'If you'll permit me?'

Morgan nodded sharply. The dragon smiled and thumbed the phone for a moment before his expression cleared and he turned it round so we could see the screen. When I realised what it showed, my stomach turned.

It was dark. It was obviously a CCTV still and the quality wasn't perfect but there was no doubt as to who the figure on the screen was. It was definitely me. I was holding aloft some kind of sword and looking down at the crumpled heap of a body at my feet. My face was in profile but, from this angle, it looked as if I were snarling. My shoulders sagged. There it was, in glorious technicolour.

I really was a killer after all.

We all stared at it for a long moment. I considered

pointing out that it could have been altered or manipulated and the sword could have been photo-shopped in but the smug look on Mendax's face gave truth to the image. It was me – and it was a real picture.

There was an unpleasant taste in the back of my mouth. I could really do with a glass of water. Scanning round, I spotted a water cooler in the corner. Without saying a word, I got up to my feet and shuffled over.

Morgan cleared his throat but, when he started talking again, his voice remained low. 'So you were following Madrona because you thought she might lead you to the sphere. She doesn't have it, though. We can assume that Rubus doesn't either or he would have used it by now. Perhaps the thing is lost.'

Mendax's eyes narrowed. I took a sip of water and watched him. There was something about the guy – I couldn't put my finger on it but he made me feel very uneasy. Maybe it was because he'd called me out as a murderer. I supposed that would do it.

Morgan continued. 'If you did happen to find it, what exactly would you do with it?'

Mendax tutted as if the answer were glaringly obvious. 'I'd destroy it, of course.'

'How?' Neither Morgan's expression nor his voice had altered in the slightest but I knew he was on tenterhooks. We all were.

'It was created with dragon magic,' the old man said, with an imperious toss of his head. 'I'll simply use dragon magic to obliterate it.'

Finn, with more rationality than I'd previously believed him capable of, leaned forward. 'Why didn't your old buddy Chen destroy it then?'

'Because it was his,' Mendax replied simply. 'We're dragons. We're hoarders by nature and we certainly don't destroy that which is ours. Chen would have been as incapable of getting rid of the sphere he created as you would be of forgetting about your homeland.'

'But if he bequeathed it to you it belongs to you,' Finn argued. 'The cycle starts all over again.'

'He bequeathed it to me in order to destroy it, not to keep it. Those are entirely different things. I do not possess the right to keep the sphere, only the right to remove it from existence.' Mendax arched an eyebrow. 'What would you do if you found it?' There was a glint in his black eyes that suggested he knew that Morgan was lying about not having it.

'The same thing,' Morgan answered. 'We would also destroy it.'

'You're not a dragon,' Mendax dismissed. 'You don't have the capabilities. Sooner or later the temptation will grow too strong and you'll use it to return to your own demesne. I have heard tales of your homesickness. You won't be able to keep those pangs at bay forever. The sphere will call to you – and you will answer.'

'That wouldn't happen.'

The dragon smiled sadly. 'Yes, it would.'

The line of tension in Morgan's spine belied his casual shrug. 'There are plenty of ways to make the sphere irretrievable.'

Mendax didn't blink. 'You have magic but so do plenty of others. Nothing is lost forever.' He glanced at me. 'Not even innocence. A simple bout of supposed amnesia and her sins are wiped clean.'

'Leave her out of this,' Morgan growled.

Amusement flickered across Mendax's face. 'As you wish.'

I moved my gaze from Mendax to Morgan. If I kept looking at the smarmy old dragon, I'd be liable to spring at him and ram my paper cup down his throat. At least Morgan was easier on the eye. He didn't once glance in my direction. Was that because he could no longer bear to look at me now that the truth about what I'd done to Charrie had been revealed?

'Did you set fire to Chen's building?' Morgan asked.

'Yes.'

'Did you take his safe?'

'That's two questions in one.'

'They're related,' Morgan said coldly.

'Yes. In fact,' Mendax added with a distinct purr, 'there is another object inside which may be of interest to you. It's not yet operational but it has … potential.'

'Go on.'

'It's an oath breaker.' He sounded incredibly smug.

I swung my eyes back towards him. The smile playing around his lips was distinctly predatory and I suddenly felt like I was catching a glimpse of the real dragon behind the pensioner's exterior.

'I don't understand,' Finn said.

'No,' Mendax murmured. 'I don't suppose you do. He does though.' He jerked his head at Morgan.

With obvious reluctance, Morgan explained. 'An oath breaker with appropriate power could be used to remove the truce. Such objects, while rare, are available in Mag Mell.'

Mendax smirked. 'One never knows when it might be prudent to go back on one's word.'

I stared at him. If we could break the truce then we could attack Rubus properly. And all his goons. He wouldn't even be expecting it. Such a thing, if wielded appropriately, could have tremendous potential. An image of Rubus splayed out with his entrails hanging out flashed into my mind. I swallowed, nauseous. Apparently I would be happy to murder again if I thought circumstances demanded it.

'I'm not part of the truce,' Finn declared. 'If we

wanted to kill a faery then I could easily do it.'

'Really?' the dragon murmured. 'Easily? If you had the ability to kill Rubus, you'd have already done so. I know that all Redcaps look like hulking brutes but in my experience your power is minimal – as evidenced by the recent deaths of your brothers.'

All three of us sucked in a breath at that. How did the slimy arsebadger know about Winn and Jinn?

At least Morgan didn't miss a beat. 'Why did you take the safe in the first place?'

Mendax rolled his eyes. 'It's obvious, isn't it? I thought the sphere would be inside it. I was rather … upset when I discovered it wasn't. I searched the rest of the house and then allowed my temper to get the better of me. The fire was not premeditated. Consider it a measure of how seriously I believe retrieving the sphere to be.' He knitted his hands together behind his back. 'It appears that we are at an impasse. I possess evidence that implicates your girlfriend in a murder, evidence that even the human police can't ignore. I don't trust you.' His gaze encompassed all of us. 'Any of you. In fact, I believe you do have Chen's sphere. It's too dangerous an object to be left in mere faery hands.'

'We don't trust you either,' Morgan said levelly. 'Tailing Madrona around the city? Tracking us here? Spying? We have no reason to believe you have pure intentions.'

'Indeed.' Mendax appraised him silently for a moment. 'Perhaps we can come up with a solution. Something which will enable us all to trust each other.'

'What do you suggest?'

The old dragon tapped his mouth as if in thought but it was all for show. He clearly already knew exactly what he was going to say. 'You were the one who initiated a bit of *quid pro quo* and it's worked well so far. Let's take it to the next stage. I will give you what exists of the oath breaker, as well as the video file proving Madrona's culpability. I won't make any copies of it. In return, you will give me an object belonging to Rubus. I haven't seen him in person but I've seen photos – human technology does have its place. He wears a ring on his pinky finger, doesn't he? Bring me that ring and I will be more inclined to trust you.'

Morgan's jaw was clenched. 'He never removes the ring and he would never willingly give it up. It belonged to our father.'

Mendax smiled. 'Then when you bring it to me, I will know for certain that you are not in his pocket.' He sighed happily. 'Once the exchange has occurred, perhaps we can build on our mutual trust and re-engage in negotiations over the sphere.'

'We don't have the sphere,' Morgan said.

'Sure.' Mendax nodded, his expression almost as sarcastic as his voice. 'You don't have it *now*. But perhaps you can be persuaded to get hold of it so that I can destroy it.'

Finn bristled. 'It seems that we are putting ourselves at greater risk than you are to achieve this trust-exchange bullshit. All you have to do is open a safe. We have to risk our lives.'

I snorted. If we agreed to this, it was obviously me who'd be doing all the risking.

Mendax shrugged. 'Do you really think that I would enjoy the fallout if the truce were destroyed? The faeries were sensible to establish it in the first place. You can't go anywhere in this city without feeling their frustration at being trapped here. Frustration leads to conflict – and that's the sort of conflict I would prefer not to happen in my own home.' He looked at Finn. 'You're a Redcap. You must understand that as well as I do. Although,' he added, 'as far as you're concerned, if you lose the truce, you'll gain the Fey back-up you require to avenge your brother's death.'

Finn's face turned a bright shade of red, caused by fury at the mention of Jinn's demise rather than embarrassment. Sooner or later he'd take a swing at Rubus whether he had support from faeries like Morgan and myself or not. He'd never win and, much as I hated to admit it, I didn't want to see the Redcap die needlessly.

Morgan got to his feet. 'How do we contact you?'

'Are you agreeing to my proposal?' Mendax enquired, without moving from his own chair.

'We will consider it. That's as far as I am prepared to go for now.'

Mendax pursed his lips. 'Then that will do. For now.' He thought for a moment then pulled a small card from his pocket and passed it over. 'I have a PO box that I use for deliveries. My lair, unlike Chen's, is sacrosanct. I don't permit anyone to visit it, so the PO box comes in handy. Leave a message there with a time, date and,' he paused, 'a neutral meeting place and I'll endeavour to see you there. If you obtain Rubus's ring, tell me and I will bring the oath breaker when I meet you. If you decide not to go ahead with this exchange then our business is concluded.' His face tightened. 'And know that if you *do* have the sphere, despite your denials, I shall do everything in my power to take it from you. It was not meant for your kind.'

'You and whose army?' Finn sneered. 'Try anything and I'll rip your intestines out of your throat, wrap them round my dick and have sexual relations with your skull.'

Nobody said a word. Well, that was one way to kill a conversation dead. I wasn't sure I could even look at Finn after that. And I was the villainous murdering bitch amongst us.

'Well,' Mendax murmured. 'Whatever floats your boat.' He got to his feet in a surprisingly lithe movement for such an old man. 'I'll leave first. Don't do anything foolish like try and follow me.'

He headed for the door then turned to look at us. 'Make sure you wipe the video evidence of this little chat this time,' he smirked at me.

A moment later we were alone again.

Chapter Ten

A considerable amount of time went by before anyone spoke. I drank more water. Finn drummed his fingers against the leather arm of his chair. Morgan didn't move a muscle. It wasn't until I'd had so much to drink that my bladder was on the point of exploding that I finally tossed the cup into the nearby bin and stalked to the middle of the floor.

'I'm a killer,' I said loudly. Too loudly. My voice echoed around the empty clubhouse, my words reverberating back at me just in case I still wasn't sure. 'But I think we need to look upon my unveiling as a good thing.'

Morgan still didn't move. Finn quirked a bushy eyebrow; given his misshapen head, the overall effect was rather startling, like a lumpy hunk of clay with random hair added. I didn't have the time to comment, however.

'How so?' he enquired.

'I have the stomach for getting the job done,' I answered simply. 'Whatever that job may be. Probably not pulling out someone's guts through their throat and wrapping them round my cock because firstly I don't have a cock and secondly even I'm not that much *of* a cock. But,' I continued, in a more sombre vein, 'I can do what needs to be done, whether that's getting rid of Mendax because he's an untrustworthy arsebadger who's planning to slit all our throats the first chance he gets, or getting rid of Rubus if this oath-breaker thing actually works.'

Finn looked me up and down critically. 'Without

wanting to disparage you, Madhatter, I'm not sure you'd have the bodily strength to succeed over either of them.'

I ignored the slight to my muscles; I'd insulted them enough myself already. 'There's more than one way to flay a feline. I have faery magic. I've only used it to deliberately harm someone once before, when I took out that sniper who was after Julie. But the ability is certainly there.' My voice was quiet. I'd never discovered if what I'd done that day had killed the sniper that had been targeting her; I'd always assumed I'd just winded him or something. Now, of course, I was no longer so sure.

I was expecting Finn to make some sort of snide remark about my black-hearted willingness to end another life. He'd probably include his brother Winn in it as I could certainly be held at least partially – if not wholly responsible – for his death, accidental or otherwise. Instead he surprised me. 'It's good that you're in this with us then,' he said.

I blinked at him and waited for him to finish the sentence with a cutting insult but he didn't seem to have anything else to say. Then a thought occurred to me. I tilted my head and I put my hands on my hips. 'Hang on one dastardly second,' I said. 'Do you feel sorry for me? Is this pity because I've finally been forced to confront the truth about myself?' I glared at him. 'Don't you dare feel that for me!'

Finn's mouth twitched. 'You know,' he drawled, 'the best way to kill a cat isn't to skin it. It's to choke it with cream.'

I saw what he was doing. I'd tried to manipulate him in a similar fashion only a few hours ago. I glowered at him accusingly. 'You think you can kill me with kindness? Because I wouldn't kill a cat like that. I'd take it by its tail and—'

'Quiet,' Morgan said. 'I really don't think this is an

appropriate conversation topic.' He looked faintly green.

'Are you a cat lady, Morgan?' I asked. 'Are you sickened by our discussion of how to murder a moggy?'

'Let's focus on more important things, shall we?'

Finn and I exchanged knowing looks then I noticed the way Morgan was studiously avoiding meeting my eyes and my short-lived amusement vanished. He'd despised me when I'd met him ten days ago and he despised me again now. My shoulders sagged and I swallowed down the pussy joke that had been on my lips. I sat down again but not next to Morgan; I didn't want to watch him recoil from me.

'I don't get a good feeling about Mendax,' I said, returning to business. 'I don't think we can trust him.'

'I agree,' Finn said, surprising me yet again. 'Let's not forget that the man's a dragon. There's never been a more self-centred species. All they care about is hoarding stuff and looking after themselves. The only reason a dragon would be bothered by an impending apocalypse is if it drove up gold prices and destroyed their treasure chests in the process.'

'Perhaps that's exactly why we *can* trust him,' Morgan said. 'His motives might be selfish but at least that sort of selfishness can be equated with honesty.'

'We don't need him,' I pointed out. 'The sphere is safe with you. Nothing else matters.'

'I don't believe he was bluffing about using the CCTV footage against you.' Morgan's jaw tightened. 'He'd hand it over to the police for no other reason than to be spiteful.'

I cast down my eyes. 'Maybe it should be handed over. Maybe I deserve to be punished.'

'Sorry? I didn't quite catch that.'

I looked up and raised my voice. 'I can find out where Mendax lives,' I said. 'I can stake out his PO box, follow him home, slit his bony throat and take back the video. I'll find this oath-breaker thing at the same time. The whole operation won't take more than a day or two.'

Morgan finally met my gaze and a ghost of a smile crossed his mouth. I couldn't tell whether it was because he was laughing at me or he thought I was just being cute.

'Except,' Finn interjected, 'his point about the sphere was valid. I'm homesick. I feel the ache for my own demesne although I know it's not as physical or as acute as what you Fey feel. It's been ten years since the borders were closed and it's got worse. It wakes me up at night and it haunts my dreams. What happens in another ten years? Or another ten after that?'

Morgan nodded grimly. 'It could get so bad that any of us will be desperate enough to use the sphere and bring on the magic that will destroy this world. It's certainly not beyond the realms of possibility.'

'I feel the ache,' I argued. 'But it's not that bad. I can live with it.'

Morgan's mouth twisted. 'I think the reason you don't feel it as keenly as the rest of us is because you don't remember anything about Mag Mell. It's as if the amnesia you suffered reset your cravings back to zero.'

I shrugged. 'It's a *fait accompli* then, isn't it? Give every faery amnesia!'

'Except,' Morgan pointed out, 'we don't know what caused yours. And I doubt that every faery in the land will queue up to forget everything about themselves.'

'Lots of faeries queued up for pixie dust. It soothed away the ache, right? I know it's addictive. I know it can be misused. But surely a small group of addicts is a small price to pay for saving the world?'

'Dust doesn't work on Redcaps,' Finn said. 'And that idea is not really a solution.'

I didn't see why not. It would even keep Rubus happy.

'You can't force people to take drugs, Maddy.'

'Well,' I answered, 'you *can*. You just don't want to.'

Morgan raked a hand through his hair and got to his feet. He walked over to one of the windows and gazed out at the shadowed, night-filled golf course. 'The easiest answer to all of this is to do what Mendax says. We learn to trust him, he learns to trust us, and together we destroy the sphere once and for all.'

'You could take the sphere and hide it,' I said. 'No one but you has to know where it is.'

Morgan didn't turn around. 'I can withstand most Truth Draws,' he said, 'even when they're conducted by very experienced Fey. I don't know that I have the strength to withstand one of Rubus's Truth Spiders. I don't know that anyone has that kind of capability. All he'd need to do is get hold of me and use one of those creatures to bring out the truth.'

'So put the sphere somewhere where no one can get hold of it even if they do know where it is! You could…' I searched around, trying to think of a way '…you could send it into space.'

Finn looked at me. 'You know many astronauts, do you?'

'All I'm saying is that we've not exhausted every possibility yet!' I threw up my hands in frustration. Saving the world really shouldn't be this damned difficult.

'Mendax was talking sense, Maddy. Nothing is ever lost forever. The sphere needs to be destroyed. We need to know without a shadow of a doubt that it's out of reach. The only way to do that is to get rid of it completely.'

I cursed loudly, even though I knew deep down he was right. I hated that he was right. 'So do we do this, then? Do we deal with Mendax?'

His answer was quiet. 'Is there any choice?' He turned and looked at me, meeting my eyes. Almost. 'Can you do it? Can you steal Rubus's ring?'

'Of course!' I snapped, though I had no earthly idea how I'd manage it.

'Then we take the first step towards the deal. We can still walk away at a later date. If there's the faintest hint that we can't trust Mendax fully, we keep the sphere to ourselves. If he keeps to his side of the bargain then, if nothing else, we might be able to break the truce so that we can remove Rubus from the equation. That'll buy us time, if nothing else.'

'You say that like we have nothing to lose.'

Morgan put his hands into his pockets. His eyes were half-closed so his expression was shuttered. 'It will be incredibly dangerous. You don't have to do it, Maddy. We can get the ring from Rubus without you risking yourself.'

His tone of voice told me that he knew his words were a lie. 'I don't think we can,' I said quietly. I sighed. 'I'll do my best.' I squared my shoulders. 'I'll do better than my best. I'll get the damned ring. You keep thinking of ways to destroy the stupid sphere or hide it away for the rest of eternity. I'll call you when I have the ring.'

'Thank you.' Then, almost inaudibly, he added, 'You're a much better person than you give yourself credit for.'

'I'm a murderer, Morgan. I'm exactly the evil bitch you believed me to be.'

I couldn't stay there any longer. I couldn't stand there knowing that he could barely look at me. And the growing sympathy in Finn's expression was becoming almost too much to cope with. Along with Morgan, I'd killed his brother, Winn, and I'd not been able to stop Rubus killing his other brother. I had no right to Finn's pity.

'Can you deal with clearing up here?' I asked. The pair of them nodded. 'Good.' I sniffed. 'I'm off. I'm dressed up to the nines and it's about time I found a suitable club to dance away the rest of the night. I'll speak to you both soon.'

I paused for a moment, waiting for Morgan to ask me to stay because I'd already promised to spend the night with him. I'd refuse, of course, but it would be nice to be asked. All he did, however, was turn away and head for the security room.

Finn actually looked concerned. I looked away. Yeah. Time to go.

***

I'd been lying about the dancing part, obviously, but I did require several stiff drinks if I was going to get any sleep. I trudged back down the hill to the main road where I could hopefully grab a taxi back to the city before finding a pub with late opening hours.

I muttered to myself all the time. Why had Charrie come to this place? Why had I killed him? Was it because the bogle had the sphere and I'd wanted to stop him from either using it himself or handing it over to Rubus to use? Or was it that I'd simply wanted to kill him for kicks? Were there others whose lives I'd snuffed out?

A mental image of Rubus casually thrusting a knife into Jinn's throat flashed into my mind. Despite my obvious shortcomings, there had been nothing about that act which had titillated me. Quite the opposite. But if I'd been pure evil before the amnesia then I had to be pure evil now; a bump on the head and a bout of forgetfulness wouldn't change my personality.

I kicked irritably at a fallen branch. Unfortunately, the ground underneath was muddier and more slippery than I'd realised and I skidded, arms flailing and legs flying out from underneath me, before landing flat on my back in true slapstick fashion.

I lay where I was for a moment, even though I could feel the damp, squelchy mud plastering the bare skin at my neck and snaking its way down the back of my corset like it had a mind of its own. Then I spread-eagled my body and moved my arms and legs. Mud angel. Maybe I could no longer believe any part of me was a superhero but I could well believe I was a dirty angel. A dirty angel with blood on her hands.

I sighed and stopped what I was doing. I could internalise my problems and fret all I wanted but I couldn't change the past, whatever it was. Charrie would still be dead and I'd still have killed him. I could only focus on the future and the way forward.

With that thought in mind, I pushed myself up to a sitting position, hoping for a low-lying tree branch that I could use to heave myself up. That was when I spotted the small chest lying against the pile of rocks only a few metres away. Huh.

I was no longer naïve enough to believe this was a coincidence. Artemesia had surmised that the magic bound into my amnesia was causing my subconscious self to seek ways to reassert my memory and rebalance the scales. My previous experiences had certainly borne that out. But I was no longer so sure that I wanted my memory back. I was looking to the future, I reminded myself. Not the past.

I already had a pretty good idea what was inside the chest and I was highly tempted to leave it where it was without checking – magical memory malarkey be damned. But I was the Madhatter. Nothing scared or intimidated me. Shadows ran from me; monsters quaked at the very mention of my name. I was no namby-pamby minion. No, I was graceful strength personified.

A strange scuttling sound reached my ears. I frowned, squinting to see where it was coming from. A moment later, a tiny spider made its way up over the side of the chest and I screamed. Very loudly. I jerked backwards, recoiling with such violence that the mud around me spattered upwards, flicking a spray of smelly gloop across my face and torso.

I wiped off the worst of it and eyed the chest suspiciously. The spider had vanished. That made me more nervous than if it were still looking at me with its creepy multiple eyes. I swung my head round, scanning the forest gloom as if I expected the eight-legged beast, which had to be at least the size of my thumbnail, to attack me with an army of its hairy buddies. I couldn't see anything; I couldn't hear anything either.

Scowling to myself, I reached for the chest again, waving my hands at it first just in case any more spiders were lurking around it. Then I flipped open the lid. The damned arachnid had put me on edge so I wasn't even pleased that my educated guess about the contents had been confirmed. I already knew I was highly intelligent; what I didn't know was where the arsebadgering spider had gone.

Still wary – as well I should have been – I dipped the tip of my index finger into the pile of sparkly dust and lifted it up to my face to examine it more closely. As far as I understood, Carduus made this crap in his lab. I wondered whether the sparkles were a side effect of whatever potions and magic spells he used or whether he put them in because he liked a bit of bling.

I stuck out my tongue, allowing myself the tiniest lick. A second later, I spat. Aniseed again. Of all the flavours in the world, why would you choose aniseed? I supposed the taste didn't really matter, given that pixie dust was designed to be snorted, but really! I shook my head, bemused, and closed the lid of the chest. Then I yanked myself awkwardly to my feet, stuffed the chest under my arm and continued walking.

Chapter Eleven

It took longer than I'd hoped to get back into the city although it was still barely gone midnight by the time I limped out of the taxi. One of Rubus's Fey henchmen was standing outside the hideout. His eyes flicked in my direction and I blew him a kiss, but he didn't react. Shrugging, I turned and walked in the opposite direction, heading for the nearest open pub.

The first one I came across displayed a curling, yellowed poster for a local band aptly named 'Mud In Your Eye'. I shrugged and entered.

It was one of those old men's pubs. No showy craft beers or artisan crisps on offer here; this was all strong ale and pork scratchings, with an invasive odour of stale Old Spice and sour body odour. I ignored the stares from the few remaining punters and took a seat on one of the bar stools.

The barman shambled over. He didn't say a cheery hello; in fact, he didn't say anything – he just looked me up and down. Perhaps I should have kept my Madhatter superhero cape and added it to my leather corset and splattered mud ensemble.

I hefted the chest of pixie dust onto the bar top. 'Vodka,' I said. 'Lots of vodka. No ice.' I look at the barman sternly. 'And make sure it's the strongest you've got.'

Mr Silent-But-Judgy nodded and turned to the shelf behind him. He poured me a double and set it down in front of me. I raised the glass and lifted it to my lips, taking only the smallest sip before choking and spluttering.

'Maybe some Coke too?' I croaked. 'Just to make it a bit sweeter.'

He smirked, finally cracking his bland exterior. 'Sure thing, duck.'

Once I could continue drinking without fearing for my life, I started to relax. The vodka, even tempered with copious amounts of sweet, fizzy cola, sent a warm buzz down through my body.

The other patrons settled back into their conversations and, thanks to my appearance, I had no worries that I would be interrupted with nonsensical flirting. Mud-caked as I was, I was still obviously far too sophisticated for the likes of anyone here. All the men must have recognised that to approach me would be to punch too far above their weight.

I tossed back my hair, inadvertently sending a few bits of dried mud behind me, one or two of which landed in a bearded fellow's pint. Oops. I hastily turned away and hunched my shoulders. Maybe if I pretended I were invisible, he wouldn't notice me.

'Enjoying yourself?' murmured a familiar voice by my side.

I jerked, spilling some of my drink. 'Rubus,' I said. 'What a joy.'

He smiled at me, although his smile didn't reach his eyes. 'You could at least pretend that you're happy to see me.'

I gave up on my invisibility attempt and flung myself off my bar stool. I wrapped my arms round Morgan's brother and squeezed him as tightly as I could without breaking the terms of the truce, then I rubbed my cheek against his like a cat. 'I'm so glad to see you,' I said breathlessly. 'All I could think about was you and how much I missed you. And now you're here!' I pulled back and clasped my heart. 'It's a miracle! A god-given miracle!'

'Hey lady,' growled the bearded man. 'You owe me another drink.'

'I'll get it,' Rubus said. He raised his eyebrows at me. 'If you'll stop acting like an idiot.'

I shrugged. I could cope with that. 'Okay,' I trilled. I hopped back onto my stool. I was pleased to note that a considerable amount of the mud that had been plastered over me was now covering Rubus.

He paid for the drinks, even going so far as to take the pint over to the whinger who, I noticed, might not have wanted mud splattered into his pint of beer but had still drunk it down to the dregs. Whatever. It was Rubus's money that was being wasted.

Rubus took several gulps of his own pint. I noticed with interest that his hands were shaking. Was he scared of me? The idea made my insides burble with happiness. Then I saw that his skin looked paler than normal and there were lines of tension around his eyes.

'Are you ill?' I enquired.

'What?' he snapped.

I pointed at his face. 'You don't look very well. You should get some vitamins down you or something. You've got a big date tomorrow night.'

Rubus's forehead creased as if he'd completely forgotten about his dinner with a star from *St Thomas Close*. He'd demanded I arrange it; the least he could do was remember it.

'I'm fine,' he answered shortly. 'No thanks to my bastard of a brother though.'

'He caused problems for you out at Chen's place?' I enquired, carefully schooling my expression to avoid yielding any truths.

'He wasn't even there.' Rubus grimaced in disgust. 'He couldn't be bothered to show up in person. He just sent a bunch of Fey flunkies.'

I tapped the side of my glass. 'Are you surprised?' I asked. 'After all, that's what you usually do.'

Anger sparked in Rubus's green eyes. They really were remarkably similar to Morgan's. 'Are you suggesting that I'm not man enough to get my hands dirty?'

'Actually,' I said, hoping this tactic would work, 'I'm saying it of both you and your brother. Aren't the pair of you supposed to be leaders or something? How do you expect people to follow you if you won't lead by example?'

'I *was* leading by example,' Rubus snapped. 'I was there – at least for a short while. Morgan didn't show his ugly face once.'

I took another sip of my drink. 'You know,' I said, 'the two of you look incredibly alike.'

Rubus glowered at me but I just smiled in return. 'I know what your game is, Madrona,' he said finally.

Uh-oh. 'Yes?' I blinked in an attempt at wide-eyed innocence.

'You're trying us both out for size. You don't remember either of us so you've spent a bit of time with Morgan and now you're spending a bit of time with me. When you've decided which one of us you like best, you'll make your choice. You won't give a shit about the other one.' He drained his glass and extended his finger to the barman to order another. 'The trouble is that if I play that game for too long, you'll end up losing us both. You're not so desirable that we'll forgive your every fault.'

'You forced me to come with you,' I pointed out.

'Yes,' he conceded. 'But you've had plenty of opportunities over the last day or two to leave, should you so wish. In fact, you've been doing the opposite.

You've been putting on quite a show for me.'

Fair point; Rubus was more canny than I'd give him credit for. I considered his words seriously. 'I'll say one thing,' I told him. 'You're certainly more intelligent than Morgan.'

Rubus laughed softly. 'Only because he could never understand what you saw in me. Everything is black and white to him. It would give me more joy than he would ever know if he and I could work together to get back home to Mag Mell but he's not interested. He won't make things happen, he'll wait for someone else to make them happen. I'm proactive, he's reactive.' He exhaled. 'He's a fool.' For the briefest second, sadness flickered across his expression.

Something twisted in my stomach. Was I actually feeling sorry for Rubus? I mentally slapped myself. Arsebadger. 'Did you and I ever fuck?' I asked.

His eyes flew to mine and he half-choked. 'You certainly have a way with words, Madrona.'

I bowed. 'Thank you very much. It's a serious question though.'

While I wasn't sure what the truth was, I knew what I expected Rubus to say. He surprised me, however. 'No,' he said. 'We did not. Although I'm sure that Morgan believes otherwise. I certainly gave him enough cause to.'

Huh. I nibbled my bottom lip, waiting until the barman had presented Rubus with his second pint and moved away again. He didn't go far; I could tell he was still interested enough to try and eavesdrop on us. Rubus did too. He glared at the barman who finally found something to do on the other side of the room.

I twiddled my fingers together. 'Did I ask Morgan to marry me?'

Rubus snapped his eyes back. 'Did he tell you that?'

I shook my head. 'No. It was a different Fey.'

His mouth thinned. 'It's true. You even went down one knee.' He shrugged. 'Or so I heard.'

'So why did I do it? Why did I leave him for you?' I was careful to keep my tone curious rather than censorious.

'The first time was for the same reason as the second time,' Rubus answered. He offered a half smile. 'Because I forced you.'

I drew in a sharp breath and he laughed. 'Look at you,' he said. 'Your little mind is whirring now, isn't it? What did I do? How terrible was it? How monstrous was I that you dumped your fiancé for me?' He gestured to my glass. 'You should drink some more. You're probably going to need it.'

I did as he suggested. Suddenly, getting drunk seemed like a remarkably good idea.

'Tell me, Madrona,' Rubus said, 'do you think honesty is a good thing? Do you believe in the righteousness of truth?'

'I guess so.' I watched him warily. I couldn't help remembering the banter about honesty that Morgan and I had engaged in. 'Though I can see when a white lie can be appropriate.'

'Indeed.' Rubus nodded. 'Because all I did to get you to leave Morgan was to promise the truth if you didn't.'

'Go on.' I'd already learned that I was a murderer tonight. How much worse could it get?

Rubus licked his lips in sudden gleeful anticipation. I felt like I was watching a car crash and I should look away. Gasbudlikins, I should *run* away. I couldn't though; I was rooted to the spot. I had to hear what he was going to say.

'There are only two people in this world,' he whispered, 'who know why the borders to other demesnes closed. Actually,' he amended, 'now that you have amnesia, there's only one person.'

Whatever I'd been expecting, it wasn't that. I blinked, too confused and surprised to work out where he was going with this. From the expression on Rubus's face, he knew it too.

'We are all stuck here because of you, Madrona,' Rubus said. 'You caused the borders to close. All this,' he swept an arm back towards the hideout, 'is your fault. You trapped us here.'

'Bullshit. There's no way that's true.'

Rubus was no longer smiling. 'I'm not lying.' He reached into his pocket. 'In fact, I'll prove it to you.'

He pulled out a box. I knew exactly what was inside it and half fell off my bar stool in a bid to get away. 'You brought one of those things here?' I spat at him.

'Relax. It's for me, not for you.' He rolled up his sleeve then opened the box lid with his other hand and let the spider crawl out. I stared in sickened fascination as it edged up his bare arm. Rubus gazed at it fondly.

I shuddered. The Truth Spider raised one of its legs and started to tap it against Rubus's skin, as if it were pondering the meaning of life. Rubus let out a mild snort.

'You weren't always afraid of spiders, Madrona,' he said. He extended one finger and gently stroked the creature's bulbous back. 'I did that.' He sounded proud of his achievement.

The spider didn't react so obviously Rubus was telling the truth. Hardly surprising. 'How many times?' I asked. 'How many times did you put those things on me?'

'I lost count,' he murmured, not taking his eyes off the spider. 'Occasionally you resisted and attempted a lie but it never went well.'

A deep-seated shiver ran through my bones. He'd told me before that the Truth Spiders only bit if you lied while one was on you – and that the ensuing pain was horrendous. Given its gleaming fangs, I could well believe it. Rubus had also mentioned that it only took three or four bites to kill a Fey. It was one way of getting round the truce.

I shuffled further back in case the hairy bastard decided to leap at me. And I wasn't just talking about the spider. I glanced around. None of the other pub customers were paying us the slightest bit of attention.

'Let's get to the point, shall we?' he murmured. 'The border to Mag Mell closed because of you, Madrona. It was your fault and you knew exactly what you were doing.'

It was probably the only thing he could have said that would have dragged my attention away from the spider. My eyes flew up to his and I realised he was watching me – and enjoying this. 'What do you mean?'

'You were somewhat … reckless when you were younger. And talented.' His smile chilled me even more than the spider had. 'You developed a spell to close the border and trap everyone here. You wanted the other Fey to stop taking this demesne for granted and you decided that forcing a large group of us to spend more time here would encourage that. Of course, you thought it would only be temporary. I believe the closure was only supposed to last for forty-eight hours. But when the deadline passed and your binding magic held,' he raised his shoulders, 'well, let's just say that you realised your mistake.'

I shot a look at the spider. I couldn't help myself. It had stopped tapping its leg and wasn't moving. I swallowed; Rubus wasn't lying then. 'How…' I licked my lips nervously. 'How did you find out that I did it?'

'You told me. You wanted to show off to someone and you knew that if you told Morganus he would not be amused. So you told me. You used me to boost your ego. It was a while later when I used that fact against you. How else do you think I got you to turn to me instead of my brother?'

'You gave me an ultimatum,' I whispered, finally realising. 'Either I went to you or you'd tell Morgan what I'd done – that all this was my fault.'

Rubus bared his teeth. 'Indeed. You were rather sullen at first but you came around. In fact, our relationship went from strength to strength when you realised how much better things were at my side. You weren't made to be angelic and pure, Madrona. You're far more interesting than that.'

What I should have done was take full advantage of the situation and the spider on his arm. I should have questioned him, trapped him in a lie or tried to find his true intentions for Chen's sphere. But the weight of Rubus's revelations had rocked me too much for coherent thought.

He smiled at me then gently encouraged the spider back into its box. 'You think I'm a bad guy,' he said softly.

I opened my mouth, wanting to protest, but he held up his hand and waved me into silence. 'There's no point lying about it, Madrona. I can see it every time you look at me. I horrify you even more than my spiders do. But you have to admit that I fascinate you too. That's because you possess the same streak that I do.'

I found my voice. 'Streak of evil?'

He laughed. 'No. There's no single word for the likes of us. Mere vocabulary can't possibly encapsulate our genius. It's a streak of cunning, of intelligence. Of pure, throbbing power and risk-taking. It's weighing up the odds and making a choice because it's the best choice available, even if some people might get hurt in the process. You and I are far more alike than you give us credit for.'

The most troubling thing about all this was that I suspected Rubus was correct and I had more in common with him than I did with Morgan. But that didn't mean I wanted it. Or him.

Rubus tucked away the box. Praise be. 'So,' he drawled, 'has this helped make your mind up as to which brother you would prefer to be with?'

Gods, yes. I jiggled my bar stool closer to him, although I made sure I was still far enough away should he release that damned spider again. I pointed at the little chest that was still resting on top of the bar. 'That should answer your question.'

Rubus reached for it, drawing it into his lap. 'There's not a poisonous snake inside here, is there?'

I managed a weak laugh. 'No. No snakes. No vipers, no adders, no cobras.' Because, I added silently, the only real snake around here is you.

He opened the chest and peered in. The surprise on his face seemed genuine. 'My pixie dust!' he exclaimed. 'You found it.'

'Well, you did demand that I search for it and return it to you.'

'I thought it would occupy you while you decided whose side you were really on. I didn't actually expect that you would locate it.' His eyes narrowed. 'Your memory…'

'Still gone,' I said. 'Artemesia had a theory about it, though. You know, Carduus's niece,' I reminded him.

'I know who she is.'

I shrugged at the growl in his voice. 'She reckons that my amnesia is magic-related and that the magic would work to return my memory by leading me to people and objects that would jolt it back into action.'

His expression cleared and he nodded. 'Of course. That makes perfect sense. That's how we were reunited so quickly. We're meant to work together – the magic demands it.'

I managed to avoid rolling my eyes. It was Morgan who I'd been drawn to, not Rubus. 'Mmm.'

Rubus delved into the box then frowned. 'What the hell is this?' he asked, scooping up a handful of dust. Amid the sparkly grey were more than a few specks of dull green.

I grimaced. 'Ah. Well, for some reason I left the chest in a small forest. A small, damp forest. I guess it got mouldy.' Either that or someone had taken a lot of moss and mixed it in so that the entire batch was unusable. I couldn't think for the life of me who that would have been though…

Rubus tutted. 'That's annoying.' He looked up. 'Which forest was this exactly?'

This was where I was on shaky ground. I'd already decided, dangerous as it was, to stick as close to the truth as possible. I had to do everything I could to make Rubus believe I was on his side – and if that meant taking risks by veering into dangerous honesty, that was what I'd do. It wasn't lost on me that he'd already pointed out this painful side of my personality tonight. I was still sure I was doing the right thing, though. 'It was on the outskirts of the city,' I answered. 'Nothing nearby, except a golf course of all things.'

I caught the faintest twitch from his eyelid. Yep, that got his attention. 'Wait a second,' he said. 'Didn't you tell me that you woke up on a golf course?'

As if he'd forgotten. I nodded. 'I did. And yes, it was the same one. I assume that I hid the pixie dust out of fear that it would be stolen or lost before whatever happened happened.'

'And the name of the golf course?' he enquired. 'I should send a team to check it out.'

He'd find it sooner or later; it was better that I controlled his discovery. I told him its name. I even gave him directions. Rubus appeared satisfied. 'Excellent,' he murmured. He closed the chest lid and tucked it under his arm. 'I should go,' he said.

My gaze dropped momentarily to his hand and to the little finger where his gold ring was proudly displayed. I was tempted to find a way to get him to hand it over right now, given that he was pleased with me, but I already had a better idea about how to nab it.

I waved him off, telling him I was going to have a nightcap. I had to tread carefully; Rubus wasn't a cardboard cut-out of a villain. In fact, he was far more complex than I'd given him credit for.

He wasn't the only one who was complex, though – and I was the murderer amongst us. I nodded to myself. He had no chance. Softly, softly catchee monkey.

Chapter Twelve

I was awoken the following morning by Morgan's gruff tones in my ear. For one pleasant moment before I was fully awake, I assumed he was lying next to me and had some morning wood that required my delicate ministrations. Then I realised it was the daft shell phone.

'How are you?' he repeated.

I fumbled groggily under my pillow for the shell and held it up. 'You're concerned about me?' I couldn't resist adding a hint of sarcasm, given the way he hadn't been able to meet my eyes the previous night. 'I'm touched.'

'Of course I'm fucking concerned, Madrona! You went back to Rubus. Have you seen him? Have you tried to get his ring?'

Ah. So that's what this was about. I suddenly had the distinct feeling that each of the brothers was using me for the same reason – to get at the other. I could hardly complain, however. Using people was apparently what I did best. I should admire the pair of them rather than feel hurt.

'I'm absolutely fine,' I told him. 'And, no, I haven't tried to get the ring yet. I'm not going to bulldoze in and wrestle it off his finger. He has to believe it's his idea to remove it or this will never work.'

'I take it you have a plan.'

'Morgan, darling,' I drawled, 'I always have a plan.' I'd had a plan to kill Charrie the Bogle and that had worked. I'd even had a plan to close the borders to Mag Mell, I thought sourly, and that had been far more successful – in a sense, anyway – than I could have hoped for. 'Just be patient.'

There was a beat of silence. 'I'm not trying to hassle you, Maddy,' Morgan said. 'I'm just worried.'

Him and me both. I sighed. Then, hearing the patter of footsteps in the corridor outside, I shook myself. 'It's too dangerous to talk now,' I told him. I bit my lip. 'Look, I need some willing pixie-dust takers.'

'Pardon?'

I ignored the dangerous edge to his voice. 'You heard me. I feel like I'm really close to getting Rubus to believe that I'm on his side and I'm a trustworthy henchwoman. Bringing him some more potential addicts will give me more leeway.'

'You want me to find you some faeries willing to turn themselves into addicts?' he asked, his disbelief palpable even through the shell's minor magic.

From what I recalled of the Fey who'd approached me when they'd thought I was selling, it wouldn't be too hard. 'It's for the greater good,' I told him. 'And it's only a short-term thing.'

'That's what you say now.' His voice hardened. 'I won't do it. There has to be a line, Madrona, and I'm drawing that line here. I won't involve innocents in our plans.'

Except innocents were always going to be in our plans because this was all about saving damned innocents. I couldn't yell that down the shell at him, though; someone would hear me. 'Fine,' I snapped. 'I'll find them myself.'

I stuffed the shell unceremoniously under the mattress. If Morgan continued to talk, I couldn't hear him.

I brushed the worst of the now fully dried mud off yesterday's clothes and reflected that it was just as well I'd chosen leather. It seemed harder to wiggle into the tight trousers today than it had been yesterday but that was good; my arse would look even better than before if the taut material hugged it snugly. I did refrain from doing up the corset too tightly, though. I still had to have a decent breakfast and I didn't want any extra flesh to pop out unless I planned for it to do so.

I combed out the worst of the tangles in my hair and hoisted it up into a tight bun. It gave me a stern look, halfway between boarding-school matron and sex-club dominatrix. I couldn't ask for more. Today I meant business.

I headed out, stalking towards the kitchen and keeping my head raised to avoid eye contact – and chitter-chatter – with any passing faeries. The smell of cooking bacon hit me long before I hit the kitchen. Excellent: I really was starving.

Recognising the chef as the bouncer who'd been positioned in front of Rubus's bedroom the previous day, I walked up and watched as he slid two perfect sunny-side eggs onto the plate next to the cooker. Beans, black pudding, three juicy sausages, crispy bacon and even a potato scone. Yum, yum, yum.

I picked up the plate and walked over to the table.

'Hey! Thass mine!' he bellowed.

I found a knife and fork and dug in. 'Oh,' I murmured, swallowing my first mouthful. 'You should have said.' I waggled my knife at him. 'Next time tell me and I'll make my own breakfast instead.' I stretched across the table and pulled the ketchup towards me before liberally dousing the whole plate.

Rubus strolled in, a lazy smile written across his handsome face. He looked much better than he had the night before, with a healthier colour to his skin. He must have had a good night's sleep. And why not? It wasn't as if he'd had to fret over the fact that he was the one who'd consigned us all to this madness.

'That bitch took my breakfast!' the other faery snarled.

Rubus raised an eyebrow. 'Are you seriously complaining to me about something so petty as bacon and eggs, Amellus?'

The way to an army was through its stomach. Rubus would have to realise that and do more to keep his troops in line, especially once the sphere was destroyed. Not that I cared. 'Yeah,' I said with a sneer, 'are you?'

Amellus glared at me and turned back to the frying pan to start cooking again. Behind his back, Rubus shook his head at me, unimpressed by my actions. I shovelled as much of the food into my mouth as I could before he decided to take it away from me.

'I thought,' I said, as I chomped on beans, 'that I might go out and try to sell some dust today. Carduus still has some, right?'

'Not much,' Rubus answered. He was watching me with an inscrutable expression. 'But enough to hook in a few extra clients. Is there anyone you have in mind?'

'When I was running around the city and trying to work out who I was,' I said, hoping I wouldn't have to name names, 'I bumped into a few faeries who asked me for some dust. At the time, I didn't know what they were talking about. Now I reckon they'd be a good place to start. They can probably lead me to other potential clients.' I smiled. 'Clients. That's a nice word, isn't it? It's better than naïve fools, I suppose.'

Rubus didn't appear amused. 'Who are these faeries?'

Gasbudlikins. I'd have to throw a few Fey under the bus after all. Greater good, I reminded myself. It was easy to see how I'd fallen so deeply into this life before my amnesia incident.

I shrugged and did my best to look nonchalant.

'Some faery woman who works at the library. And a guy who runs a hotel.'

'Begonius,' Rubus said instantly. 'I thought you probably talked to him since that's where I found you. And Paeonia, I assume.'

'That might have been their names,' I said unconvincingly.

Rubus rubbed his chin. 'They've dabbled in dust before but not enough to become true addicts.'

'Well, maybe I can change that.' I met his gaze head-on. Trust me. Believe in me.

He waved a hand. 'Very well,' he said, as if it were of no real interest to him. 'There is another name you might wish to throw into the mix.'

'Who's that?' I asked, with a sudden feeling of trepidation.

'A Fey called Vandrake. He used to be one of ours.' Rubus scowled. 'Then Morganus got involved. Vandrake's been off dust for a while but he possessed certain talents which are … useful. It would be good to have him back in the fold again.'

I winced internally. I'd actually met Vandrake – Morgan had taken me to meet him in a bid to educate me about the damages of pixie dust. Vandrake had been terrified of me – and even more petrified of becoming an addict again. I strongly suspected it wouldn't take much to tip him back over the edge. Was I really callous enough to be the person to achieve that?

'The more the merrier,' I said to Rubus, hoping my expression didn't betray my inner turmoil. 'Where might I find him?'

'Carduus has records of all our … clients. Past and present. When you pick up the pixie dust from him, make sure he gives you Vandrake's address too.'

I nodded and returned my attention to my plate. At

least my breakfast wasn't going to make any criminal demands on me, even if it did cause a bout of heartburn later on.

Rubus ambled over until he was right next to me. It was just as well I'd almost finished eating because I could swear his aftershave was even stronger today than usual. 'Do this for me, Maddy,' he said quietly. 'And I might be more inclined to trust you properly again.'

Again? From what I'd heard from Artemesia, he'd never really trusted me the first time around and that had been after years of this sort of shit. I sighed. 'I just can't stop thinking about what you told me last night. That all this…' I sneaked a look at the other faery in the room. He appeared absorbed in crisping up his bacon but I couldn't be too sure he wasn't earwigging at the same time. I dropped my voice. 'That all this is my fault.'

'Don't worry,' Rubus said, clapping me on the back. 'I didn't tell anyone then and I won't tell anyone now. Not if you stay in your place.' He winked at me as if all this were nothing more than a great joke. Ha bloody ha. Then he strode over to the cooker. 'That bacon looks good,' he murmured. 'I'll have it.'

I really wanted the Fey to kick up a fuss and complain at losing his second batch of food but he was too eager to please his lord and master. I watched him bob his head eagerly and rolled my eyes, before pushing back my plate and standing up. It appeared I had a mission to complete, as distasteful as it was.

Drug dealing was just so … dirty. Murdering innocent bogles and sending a thousand Fey into exile were more my kind of business. Apparently.

***

Carduus was in the laboratory when I arrived,

wearing a pristine white coat as if he were some kind of vaunted scientist and frowning at a steaming beaker filled with nasty-looking purple gunk.

'Cardy, baby! How's it hanging?'

He didn't even deign to answer me with a glare, so he went up a notch in my estimation. 'Here,' he said. 'Try this.' He took a spoon and pulled out a gloop of purple and offered it to me.

'Uh, no.' I smiled sweetly. 'My mother told me never to accept sweets from strangers.'

He frowned. 'You remember your mother? Has your memory returned?'

I mentally lowered that notch back a level again. 'I thought scientists were supposed to be smart. You have the IQ of lint.'

Carduus still looked confused. 'What's lint?'

'You spend far too long inside this laboratory, Cardigan,' I told him.

He sniffed. 'That is not my name. And I do whatever my lord requires.' I could only presume by 'my lord' he was referring to Rubus. This place was like a damned cult.

He jiggled the spoon at me. 'Now,' he said, 'try this. It's mugwort enhanced with a sprinkle of lavender and essence of anemone and bound up in an old spell. It doesn't taste as bad as it looks.'

Somehow I doubted that. I folded my arms defiantly. 'I'm not putting that inside my mouth.'

'You've had worse.' This time I definitely registered a leer. 'It's something I've put together myself. It might help your memory to return.'

'You're going to have to do better than that before I slurp it, mate.' I patted by belly. 'Besides, I've just had breakfast. I'm really not hungry.'

Carduus pushed his glasses up his nose in irritation.

'It's supposed to be taken on an empty stomach.'

'Well, that is a shame.' I couldn't have sounded more flat than a pancake on Shrove Tuesday. 'Another time.'

'Tomorrow morning,' he ordered. 'First thing.'

'Yeah,' I murmured unconvincingly. 'Sure.'

He emptied the contents of the spoon back into the beaker. There was a definite acidic hiss when the gloop landed and I stepped backwards. It seemed prudent to put as much distance as possible between the foul concoction and myself.

'I need some pixie dust,' I informed him. 'I'm going to hit the streets and do some selling.'

He gestured at the shelf. 'It's over there. Help yourself.'

I did as he bade, locating the familiar sparkly grey dust quickly enough. Rubus had been right; there wasn't much of it. In fact, by the time I found Vandrake I doubted there'd be any left. 'Do you have a bag?'

Carduus muttered and pointed behind him. I located a crumpled pile of old plastic bags and selected one at random. As I did so, my eye was caught by three large jars filled with a colourless liquid. I tapped the nearest one. 'What's this?'

He glanced up and his nostrils flared slightly. 'Nothing that concerns you.'

I doubted that; his response meant that it was something that concerned me very much. Without asking him for permission, I leaned over, uncorked the nearest jar and took a deep sniff. Huh. It was an oddly familiar smell but I couldn't place it.

'Get away from that!' Carduus snapped. 'It's not for you! You'll contaminate it.'

Curious. I returned the stopper to its original position but he still didn't relax. I couldn't risk raising his suspicion when the liquid might be completely innocuous so I smiled at him benignly. 'Okay-dokey. Before I go, I also need a copy of the file with all the past and present clients. Rubus told me to get it so I know who to target.'

Carduus insinuated himself between me and the jars, as if he were still afraid that I was going to lunge for one of them and try to escape with it. I almost laughed. All three of them were enormous – I'd be lucky to lift one of them, let alone sprint away and liberate it from his clutches.

'I don't tend to call them clients,' he told me.

'What do you call them?'

He grinned. It wasn't pleasant. 'Cannon fodder.'

'Well, you're just charm personified.'

He bowed. 'The list is in the second drawer to the right. Help yourself.'

I extricated a manila folder and glanced inside. There was a crapload of names. Some had smiley faces scratched next to them, some had question marks. A far smaller number, Vandrake's included, possessed crosses. I slid it into the bag together with the dust. This would come in useful.

'Thank you.' It probably paid to be at least slightly polite to the mad scientist.

He waved me off. 'Get out of here. I need to concentrate.' He spat onto the floor, a long stream of green phlegm of a similar consistency to his potion. 'And don't forget to come back first thing tomorrow!'

I grimaced and made my exit. Bleugh. No chance.

Chapter Thirteen

I'd assumed that I'd be free to leave on my own as I had the previous day; in fact, I was counting on it. Unfortunately, I was only halfway to the door when Lunaria bounced up. She was, I noted, no longer wearing the red-leather number. Chicken.

'I'm to come with you!' she trilled, a delighted smile stretching from ear to ear. 'Maybe I can learn something. You are the master at selling, after all.'

'I'm a masterful sort of person,' I murmured. I had to stop her tagging along, she would only get in my way. 'But I don't think…'

I was only halfway through my sentence when Rubus appeared and stopped to watch us, a tiny smile playing around his lips. Gasbudlikins.

'…I don't think I'll have much to teach you,' I said, altering my original statement in the nick of time. 'After all, I don't remember ever doing this before.'

'It's like riding a bike,' she told me. 'You'll pick it up again in no time.'

And if I didn't, no doubt she would report it back to her lord and master. I forced a smile. 'Then it'll be wonderful to have you along for back-up,' I said.

Lunaria beamed and took my arm. I thrust the bag at her; if she was going to be this much of a pain in my arse then at the very least she could caddy for me. 'Here,' I said. 'I trust you to keep this and not lose it.'

She was far too delighted with the sudden burden. 'Great!'

As we walked out together, I could feel Rubus's eyes burning into my back. The scowl on my face remained.

This was most definitely not how I wanted my day to begin. I created a mental image of myself pushing Lunaria under a bus but it didn't really help.

Outside, the sun was shining, entirely at odds with my sudden change in mood. I twisted right, marching so quickly that Lunaria was forced to jog to keep up.

'Rubus was looking very dark and handsome just now, don't you think?' she twittered.

'Just about the only time I find him handsome is when it's dark,' I retorted.

Lunaria squinted at me. 'But when it's dark you can't see him properly.'

I was surrounded by fools. Sighing, I crossed the road. 'We're going to the library first,' I said. 'There's a Fey woman there called Paeonia who will be an easy mark.'

Lunaria clapped her hands. 'Excellent!'

I was starting to feel like I had my own personal cheerleader. Everything was 'wonderful' and 'great' and 'fantastic'. Maybe that was why she wasn't wearing the red-leather outfit today – it didn't match her pompoms. Deciding that the least I could was to take advantage of her beaming friendliness and do some digging, I slowed my steps to allow her to draw level and have a proper chat.

'So, Looney Tunes,' I said, 'how are things going with you? I've not seen you since our shopping expedition yesterday and that feels like a lifetime ago. Have you been busy? Weren't you doing some kind of hush-hush investigation for Rubus?'

It was like I'd taken a cloth to her face and wiped off her expression. Her smile vanished and even the sparkle in her eyes appeared to dim – although her cheeks reddened considerably. 'Oh yeah,' she said. She fidgeted with the bag. 'I've been taken off that. It's why I can come with you today instead.'

'Mm-hmm. Has everyone been taken off it?' After all, I'd told Rubus exactly where to go. There was no point searching every golf course for miles around when he already had the answer.

She chewed her bottom lip. 'I really don't know.'

For someone with the effervescence of a shaken Pepsi can, Lunaria could be remarkably tight-lipped. I wasn't going to get anywhere by pursuing this line of questioning; I had to be smarter. That was okay. I was the Madhatter. I was intelligence personified. Most of the time.

'There's still a lot about this world that I don't know,' I confided. 'I mean, I understand we're all trapped here but how exactly did that happen? What made the borders close like that?'

Obviously relieved to be on safer ground, Lunaria's full-wattage smile returned. At least, that was, until she remembered I'd asked her about the worst thing to happen to us faeries since Tinkerbell. She quickly replaced her grin with a serious expression. 'No one really knows what happened. It took a while for us to realise that the borders were closed in the first place. It was never easy to get here so once you did you had to make the most of every minute. To get approval to travel, you had to get a visa from the authorities in Mag Mell and there was always loads of red tape. They were concerned that too many faeries in this demesne would upset the balance so they tried to limit the numbers.'

I absorbed this, comparing it to what Rubus had told me the night before. 'So the faeries in charge were concerned about this demesne?'

'Sure! Although,' her eyes clouded slightly, 'there was a rumour going around that they were going to relax the bureaucracy and let more people travel because there hadn't been any problems with us coming across. Not everyone was happy about that. In fact, *you* complained a lot. You had a strong personality when you were a teenager.'

Strong personality? There was a euphemism for bitch if ever I heard one. 'You mean I'm not like that now?'

Lunaria just laughed. 'In any case, there was no single event that any of us knew of that caused the borders to close. We thought at first that it was a problem with Mag Mell itself, but all signs point to something on this side that created the issue.'

There wasn't the faintest trace of guile on her face. Lunaria didn't suspect for a moment that all this was down to me. I wondered what she'd say if she knew. I doubted she'd be so happy to trip the street beside me. 'Why did I come over?'

'You gave a reason at the time, something about observing human behaviour in cities to see if we could apply any new techniques to our own behaviour back home which would have a positive effect. Everyone knew you were really just tagging along behind Morgan.'

'Uh-huh. And Rubus? Why did he come over?'

She gave me a lopsided smile. 'Anything Morgan did, Rubus wanted to do too.' It was a surprisingly honest statement from someone who thought the sun shone out of Rubus's arse. It also sounded like Rubus and I had even more in common. We'd both crossed the border to this demesne for the same reason – but only one of us had trapped everyone here.

I fell into my own thoughts for the rest of the journey, turning everything over and over again in my head. I reckoned I must have been about nineteen when I came over. Young enough to make a stupid mistake but still old enough to know better. I wondered how long I'd feel guilty about something I couldn't even remember. It wasn't an emotion that suited me at all well.

We swung into the library and I saw the top of Paeonia's head in front of the queue of customers. I could have waited patiently in line for my turn but my mission was more important than theirs.

I strolled up to the front, ignoring the angry tuts as I barged my way in. Lunaria, looking vaguely ashamed, loped up behind me.

Paeonia glanced in our direction with her faery green eyes and stiffened. We'd only met once before and Morgan had marched me away from her before I could do much of anything. She had recognised me and petitioned me for some dust, halting only when Morgan had told her off. She was listed as a potential pixie-dust user on Carduus's list but I didn't think she was actually in thrall to Rubus. I didn't know many people I could turn to right now so I had to use every possible contact. It was the only way.

'Excuse me!' Someone tapped on my shoulder.

I half turned. It was a little old lady holding a pile of books in one hand and a walking stick in the other. 'What?' I snapped.

'There's a queue!'

'I know,' I informed her. 'I'm not an idiot. I just don't have the manners to wait.'

Her blue eyes widened in shock. 'This is a library!'

I stared at her. Was that supposed to make a difference? Were the surrounding books supposed to imbue me with a sense of inferiority? I opened my mouth to answer her but Paeonia was already stepping in. 'Ernest, take over from here.' She glared at me. 'I'll deal with this customer.'

She beckoned Lunaria and me well away from the snooping ears of the other book borrowers who were sending me narrow-eyed evil looks. I curtsied dramatically.

Paeonia hissed, 'What are you doing? I don't want to lose my job because you're being a bitch! Why are you here?'

'Last time we met,' I said, 'you were looking for some pixie dust.'

Her face whitened. 'I changed my mind. I don't want any. You can't come here selling that stuff.'

'Why?' I enquired. 'Because Morgan told me I couldn't?' I shrugged. 'I suppose in the land of the witless, it's the half-wit who's king.'

Even Lunaria drew in a breath at that. Perhaps insulting my would-be customer and all her buddies wasn't the way to win her over. I pasted on a disarming smile but that only seemed to petrify Paeonia even more. 'Look,' I said. 'Several days ago, you asked me for pixie dust and I promised I'd get you some. I'm here to fulfil that promise. It's high-quality stuff that I've got.'

'I don't want it.' The expression in Paeonia's eyes belied her words.

I held out my hand to Lunaria, who solemnly handed me the bag. Reaching inside, I drew out the bottle containing the pixie dust and held it up. 'Look,' I cooed. 'So pretty.' I unscrewed the top and dipped my finger in before holding it up to Paeonia's nose. She was mesmerised by it. I smiled at her. This was where things were going to get tricky. 'It's incredibly high quality,' I said. 'We've never had a batch quite like it. Lunaria will demonstrate.'

At my side, Lunaria stiffened. 'Will I?'

I nudged her. 'Just a wee bit to show Paeonia what she's missing.'

I could see that Lunaria was desperate to refuse. For all that dust might soothe the physical ache of homesickness, she was too intelligent to want to become an addict to the stuff. She was already addicted to Rubus – why would she need a drug at the same time? All the same, she'd know that if she refused Paeonia would have the excuse she needed to do the same. The thought of failure – which would not endear Rubus to her in any way, shape or form – was enough to tip Lunaria over the edge and into reluctant agreement.

Reaching into the jar, she took the tiniest amount on the tip of her index finger then lifted it up to her right nostril. 'Bottoms up,' she said shakily. Then she snorted.

Both Paeonia and I leaned forward. I had to admit that I was eager to see what the effects were as much as the librarian was. It took scant seconds. Lunaria's eyes glazed over and she breathed out. 'Oh. Oh my.' Her whole body juddered as if in ecstasy. 'Man, that's good.'

I visibly stiffened. 'Gasbudlikins,' I muttered. 'That old woman who was complaining at me is heading over here. She might have seen you snorting. Looney, you need to head to the toilet and freshen up before she gets here and decides to call the police because someone is taking drugs in the middle of her precious library.'

Lunaria started to turn to check. I grabbed her arm. 'Don't look! It'll only make her more suspicious.' I gave her a nudge. 'Go on! Go now!'

Fortunately, she did as I asked, stumbling away from us. I had a few minutes at best. I'd have to work quickly.

'There's no one there,' Paeonia said, puzzled. 'And no one can see us here.'

'I know that, you jumped-up book shelver!' I snapped. 'I needed Lunaria out of the way. She's in Rubus's pocket and she'll report anything I do back to him. Look, you have to take some dust. Throw it away or flush it down the toilet, I don't really care. But I need it to look like you're on board and buying it from me.'

I knew deep down that Paeonia wouldn't be able to

resist the pixie dust's lure once she had it in her possession. That was her look-out, however, not mine. I had more important things to worry about.

'As soon as we've gone,' I said, 'you need to get in touch with Artemesia. I have to find her, and find her fast. We're heading to Begonius at the Travotel next. Tell him to tell me where Artemesia is without Lunaria realising. It's vitally important that you do this before we reach him. It'll take us about thirty minutes to get to his hotel so that's all the time you'll have. You also need to get in touch with a Fey guy called Vandrake. He's—'

'I know who he is.'

'Good. Tell him to get out of the city. Or to hide. Or to go to Morgan's place for the time being. I don't care. He just needs to get out of the way.'

She stared at me. 'I don't understand.'

'I don't need you to understand, I just need you to follow instructions.'

'Why are you trusting me with this? You've only met me once and you don't even seem to like me.'

'I don't like anyone. And I don't have anyone else to trust,' I said simply. 'Billions of lives might rest on what you choose to do and how you choose to do it, Paeonia. You need to step up to the plate.'

For the first time, she seemed to straighten up and puff out her chest. I knew in that instant that she'd do what I asked. She was even proud that I'd asked her. She would set aside her own desires, if only momentarily, and do what was needed.

Paeonia didn't know enough to trust me, and she had no real reason to do as I asked, but part of her sensed the truth of my words. Regardless of who we were and what we were like, maybe we all had an inner hero that was waiting to be nudged to come out from the shadows of our deepest souls. At least people like Paeonia did; I couldn't say the same for myself.

A movement flickered in the corner of my eye. Gasbudlikins. 'Lunaria is coming back. Can you do this, Paeonia? You can check with Morgan if you want. He'll tell you to trust me.' I crossed my fingers. He might. He knew what I was doing and he'd understand what I'd asked her to do was going to help people, not hurt them.

'I'll do it,' she said. She nodded her head and I knew that she would keep her promise. I breathed out. Maybe this day would be successful after all.

'Are we in the clear?' Lunaria asked, re-joining us. Her pupils were dilated and she was blinking rapidly. She looked more manic than happy. You gotta do what you gotta do, I told myself.

'We got rid of the woman,' Paeonia said. 'She's a regular here so it wasn't too difficult. She trusts me.' As she said this last part, her eyes were on mine and I was fully aware of who she was really referring to. 'How do you feel?' she asked Lunaria.

'Bloody amazing.'

Paeonia sighed. 'Fine, then. I'll take some dust. I don't have much money, though.'

I glanced at Lunaria. 'Actually, if my fabulous colleague here agrees, we can give you a free sample.'

Lunaria smiled. After all, the objective here was to supposedly create loyal addicts, not to bankrupt faeries across the city in a bid to make ourselves rich. 'I think I can agree to that,' she said dreamily.

It belatedly occurred to me that I didn't have a way of passing over the dust to Paeonia. I should have brought some empty ziplocked bags. Some drug dealer I was. 'Hold out your hands,' I instructed.

With a wary expression, Paeonia did as I asked. I took the dust bottle and tipped it up, pouring a large amount onto her palms.

Paeonia stared down at it, her eyes almost as wide as Lunaria's.

'Time to go!' I said. I waved and smiled then nudged Lunaria in front of me and we headed for the library's exit. We were less than a metre from the door when I looked round, just in time to see a man with a book-laden trolley appear from round the corner and bump into Paeonia's frozen body. She jerked – and the pixie dust went flying everywhere, scattering into the air and onto the floor as well as over a lot of the books shelved nearby.

For a brief moment, her expression was stricken. Then her mouth tightened and she nodded. Her eyes met mine and I could see the resolve reflected in their depths. All's well that ends well, I decided. For now, anyway.

Chapter Fourteen

We'd barely gone a hundred yards from the library when I started to think that encouraging Lunaria to snort pixie dust had been a hellish mistake. She stopped halfway across the road and bent down to start a conversation with a puddle, or maybe it was her reflection that she was talking to. Either way, I had to yank her viciously to get her out of the way before she was mown down by the oncoming traffic.

'Hey! You hurt me!' she complained. 'Again!' She squinted. 'Does the truce not work for you? You're not supposed to be able to hurt me.'

I sighed. 'I wasn't trying to hurt you,' I muttered. 'I was trying to save you. You were almost squished by that Range Rover.'

Instead of telling me she was grateful that she wasn't road kill, she glanced over my shoulder. Her eyes caught something that flooded her expression with delight. She clapped her hands. 'Whirly!' she shrieked.

She skipped away from me towards the revolving door leading into one of Manchester's grander department stores. Clearly, Lunaria had no desire to go into the shop; all she wanted to do was to spin round in the door. Again and again and again.

I gritted my teeth. I had no one to blame for this but myself. It was tempting to use her drug-addled state as an excuse to abandon her but I feared for Manchester and the fate of its revolving doors if I were to do so.

When Lunaria spun past me for the sixth time, I reached in and dragged her out just before the door whirled away again. All Lunaria did was pout. 'You used to be fun, Mads,' she said. 'Since you lost your memory, you've gone all serious.'

That was not a word I would ever choose to describe myself and I wasn't sure anyone else would either. All the same, standing over Lunaria as she tugged at me to be allowed to go back in and whirl round the revolving door again, I felt a bit like I was sucking all the joy out of her life.

I half turned my head, as if glancing down the street. 'Is that Rubus over there?'

She immediately stopped and whipped round. 'Where?' she demanded. 'Where is my love bunny?'

I waved my hand vaguely in the direction I wanted to go. 'Over there. I might have been mistaken…' I barely managed to finish my sentence before she took off.

I caught up to her when she paused in front of a guitar-strumming busker. She was still scanning the street as if Rubus would appear at any moment but she also looked deflated. 'He's gone, hasn't he?' Her bottom lip jutted out and started to tremble. 'He ran away from me.'

Gasbudlikins. She was going to have a complete meltdown. 'It wasn't him,' I said hastily. 'I made a mistake.'

Her head drooped. 'He doesn't want me.'

'Then he's a fool.'

'He didn't even notice my new outfit. Skin-tight red leather and he didn't even say I looked good.'

Wow. She had it bad. 'Pull yourself together,' I snapped. 'You're obviously too good for him. It's his loss, not yours.'

Lunaria sniffed. 'I'm too good?'

'Of course!'

The busker, who'd given up strumming to watch our byplay, apparently agreed. 'She's right,' he said. 'Whoever this guy is, he's not worth it.'

‘I want to be a good faery,’ she told him. ‘I *am* a good faery.’

I gave the busker a tight smile and steered Lunaria away before she could say or do anything else. ‘Watch what you say,’ I warned. ‘He’s a human. He’s not supposed to know about us.’

She didn’t even hear me. ‘If I’m good,’ she said, ‘maybe I should go to Morgan instead. Maybe he’ll want me. He looks like Rubus. He’s got to be the next best thing. Isn’t that bar of his round here somewhere?’

‘No. And you can’t fling yourself at Morgan.’

Lunaria blinked. ‘Why not?’

‘Because … because…’ I banked down the sudden wave of jealousy that tore through me at the thought of Lunaria with Morgan, of anyone with Morgan. I took several deep breaths; I had no right to tell her what she could or couldn’t do. Much as it killed me to do so, I veered away from forbidding her to go anywhere near my green-eyed lust bucket and sighed. ‘You have to make your own choices and do what you want to do, Looney. But those choices have to be for the right reasons.’

A brief flash of clarity entered her eyes. ‘Did you leave Morgan for the right reasons?’ she asked.

I ran a hand through my hair. ‘I wish I knew.’ Somehow I doubted it, even knowing everything that I did now. ‘Come on. We’ve still got several ounces of pixie dust to offload.’

‘I’ll take it,’ Lunaria said brightly.

‘That’s probably not a good idea.’

I sighed again. I didn’t like thoughtful Madrona, I decided. She always took the difficult way out.

***

By the time we reached the Travotel, the worst

effects of the pixie dust seemed to be wearing off. Lunaria was now groaning and clutching her head. Her skin had a tinge of yellow about it and I made sure not to walk too close to her, as I was sure she was on the verge of heaving her guts up.

'I have the mother of all hangovers,' she groaned. 'Why on earth would anyone willingly take this stuff? It doesn't last nearly long enough to be worth it.'

That was probably why so many ended up taking more dust. 'I'm sorry I made you do that,' I said, actually meaning it. 'It won't happen again.'

Lunaria winced. 'I obviously still have too much of it in my system because I could swear you were just nice to me.'

I glanced at her hopefully. 'Would you prefer it if I were mean?'

'Honestly, Mads, I'd prefer it if you just stayed quiet. My head is pounding.'

Fair enough. At least I'd have a good excuse for talking to Timmons – or rather Begonius, as was his Fey name – alone.

I left Lunaria on a small bench in front of the hotel and ambled in. Begonius was already waiting in the lobby, wringing his hands.

'Hey!' I stretched out my arms in greeting. 'Did ya miss me?'

The fact that he took a step backwards was all the answer I needed. He jerked his head at the door leading to his office. I shrugged and went that way, throwing a wave to the receptionist as I passed her. She gave me a puzzled look.

'You've got new staff,' I commented, once the office door was shut behind us.

'I had to have the others transferred to different venues after your little stunts,' he hissed at me. 'I couldn't risk them getting suspicious about who I really am – or what I really am.'

'Sure,' I said sarcastically. 'Because having a strange woman stay *once* in your hotel and a strange man visit you *once* would lead them to all to immediately believing you're a faery in human disguise.'

'Shhh!'

I tutted. 'I don't think they can hear us.'

'You never know. Besides, you might think I'm being paranoid but you've forgotten about all that shit that happened right outside here with Rubus. Murders, Madrona. Several of them!'

'Those weren't my fault.'

He glared. 'I didn't say they were.'

He was certainly very uptight and prickly but I couldn't really blame him. 'Look, Begonius,' I began.

'Mike. Or Timmons.' He heaved himself into his chair with a thump. 'Not Begonius.'

I gave him a curious look. 'You like it here,' I said, realisation dawning.

'It's a Travotel. There are hundreds of other hotels exactly like this one up and down the country. It's hardly unique but it's not a bad place to work.'

I shook my head. 'No, I mean *here*. This demesne.' I watched his expression. 'You don't want to go back to Mag Mell.'

He shifted uneasily. 'I don't know where you got that idea from,' he said stiffly.

I took the chair opposite him. 'It's nothing to be ashamed of. I'm just … surprised. Every other faery in the world can't seem to wait to get back.'

Timmons fidgeted with a pen. 'It's not that I don't feel the ache.' He briefly touched his chest. 'It hurts me to be away as much as it hurts everyone else. Why do you think I wanted pixie dust from you? But,' he continued, 'just because I miss home physically doesn't mean I'd rather be back there. Here in this hotel I'm respected. It's my own little kingdom where there are clean sheets and hand soaps and those cute little sachets of instant coffee. I'm in charge. It's not perfect – but nowhere is. Back in Mag Mell, I'm a nobody. Here I have a purpose.' The pen snapped in his hands and his mouth twisted. 'I don't know why I'm telling you all this.' He glared at me as if his confession were my fault.

'Kebabs,' I said suddenly.

Timmons frowned. 'Huh?'

'I can't remember anything about Mag Mell,' I told him, 'but I'd bet my stunning good looks that there aren't any doner kebabs to be had for love or money.' I smacked my lips.

'No,' he agreed. 'There's not. Some bright spark tried to introduce chillies, which should have been easy given they're just another plant. They didn't take, though.' He shrugged. 'Too spicy.'

'You can't have a kebab without chilli sauce,' I said, utterly horrified.

Timmons nodded. 'Exactly.'

'Rave music. I bet there's no rave music.'

'Only folk,' he said morosely.

The horror. 'Chocolate?'

'There's chocolate, but only dark chocolate. And you'd never find a Mars Bar.'

'I'm guessing there's no Candy Crush.'

'Nope.'

'Or Uber.'

'Nope.'

'Or YouTube.'

'Nope.'

It made one wonder what exactly the point of Mag Mell was. 'Probably no vibrators.'

Timmons visibly winced. 'Too much information.'

Fair enough. 'I get it,' I told him. 'It's not so bad here.'

'It's pretty good. I like it.' He sniffed. 'And I don't want anyone to mess it up for me.'

'Meaning me. You don't want *me* to mess this up for you.'

He shrugged. 'You're not exactly a selfless angel who puts the needs and desires of others first.'

'I'm fighting for the greater good. Sometimes the end justifies the means.'

'Does it?' he asked quietly.

Suddenly I was unable to meet his eyes. That was weird. And uncomfortable. 'I have pixie dust if you really want some,' I offered, glad to change the subject. 'I'm going to tell Rubus I gave it to you and you're more than welcome to have it if you want. I don't think you should take it but I also believe in free will. It's your choice.'

Timmons' expression was open with hungry desire. 'Give it to me.'

I hesitated. 'Are you sure?'

'You just said it was my choice.'

'It's addictive. I just watched Lunaria go nuts in the middle of the street because of it. Rubus will have you over a barrel and—'

'Please.'

I sighed. Fine. I passed him the bottle. 'I'll need to keep a bit back,' I told him. 'I'm supposed to go looking for Vandrake and get him to come back into the drug-addled fold.'

'So I heard.' He decanted a large quantity of the sparkly dust into a plastic container and passed the bottle back. 'Paeonia called me. Vandrake's gone to Morgan.'

I breathed out. Good. I'd be responsible for Timmons' potential collapse – and Lunaria's – but at least one faery was safe from my talons. 'And Artemesia?'

Timmons slid over a piece of paper. 'She's here.'

I glanced down at the scrawled address, memorising it before passing it back. 'Thanks.'

He cleared his throat. 'She says that if you go anywhere near her with Lunaria in tow, she won't have anything more to do with you.'

I nodded; I'd expected as much. I'd have been disappointed if she hadn't threatened that.

'She doesn't want you inside her lab either.'

That was just stupid but I was sure I could persuade her otherwise. 'I do appreciate your help,' I told him.

Timmons looked at me without saying anything.

'What?' I asked.

He pursed his lips. 'I'm waiting for the insult that follows.'

That was twice in one day that I'd been told to be meaner. I folded my arms and huffed. 'I'm not going to insult you,' I said. 'There's more to me than bitchiness. Besides,' I added at Timmons' incredulous expression, 'I don't want you to have to feel forced into turning the other cheek. It's even more grotesque than the one I can see now.'

He spluttered but he also looked rather pleased. 'You know,' he told me, 'word on the Fey street is that if you've not been personally slagged off by the Madhatter you're not worthy of notice.'

I considered this before deciding to take it as a compliment. I'd heard worse. 'I guess that's just the sort of legend I am.'

I stood up and leaned over, kissing Timmons' cheek. 'Tell whoever you like about the insult. Tell anyone that I kissed your cheek and I'll have your scrambled brains for breakfast.'

He looked utterly delighted. Gasbudlikins. I really was losing my touch.

***

'Okay-dokey!' I beamed at Lunaria, who was looking worse and worse by the minute. 'It was right here where I saw Vandrake. All we need to do is search the streets and I'm sure we'll find him. He uses the AA meetings in that church to stay clean so I'm betting he won't venture far from here. He probably lives in the vicinity.' I tapped my temple. 'In fact, I have a great idea. The next meeting is scheduled for four o'clock. If we don't find Vandrake before then, we can crash the AA and spike his coffee while we're inside. There might even be other ex-dust addict faeries who attend. We'll be able to nab them too.'

Lunaria shuffled her feet but she didn't say anything. I'd have to push just a little bit harder. Hopefully not too hard.

'Last time,' I confided, 'I thought I saw some kids hanging around. Pixie dust doesn't work on human adults but I bet no one's tried it on human kids. Their biology is different. There's probably enough dust left for us to reel Vandrake back in and experiment on a few kiddies. It's better to get them while they're young.'

Lunaria turned a shade paler but she still didn't say anything. This was getting ridiculous. I knew from her daft shenanigans about Rubus that she didn't often stand up for herself but I'd just suggested we gatecrash an AA meeting to peddle our wares to the people trying desperately to stay clean and that we pressgang children into trying dust too. Lunaria wasn't a bad person; she was, as she'd so doubtfully said herself, a 'good faery' at heart. What exactly would it take to make her fight back?

I shook the bag containing the bottle of dust.

'Yummy yummy dust,' I cooed. 'We should come up with a tagline. All the best firms do it. Yummy yummy dust. It will take away your … rust.' I frowned. 'It's not the best. Can you do any better?'

'Actually, Madrona,' Lunaria said weakly, as she passed a limp hand across her forehead, 'I'm not feeling very well. Do you think you can manage without me?'

Praise be. I exhaled silently in relief. I didn't want to appear too disappointed that she was bailing on me but I could hardly show her what I was really thinking. 'Well,' I said, 'I've really been enjoying your company but you do look kind of dead on your feet. Maybe it's best if you go and lie down for a bit.'

'Yeah. Maybe.' Her shoulders slumped. 'Do you think Rubus will be very angry?'

Him again. 'Honestly,' I said, without lying, 'I doubt he'll even notice.'

Lunaria looked as if she were going to start bawling. Alarmed, I reached out and drew her into a hug. Please, anything but tears. Unfortunately, the hug had the opposite of its intended effect and set her off.

She hiccupped and started to sob. 'I don't know how you do this all the time,' she said. 'I mean, I know you've got brain damage and all, but it's just so hard.'

'I don't have brain damage,' I said into her shoulder, unable to extricate myself from her tight hold. 'I just have amnesia.'

'Yeah,' she sniffed. 'But we all know how weird you're acting. You're not quite … right.'

Score one to Looney Tunes. 'There, there,' I told her. 'Maybe one day you'll end up with total memory loss too and you can experience the wonder of not knowing your own name.'

'You're so lucky,' she gasped, pulling back and wiping her eyes.

Yeah, I thought, eyeing her sourly. The trouble was that she was right. I was lucky I didn't remember killing Charrie the Bogle; I was lucky that I didn't remember dumping Morgan when it suited me. Memory loss did indeed have its advantages. And perhaps I was brain damaged. Perhaps I even deserved it.

'Go on then,' I said, not entirely unkindly. 'Get yourself home.'

She sniffed again and nodded. 'See you later.'

I raised a hand in farewell. 'Can't wait.'

I watched her turn round and toddle off. As soon as she was out of sight, I jumped into action. I'd have to be back at Rubus's place before too long. After all, there was the big dinner with Julie tonight and I had loads to do before then.

Brain damaged or not, it wasn't easy being me.

Chapter Fifteen

I spun away from the church and headed for the address that Timmons had given me. I didn't know if Artemesia would be able to help me or not but it was more than worth a try.

Although this time her laboratory-cum-potion-shop-cum-shed was located close by, it took far longer than I'd anticipated to reach it thanks to a combination of steady drizzle, slow-moving pedestrians and winding streets. I actually walked past the damn place three times before I spotted it. Last time she'd used magic to make her place look like a ramshackle shed from the outside; now, no doubt in order to blend in more effectively with her new surroundings, the exterior of her lab appeared to be a small, boarded-up pawn shop.

I knocked on the rusting door then, without waiting for an answer, pushed it open and entered. I'd barely put one foot inside when a viciously loud klaxon sounded. She'd amped up her security after my last visit. This was confirmed when, a few heartbeats later, Artemesia appeared wielding a long steel bar.

I raised an eyebrow. 'What are you planning to do with that?' I enquired. 'Only a faery would enter this place and only faeries are affected by the truce. All you can do is swing it around and look threatening.'

She glared at me. 'Usually that's enough. After all, I am a highly skilled potion maker. You never know when I might find something that will work around the truce.'

I immediately brightened. 'Really? Are you searching for something? Because that would be a game changer.'

'The truce binding is too strong.' She dropped the steel bar. 'But I heard about the oath breaker that the dragon is prepared to hand over. I can't be sure without examining it – and with that sort of magic there's always some sort of catch – but it has potential.'

I grunted. 'Even mould has potential. I won't hold my breath.'

I moved further inside but Artemesia sprang in front of me. 'You can't come in here. I gave Timmons my address for you but that doesn't mean I want you inside. There's a café round the corner. We'll go there.'

I spread out my arms in a gesture of peace. 'I'm already here. We might as well stay. I understand you might not trust me—'

'Trust you?' Her expression was one of total incredulity.

'You'd already moved on from that last place,' I pointed out calmly. 'And you admitted that you expected me to tell your uncle where you were.'

'That's not the point.'

Of course it was the point. There had been no harm done and I had the impression when we last met that we'd got on alright. Maybe we weren't bosom buddies but, if Artemesia played her cards right, I might allow her to become my friend one day.

As if she could tell what I was thinking, Artemesia's mouth tightened. 'It's one thing to meet you in a neutral location but it's quite another when you enter my home and snoop around.'

'Even if you kick me out,' I said, 'I still know where you are. And you did allow Timmons to tell me your address. Not that I'm going to reveal your location. I told Carduus where you were last time because I was sure that you'd have already left and it gave me an opportunity to gain both his and Rubus's trust. I have no reason to blab again and I'm not going to snoop. But we should stay here because all your equipment is here and we might need it. Besides, I did as you requested: I didn't bring Lunaria.'

Artemesia's lips moved silently. I peered at her. 'Are you counting to ten?' I asked. 'Does that actually work?'

'Not in your case, no.' She sighed. 'It's so much freaking work to pack up everything. I'm going to have to do it all again now.'

'You really don't need to.'

Her shoulders sagged. 'I really do.' She shook her head. 'Even if you promised not to say anything about where I am or what supplies I have and what experiments I'm doing, those Truth Spiders…'

I grimaced. 'The Truth Spiders only work if you ask the right questions. So far, Rubus hasn't done that.'

'All the same, you're still Madrona the Madhatter. You betrayed our side once before.' She bit her lip. 'I want to trust you. I think that even Morgan trusts you again now, and if he can manage it then the rest of us probably should.'

I ignored the sudden leap in my chest. 'But…?' I prodded.

'But there's too much at stake. You're still with Rubus.' She looked away. 'It's too risky to have you here. There are things I'm working on that Carduus would kill to get his hands on. If he got even an inkling about some of my projects, we'd lose more than you could imagine.'

I could imagine a fair bit. I gnawed the inside of my cheek. 'How about,' I said quietly, 'if I gave you information that you could hold over me? If I allowed you to have the upper hand?'

'I don't possibly see—'

'I'm responsible for the borders closing,' I

interrupted.

Artemesia's jaw dropped. Yep. Of everything she might have expected me to say, I bet she hadn't thought it would be this. 'What?'

'I have even more power and ability to be evil than you could imagine,' I told her.

'I …' She shook her head. 'I don't believe it.'

I laughed harshly. 'Well, I can assure you that it's true. Rubus told me.'

'And you trust him? Seriously?'

I dropped my gaze. 'He used a Truth Spider on himself.'

Artemesia didn't say anything. I looked up, expecting to see both horror and disgust displayed on her face but she seemed more fascinated than appalled. 'What did you do?'

I told her everything that Rubus had told me. I was taking a massive gamble but somehow I had the feeling it would pay off.

When I'd finished, Artemesia took several steps backwards. I thought at first that it was because she wanted to put as much distance between us as she could then I realised that she needed to sit down.

She half fell onto a stool. 'It's all making sense now,' she breathed. She turned her head towards the back of the room. 'Did you hear all that?' she asked.

I stiffened. What the gasbudlikin bastard…?

There was a faint thud and Morgan appeared from round the back of a set of shelves. 'I did.' His expression was grim.

I put my hands on my hips. Unbelievable. My gaze swung from Artemesia to Morgan and back again. 'This is why you didn't want me to come in! You're having an affair! Were you naked back there, Morganus?' I demanded. 'Is that why it took you so long to appear?'

Without giving him a chance to answer, I glared at Artemesia. 'How long has this been going on for? I hope the sex is worth it. I hope he's bringing a good al-dente noodle to your spaghetti house and that he's properly cleaning your cobwebs with his womb broom.'

I couldn't bring myself to look at Morgan. 'He's got the body for masterfully negotiating the forest chasm, so if you're not squealing when he's paddling up coochie creek then I want to know about it. You deserve only the very best, Artemesia. You could have told me, though. I might be the Madhatter but I only want everyone to be happy.'

Unbidden, tears rose to my eyes and I dashed them away furiously. 'I'm not angry. I'm happy that you're together. I'm thrilled.' I jiggled around. 'See? This is my happy dance.' I used the tips of my fingers to push my mouth into a smile. 'When's the wedding? Can I get an invite? Can—?'

Morgan walked over to me and put a finger against my lips. 'Hush. I was here because I was meeting Artemesia to talk about what we can do to guard against any potential betrayal by Mendax. And to discuss whether his oath breaker will actually work or not.' Something indefinable glittered in his eyes. 'We're not together.'

I hiccupped. 'You're not?'

'No.'

I stepped back and sniffed. 'It's not like I care. The pair of you can do whatever you want, it's got nothing to do with me. Some people would say that you're perfect idiots but I say you're not perfect. In fact—'

'Maddy,' Morgan said. 'Shut up.'

I snapped my mouth closed. Well, someone got out of the wrong side of bed this morning.

The corners of the lips crooked up. 'So much for all

that open honesty,' he murmured.

Artemesia cleared her throat. 'Perhaps we should get back to the revelation that Madrona is responsible for all the border closures.'

I'd forgotten my admission in the wake of her and Morgan's non-sexual relationship. Uh-oh. I scratched my head awkwardly. 'I don't remember any of it,' I said. 'Obviously.'

Morgan's eyes held mine. 'You were nineteen. And foolhardy.'

'Nineteen,' I argued. 'Not nine. I should have known better.'

'I can imagine,' he said softly, 'that the guilt over your mistake was tremendous. I could feel you pulling away from me, you know. As the months passed and the borders didn't re-open, you became more and more distant – and more and more nasty. You already believed you were villainous so it wouldn't have taken much for Rubus to persuade you on to his side.'

'He *blackmailed* me on to his side.'

'Yeah,' he said. 'But I reckon you were relieved to go. You wanted to punish yourself for what you did.' He raised his shoulders in a heavy shrug. 'We can't change the past, Maddy. You did what you did. We can only do better in the future.'

I stared at him. 'That's it?'

'What do you want me to say?'

I threw my hands up in the air. 'That this is my fault! All this is my fault! All these faeries are trapped here because of me and a stupid stunt that I pulled! If Rubus gets his hands on the sphere, floods this place with magic and kills all the humans in the process, then that will be my fault too.'

'No,' Morgan said, with the apparent patience of a saint. 'That will be down to Rubus. No one is forcing him to be a genocidal prick.'

'I caused this situation, Morgan. Me. He's just reacting to it.'

'Actually,' Artemesia interrupted, 'as much fun as it would be to place you in the villain's box, I'm with Morgan on this. You made a mistake and you've been paying for it ever since. You didn't deliberately shut us all in here. It was an unintended consequence.'

'Maybe I did do it deliberately. Unless my memory returns, we'll never know for sure what I did.'

'If you did it deliberately, Rubus would have made sure that you knew it.'

'So I committed manslaughter rather than murder,' I said. 'Go me.' What I didn't add was that I waited a decade before escalating my sins to premeditated murder by killing Charrie. I was irredeemable. Both Morgan and Artemesia must see that.

'You screwed up,' Morgan told me. 'Everyone does at some point or other.'

Artemesia's eyes travelled to Morgan. 'If only we'd known…'

I huffed. 'If only you'd known what?'

'We couldn't know the reason for the border closure. We thought that maybe we'd displeased the authorities in Mag Mell. Maybe something was terribly wrong in this demesne and we just couldn't see what. Now that we know the real reason why we're stuck here, I feel a whole lot better.'

'So it's a good thing that I fucked us all?' I demanded. 'Is that what you're saying?'

Her expression remained calm. 'You forget that we've lived with this situation for ten years. Knowing the reason behind it doesn't change the situation but potentially it makes it easier to fix. If we can get your memory back and find exactly what it is you did,' her face glowed, 'we can work to re-open the borders ourselves, without any freaky sphere crap. Truthfully, Madrona, this is fantastic news.'

'You don't want to kill me?' I asked her doubtfully.

'Of course I want to kill you. I kind of want to hug you too.'

I stepped to the side just in case she dared. 'I'm evil,' I said in a small voice.

'Yeah, you are. But maybe only a tiny bit.' She grinned at me.

This wasn't going at all as I'd expected. It was my turn to sit down before my legs gave way.

'So what do you need me for?' Artemesia enquired.

'Huh?'

'You came to see me for a reason,' she prompted. 'What is it?'

Oh. 'There are two things. Your uncle reckons he might have an amnesia-curing potion.' I screwed up my face, trying to remember what he said he'd used. 'Uh, with anemone and mugwort and, uh…'

Artemesia rolled her eyes. 'Lavender?'

I nodded. ' I think so.'

She sighed. 'I know both the spell and the magic he'll have bound the potion up with. It won't do a thing to help your amnesia but it will give you the runs for several days. Carduus is a moron.'

The runs? Nice. I wasn't surprised, though. I shrugged, lifted up the plastic bag and pulled out the dust bottle. There wasn't much inside but I was hoping there would be enough. 'The other thing is that you created dust,' I said. 'You made it to help us.'

'And my uncle changed it to harm us.' Her expression hardened. 'There's an example of someone not making a foolish mistake but a deliberate act designed to induce pain.'

'Can't you just flood the market with your version, rather than his?'

Artemesia ran a hand through her hair. 'But my version isn't addictive. That's the reason why his pixie dust worked and mine fell by the wayside. He got everyone hooked until his dust was the only one they wanted.'

'I have some of his here. I thought that maybe you could try and reverse-engineer it. Find out what's in it that makes it addictive and I can do something to pollute the ingredients in Carduus's lab so that his pixie dust is weaker than yours. Then everyone will come back to you and, more to the point, their addictions will fade away.'

Artemesia rolled her eyes. 'It's really not that simple. You say it like all I have to do is wave a magic wand and, hey presto! Frankly, if it were that easy, I'd have already tried it.'

Morgan rubbed his chin. 'Maybe you can't reverse-engineer it, Arty, but I bet that with that original sample you can find a way to counteract its addictive qualities.'

'You mean find an antidote? I'm a one-woman band here, Morganus. I can't do everything at once! You two aren't the only faeries in the city, you know. There are others who have needs as well as you two.'

I placed the bottle on the nearest table. 'I know it's a long shot,' I said. 'But I thought that it would be worth a try.'

'I can't create more time. There are only so many hours in the day.'

'I can slow down time!' I beamed. 'I can help with that.'

Artemesia looked horrified. 'Have you been doing that? You have to stop. It's terribly risky.'

I'd been hoping for a bit more adulation. 'I've only done it a few times.'

'Well, stop! It'll cause havoc. The more you do it, the more chance there is that the magic will adversely affect this realm.'

'Morgan did it once too,' I said sulkily. 'It's not just me.'

She glowered at him. 'You know the risks.'

'It was a one-off situation,' he said. 'Sometimes, just sometimes, the ends justify the means.'

I gazed at him. 'Have you been eavesdropping on me?'

Morgan just looked confused. 'Huh?'

I dismissed it. 'Never mind.' But it vexed me that Morgan sounded heroic when he said that to Artemesia; when I said it, I sounded like I was making an excuse.

Artemesia picked up the dust bottle, holding it gingerly as if were some kind of nuclear bomb. 'I'll do my best,' she said. 'But it won't be quick. You lot keep giving me more and more things to do and I can't possibly do all of them. Reverse-engineering my uncle's pixie dust, as satisfying as it would be to ruin all his work, is at the bottom of my to-do list.'

She turned. 'I'm taking this round the back,' she said pointedly. 'It'll take me ages to label it properly and make sure it's safe. You two will have plenty of time alone to sort out whatever crap is going on between you. I don't have time for this dust – and you two don't have time for this dance.' With that, she disappeared.

I shuffled my feet as silence descended between Morgan and me. 'You hid from me,' I said quietly. 'You conspired with Artemesia to keep me away from this place so I wouldn't discover you were here.'

Morgan didn't move a muscle. 'You decided you were a bad person because you made a mistake.'

'A catastrophic mistake.'

He waved his hand. 'You made a catastrophic

mistake and then decided it defined who you were. You thought that one mistake made you a villain so that's what you became. It's still in you now – I can see it inside you. Deep down, you don't believe you can be good so you make the effort to be bad because that's all you think you deserve.'

'Hey!' I protested. 'I'm not all bad! I am trying to stop Rubus, after all.'

He smiled slightly. 'You are. Maybe, just maybe, there really is a superhero inside you.' His expression sobered. 'I felt guilty,' he said. 'I asked you to come home with me and a couple of hours later all but demanded you return to Rubus instead. I have no right to make demands of you but I did it because my brother has to be stopped. You might be the only person who's capable of doing it. I asked Arty to keep my presence quiet because I didn't think you'd want to see me. I wouldn't blame you for that.' He sighed. 'I expect it.'

I stared at him. *He* felt guilty? I was the one who'd consigned us all to a lifetime trapped in this demesne. I was the one who'd dropped him the first time around to be with Rubus. A trickle of discomfort filtered through me. I didn't deserve Morgan. He was far too good for me.

Then I remembered that I was the Madhatter. He was lucky I was even deigning to have this conversation with him, let alone entertain visions of hot-blooded, sweat-soaked sex.

I sniffed. 'I'll permit you to grovel.' I looked him up and down. 'On your knees.' Morgan laughed. I put my hands on my hips. 'I mean it!'

His lazy smile returned. He took a step towards me. 'I'll get on my knees if that's what you really want, Maddy. Or I could stay on my feet and run my hands through your hair, down your back, across your breasts…' He licked his lips. 'I could press my body against yours so you can feel just how hard you make me. Even just the thought of you affects me.' His voice was growing huskier by the second.

Involuntarily, my eyes drifted downwards. Oh. I swallowed. I supposed it was only natural. I was indeed remarkably sexy. I looked up again, losing myself in Morgan's mesmerizing emerald gaze. Then I bit my lip. 'I'm sorry,' I whispered. 'But will you just hold me?'

If I'd thought that Morgan was going to be disappointed that I wasn't ordering him to strip off, I was mistaken. Despite his body's physical response, his features softened with warmth and kindness. He covered the distance between us and wrapped his arms round me. I put my head on his shoulder and inhaled, closing my eyes.

Orgasmic.

Chapter Sixteen

'So you still won't tell me which actor I'm meeting?' Rubus asked from the back seat of the car. 'I won't be happy if it ends up being Sammy.'

'I've never watched the show,' I admitted. 'But I do want to.' As soon as I had some time and I wasn't running around trying to save the world. 'I don't know who Sammy is.'

'The dog. Sammy is the dog.' Rubus wrinkled his nose. 'I can see how you might find it amusing to sit me down in front of a bowl of Pedigree Chum but I assure you, Madrona, it will not go well for you if you do.'

I was almost disappointed that I'd not asked Julie if there were any animals on *St Thomas Close* that I could pressgang into meeting Rubus instead of her. I rather liked the idea of seeing him trying to engage a pooch in artful conversation. 'It's not the dog,' I told him. 'I think you'll be pleasantly surprised.'

'I hate surprises,' he growled.

That's what I was counting on. 'You're going to meet her in ten minutes. I suppose I can tell you who it is now.'

Rubus leaned forward, green eyes wide. 'Go on then.'

I used the dashboard to beat a drum roll and build up tension. Rubus looked irritated, as if he was worried that I'd leave fingerprint smears on his pristine interior. Not much of a music lover then. 'It's the one you mentioned. The one you wanted it to be.'

His mouth formed a perfect O. 'Stacey?'

'Well,' I demurred, 'that's her character's name.

She's Julie.'

He couldn't hide his excitement. 'Really? That's amazing!' He beamed, his eyes lighting up like a giddy schoolboy's. 'She's the best one!'

Somehow I couldn't quite connect my image of Rubus as an evil drug lord with that of a soap-opera addict. I supposed it took all sorts. 'How much do you love me now?' I enquired.

He sighed happily. 'I won't deny that I'm impressed, Madrona. Good work.' He said that last part as if I'd befriended Julie purely so that I could introduce him to her. And I'd thought I had an ego the size of a barrage balloon; I had nothing on him.

'You're going to have to be careful,' I warned him. 'She's a creative and she's used to getting what she wants. You know what these actors are like.'

'Of course, of course.' He nodded like he spent all his time hanging out with Hollywood types. 'Give me some tips.'

'She loves gin and tonic.'

He made a face. 'Yuck. But okay.'

'And she's very skittish. She's still worried about those stalkers of hers.'

He waved a hand dismissively. 'But I took care of those for her.'

He took care of them because it suited him at the time to show off his leadership skills while acting like a homicidal maniac. 'I'm sure she's very grateful,' I murmured. 'But there still might be more like them out there.'

'I always had the impression that human stalkers worked alone. A whole group of them has got to be unusual.'

'I blame the internet,' I said cheerfully. In a way that was true: the internet meant that the vampire hunters had ways and means of tracking their prey and coordinating their efforts to abduct bloodsuckers like Julie. But I couldn't tell Rubus that, even if I wanted to, because I was still bound by the terms of Julie's blood-enhanced NDA.

'Anyway,' I continued, 'because she doesn't know who you are, I'll have to be present at the dinner as well. Just to reassure her, you understand.' And to stop Finn from potentially going postal. 'You won't even know I'm there.' I could barely keep a straight face as I said the last part. As if.

'Fine, fine.'

Rubus was so excited that he'd have agreed to anything. I mentally crossed my fingers. I needed this next part to work so I was going to have to tread carefully. That was okay. I was the Madhatter; I had cunning and guile in spades.

'She takes her appearance very seriously,' I said. 'Not a hair out of place, no unsightly facial blemishes or spots. After all, she's got paparazzi following her as well as stalkers. She's got to look her best at all times – and she expects her companions to do the same.'

Rubus grinned. 'She'll be happy with me. I photograph well.'

'Mmm-hmmm.' I nodded. 'So do I. But you'll notice that I'm not wearing any jewellery either.'

His brow creased. 'I don't understand.'

'She hates gold. And silver. She says she's allergic to both but I think she just doesn't like anything that glitters more than she does. She seems to have a particular aversion to men who wear jewellery. I wasn't with her very long, you understand, but even I had time to see what she did to men who wore necklaces and earrings in her presence. She can be very … cutting.'

It was so ridiculous that Rubus fell for it

wholeheartedly. 'That's not a problem. I don't wear any jewellery apart from…' He hesitated. 'Oh. How does she feel about rings?' He held up his hand, displaying his pinky ring. 'I never take this off. It was a gift from my father.' For a brief second his eyes gleamed with smug satisfaction. 'Morgan doesn't have one.'

I let my expression fall. 'Oh.' I swallowed. 'Well, it's not very flashy. Maybe she won't notice it.' I bit my lip. 'I'm sure it'll be fine,' I said, making it clear with my tone of voice that it would be anything but.

All of a sudden, Rubus looked anything but happy. 'I never take it off,' he repeated in a low mutter.

'I'm sure she'll understand.' My fingers twitched and I dropped my eyes to my lap.

'It's only temporary though. It's only one meal.' He pursed his lips and considered. Then he yanked off the ring and leaned across me, dropping it in the glove box. 'Anything to keep Stacey happy.'

'Julie.'

He rolled his eyes. 'Whatever.' His smile returned. 'I'll dazzle her with my good looks and charm instead of my gold.' His mouth took on an unpleasantly lascivious twist. 'Easy. She's going to love me.'

'They do say that opposites attract,' I agreed. 'And Julie is cultured, intelligent and attractive.'

It was probably a good thing that he wasn't paying me any attention. He checked his appearance once more in the mirror. Then he sniffed his armpits. 'I should put on more aftershave. Just in case.'

'You don't want to overdo it,' I advised. Especially given it was already hard to breathe. 'She's an actress. She'll appreciate some subtlety.'

Rubus didn't look entirely convinced but at least he refrained from adding more of the noxious scent. He stepped out of the car, adjusted his tie and his cuffs, and headed for the door of the restaurant. I followed, watching as he used the remote to lock the vehicle before pocketing the keys. With any luck, Finn would possess more skill than just the ability to scowl. I'd played my part. It was up to him now. I turned my head as Rubus walked inside the restaurant and spotted the waiting car on the opposite side of street.

'Glove box,' I mouthed. Then I smiled. This was just too freaking easy.

***

The restaurant was half full. We were directed to our reserved table in the corner, which I'd made sure was away from the window and any view of Rubus's car. I had to admit that he was acting like a perfect gentleman – he even pulled out my seat for me. Rather than put me at ease that made me feel slightly wary, as if at any moment he was about to leap up and start slamming pixie dust down the waiters' throats. I didn't let my worry show, of course. I was far too super a spy for anything like that.

'She's not here,' Rubus said.

'I'm sure she's on her way.'

He swung his head round, eyes flashing at the other diners as if Julie's lack of punctuality was their fault. 'As much as I like you, Madrona, I've got better things to do than have dinner with you by candlelight. If she doesn't show, I'll hold you personally responsible.' He leaned forward and licked his lips. 'Despite the truce, I can still make your life very unpleasant.'

'Seriously?' I stared at him in disbelief. 'I'm making your dreams come true and you're making threats? I thought that you were a great asset. It turns out I was off by two letters.'

He knitted his fingers together under his chin and

regarded me. 'A sharp tongue is no indication of a sharp mind. You would do well to remember that. Morganus didn't have to put up with this kind of bullshit. You have to watch your mouth.'

Not for the first time, it occurred to me that there were substantial differences between the two brothers. I probably insulted Morgan more than I insulted Rubus and yet Morgan, even if he didn't really like me, didn't patronise me or treat me like a child in the way that Rubus did.

Despite Rubus's promises to re-open the borders, I was befuddled that so many faeries chose to follow him. Where was the supposedly suave intelligence and forward planning that I kept hearing so much about?

I toyed with the stem of my empty wine glass. 'Do I intimidate you, Rubus?' I asked softly.

'I have more power in my little finger than you have in your entire body, Madrona. Do *I* intimidate *you*?'

I was saved from answering by the tinkle of the restaurant door opening and Julie's blessed appearance. Every head turned towards her and a rippling murmur of awed surprise drifted through the restaurant. It wasn't only because she was instantly recognisable; she was also looking remarkably glamorous.

I got to my feet and started clapping. I just couldn't help myself. Several waiters sprang over to help her with her coat – just as I belatedly realised that she was wearing a dramatic diamond necklace. Before Rubus spotted it, I jumped over to her and blocked her from his view.

'Darling!' she beamed, drawing me into a loose hug and planting an air kiss near my cheek.

'Lovely to see you again!' I chirped back. 'Take off the damn necklace,' I hissed in her ear. 'I told him no jewellery.'

She blinked, startled. I growled at her under my

breath and she turned round. 'Where's the powder room?' she enquired.

With a star-struck expression, the maître d' gestured to the left. Julie smiled prettily and headed that way. I crossed my fingers that Rubus hadn't noticed anything untoward, especially since he no doubt had the same enhanced Fey super-hearing skills that I did. With any luck, the whispered delight of the others in the restaurant had drowned out my whispered command.

I returned to the table. Rubus was also on his feet, looking slightly nonplussed. 'Where did she go?'

'To take a piss.'

He grimaced. 'You might take a piss, Madrona,' he scolded. 'Ladies like Stacey powder their noses.'

I rolled my eyes. 'I'm pretty certain her bladder works the same way mine does. And, as I keep telling you, her name is Julie.'

Rubus gestured to the waiter. 'A bottle of your most expensive champagne,' he said grandiosely.

'Of course, sir.' The waiter bowed. Now that he'd realised who we were meeting, he was falling over himself to please. There was a lot to be said for this celebrity business although, I conceded, that was probably what life felt like for Rubus all the time, given how many loyal hangers-on he had.

Rubus sat down again just as Julie emerged, her neck thankfully now bare. He immediately shot back up again and trotted over, obsequiously taking her hand and leading her to the table as though she couldn't possibly cover the ten or so steps on her own.

'Julie,' I murmured, 'this is Rubus. He's a big fan.'

She laughed lightly and patted her carefully coiffured hair. 'It's so lovely to meet you. Normally I don't meet fans in this way but darling Madrona said you were a wonderful man. I'm sure we'll get on famously.'

To my astonishment, Rubus's cheeks turned red. He was genuinely smitten. He pulled out the chair next to his. Like a queen, Julie smoothed down her dress and sat down gracefully. I could only marvel; she was truly a consummate actress. Almost as good as me.

The waiter returned with the bottle and presented the label to Rubus with an overly dramatic flourish while another brought over an ice bucket. When the first waiter received the nod, he popped the cork. Julie let out a delighted giggle. Rubus blushed a deeper red.

We waited until our glasses were full and the eager wait staff had left us in peace. Julie raised her glass by the stem in a fluid, elegant motion. 'To new friends,' she purred.

'To new friends,' I agreed, copying her action.

'And maybe something more,' Rubus murmured. He didn't exactly leer at Julie but there was a definite aura of sleaze to both his words and his expression. Surprisingly it discomfited me, as if somehow I'd expected better of him.

I took a sip of the champagne, barely pausing to savour it. 'I had a lovely day today,' I said, with fake warmth. 'I was out with Lunaria.'

Rubus looked irritated that I'd attempted to start a conversation but Julie was on her best behaviour. She leaned forward, looking interested. 'Oh yes? Who is Lunaria? Should I know her?'

'She works for Rubus,' I said. 'She's a wonderful person. Incredibly attractive, both inside and out, not to mention funny and smart. Obviously. I wouldn't be friends with a lesser person.'

Rubus snorted. A heartbeat later he seemed to realise how derogatory he sounded and that it might not endear him to Julie. He hastily explained himself. 'Madrona only knows the best people,' he said. 'After all, she's friends with you.' He puffed out his chest. 'And me.'

Julie put her hand on his arm and leaned towards him. 'Tell me more about you,' she said. 'I know all about Mads but she didn't tell me much about you.' Her voice had taken on a low, husky quality, as if she were conducting steamy phone sex or voicing an advert for flaky chocolate. She certainly seemed to be making Rubus melt.

'Oh,' Rubus laughed, 'I have fingers in many pies. I like to think of myself as diverse. My company has several branches. We produce pharmaceuticals, which are designed to truly help people. Then there are sales which, if I do say so myself, are going incredibly well. We also have a pro-bono section,' he added. 'It's so important to give back to the community, don't you think?'

Julie's fingers stroked Rubus's arm; it looked as if it were nothing more than an unconscious action but there was no doubt in my mind that it was entirely calculated. 'Oh, I agree,' she said. 'I so agree. There are so many people who need that bit of extra help. The more people there are like you and me, the better place this world will be. It is only through helping others that I think you truly help yourself.' She moistened her lips with her tongue and held Rubus's gaze. He was almost drooling.

'Indeed,' he said, 'indeed, indeed.'

'Yes,' I agreed. 'In deed is quite as important as in voice.' I gave Rubus a hard look but he wasn't paying me the slightest bit of attention so the effort was wasted.

'Well,' Julie giggled to me, 'you should make sure to invoice me later. I owe you for introducing me to such a charming man.' She took a delicate gulp of her champagne, pretending not to notice that Rubus's tongue was hanging out as if he were closely related to a Labrador who had just spied a tasty sausage. 'I really shouldn't drink this,' she said, patting her cheeks lightly with her free hand. 'Champagne makes me frisky.'

Rubus laughed so loudly that the customers on the other side of the restaurant turned round and stared at him. 'We'll have to make sure that they have enough bottles in their cellar then, won't we? I do like frisky.'

As if to give weight to his words, Julie drained her champagne in one gulp.

Delighted, Rubus rolled up his sleeves, reached across her and took the bottle to refill her glass. 'Do you know,' he said, with a stomach-churning wink, 'I always thought I would make a good actor.' He tossed back his head. '*To be or not to be, that is the question.*'

I rolled my eyes. What an arsebadger. Then I glanced down at his bare arms. Hang on a gasbudlikin minute – were those needle track marks?

Julie clapped her hands in delight. 'Shakespeare,' she trilled. 'I simply love Shakespeare. There's nothing quite like treading the boards. You know,' she confided, 'as much fun as it is being in a soap opera, I do miss the thrill of the theatre.'

Rubus appeared horrified. He dropped his hands under the table, angling his body towards Julie. Whatever marks were on the underside of his arms, I could no longer see them. 'But think of all the people who wouldn't see your talent. You can reach a far wider audience through television. Besides, I just love Stacey. She is such a fabulous character.' He tilted his head. 'Tell me, is she going to stay with her husband?'

'Oh,' Julie said. 'I'm really not allowed to say. It's all very hush-hush. We have to keep the storyline secret, you know.'

Rubus waggled his eyebrows. 'I wouldn't tell a soul,' he said. 'You can trust me.'

'Hmm. I could tell you,' Julie drawled, 'but then I'd have to kill you.' Both she and Rubus burst into peals of laughter. I stared at both of them. That really wasn't very funny.

I looked round for the waiter; we were going to need more than just champagne if I was going to make it through this evening. Unfortunately, every eye in the place was on Julie rather than on me. If I wanted a bottle of tequila I'd probably have to get her to order it. From what I knew of her, I doubted that it would be difficult to persuade her that we needed more alcohol.

'Speaking of secrecy,' Rubus said, 'Madrona told me that you asked her to sign a nondisclosure agreement. She also said that you're having a terrible problem with stalkers. Perhaps I can help with that.'

A brief calculating flash passed across Julie's eyes. It instantly put me on edge. Rubus hadn't appeared to notice it – not that it mattered because, before I could jump in and ward off any potential damage, she was already answering him.

'Actually,' she said, 'that's why I've agreed to meet with you. Handsome as you are, I don't normally meet with strange men. One never knows what might happen. I know what you did for me, though. I know you stopped those men who were after me. If I had realised that faeries existed, I would have come looking for you sooner.'

Her words took a moment to sink in. While I kicked her under the table, Rubus's face slowly filled with dawning realisation. He paused long enough to glare at me and turned back to Julie. His fawning expression all but disappeared and in its place was a hard-eyed nastiness that was far more like the Rubus I had come to know.

'I was not aware that Madrona had revealed our ethnicity to you. In fact, she said quite the opposite. She said you did not know what we were.'

My heart sank. It felt like all the good I had done in

getting Rubus to trust me has been undone by one simple sentence. Now he'd see me as nothing more than a liar – and a loose-lipped liar at that.

Julie didn't miss a beat. She waved an airy hand in the air and smiled benignly. 'Oh,' she said, 'don't blame darling Mads. It's not her fault. Truthfully, this is all down to me. Those men you took care of were not stalkers, at least not in the sense that you think they were. They were hunters. You see,' she said running her tongue across her top lip in a manner that was almost predatory, 'they were after me because I'm a…'

I whipped my hand across the table, causing all three champagne glasses to fall and spill. Rubus leapt to his feet. Several waiters appeared with napkins in hand and concerned expressions on their faces.

'What the hell, Madrona?' Rubus yelled.

Julie put a calming hand on his shoulder.

'I'm so clumsy!' I blurted. 'And look, Julie! I've stained your beautiful top.' I reached across the table and grabbed her hand, pulling her up to her feet. 'Let's head to the ladies room and I'll dry you off.'

I didn't give anyone a chance to reply. There certainly wasn't anyone around here who was happy. Rubus looked at me with a serial-killer stare as I hauled Julie off. The waiters were in a panic at the mess I'd created, while the maître d' was literally wringing his hands. Even the other restaurant patrons appeared unimpressed. They at least should be happy – I was giving them a show. All they had to do was whip out their mobile phones and sell the footage to one of the tabloids and their mortgage would be paid for a month. Honestly. People ought to be more grateful.

Aware that Rubus possessed the same fine hearing skills that I did, I pushed Julie to the back of the toilets and turned on all the automatic hand dryers to mask our voices. 'What in gasbudlikin hell are you doing?' I hissed at her.

She gazed at me coolly in return. 'Taking a leaf from your book, darling. I'm getting the monster to trust me. He's already gaga at meeting me. Maybe I can be the heroine for once, instead of the damsel in distress.'

The last thing Julie had ever struck me as was a damsel in distress. I put my hands on my hips. 'You are going to tell him you're a vampire. Aren't you?'

'I am. It is not a spur-of-the-moment decision, Mads. This is a calculated manoeuvre.'

'You made me sign an NDA! A magical NDA! And you're just going to tell him over dinner that you're a member of the undead? Just casually drop it into conversation?'

Julie didn't flinch. 'I requested that you sign the nondisclosure agreement because at the time I believed you were human,' she said. 'Now I know otherwise. By telling Rubus what I am, I will distract him. And that's what you need, isn't it? You need him distracted.'

Her eyes met mine. 'If he gets his hands on that sphere that you are all so anxious about,' she continued, 'it's people like me who will suffer. Not people like you. You will get to trip off back to your homeland but I will die. This is my home, Mads. I have as much of a right to defend it as you do. Don't underestimate me. I'm a great deal older than you and a great deal wiser. I know what I'm doing.'

She reached behind her, grabbed a paper towel and dabbed at her top. 'At least it's not red wine,' she muttered. Then she pushed past me and left. All I could do was watch her go.

I heaved in several breaths, trying to stay calm. Julie was indeed older than me; she also had her own mind and was her own person. But that didn't mean she shouldn't recognise my obvious superiority and do everything that I told her to do. I had no idea how Rubus would react upon discovering that she was a vampire – and I had a very bad feeling about it.

I considered hiding out in the bathroom for the next hour. I could make like an ostrich: what I couldn't see and what I couldn't hear couldn't hurt me. I sighed. If only that were true. Madrona the Madhatter was many things and had many faults but she was not a coward. I straightened my shoulders and headed out after Julie.

The restaurant had worked fast. Not only had both the champagne and the glasses been replaced, but so had the tablecloth. All the same, I still received plenty of glares as I wound my way back to our table. Anyone would think I tried to assassinate a national treasure instead of trying to save her from herself.

From the expression on Rubus's face when I sat down, Julie had already told him. I poured myself a glass of champagne and gulped it down.

'You knew about this,' he said accusingly.

I shrugged helplessly. 'I told you, I signed an NDA. And not the sort of NDA where I might simply be sued for breaking the terms. It was the sort of NDA that make your damned Truth Spiders look like cuddly teddy bears.'

At that last part, keen interest lit Rubus's eyes. That was all we needed, for him to work out how to replicate Julie's blood-enhanced contracts. Who needed pixie dust when you could turn your entire community into slaves by getting them to sign on the dotted line?

I cursed inwardly but, because I was also a brilliant actress, I gave him a fawning smile. 'I really wanted to tell you,' I said. 'But I was physically incapable of doing so.'

Julie nodded. 'It's true,' she said. 'I didn't give her any choice.'

He glanced at her. ‘You are fabulous,’ he breathed. ‘I thought you were fabulous before all this, Stacey. Now I know that you are truly a woman after my own heart.’

‘Her name is Julie,’ I said tiredly.

Julie smiled at Rubus. ‘You may call me whatever you wish,’ she husked as she leaned in closer to him.

‘Leave us, Madrona,’ he ordered, without even looking at me.

I folded my arms. ‘That was not our agreement.’

‘I assume you felt you had to stay here in order to protect your friend, given her true nature. But now I know her true nature and she knows mine, no one has anything to fear. I will not hurt her. Far from it.’ The intensity of his gaze deepened. ‘I will not hurt you, Julie,’ Rubus promised.

‘We'll be fine, Mads,’ she said. She appeared to be as focused on Rubus as he was on her.

I couldn't argue. I had no good reason to argue – other than the fact that Rubus was a genocidally inclined maniac, of course. I was supposed to be on his side; if I protested, I’d only lose more ground with him. The vampire was already out of the coffin. I'd just have to leave them to it.

‘Fair enough,’ I told them, trying to look like I wasn't in the slightest bit bothered. My presence would only outshine them anyway.

I picked up the champagne bottle from the ice bucket, tilted it up to my lips and took a swig. ‘I'm taking this with me,’ I said. It was rather galling that neither of them paid me the slightest bit of attention so I took another long gulp and sashayed out. No one watched me go.

Good grief. I had to get myself some less attractive and less famous friends.

Chapter Seventeen

Rubus's car had vanished but, unfortunately for me, Finn hadn't. I'd barely gone three steps from the restaurant before he marched over to me, his long arms swinging. I took another swig from the bottle of champagne and eyed him.

'Have you ever been mistaken for an orang-utan?' I enquired. I could imagine some well-meaning zoologist capturing him and returning him to some deep Sumatran jungle.

'Where's Julie?' he snapped, ignoring my eminently sensible question. 'What's gone wrong?'

I sighed. 'Julie's still inside with Rubus. They've not even ordered their meal yet. They have, however, ordered me out.'

He snarled under his breath. 'Why? What did you do?'

I spread my arms innocently. 'I didn't do anything, other than try to save Julie from herself. The fact that I failed epically is not because my powers are weak but because her powers are so strong.'

'She has no powers,' he snapped.

'She has no *magical* powers,' I agreed. 'But her powers of wilful stubbornness and her ability to charm the pants off bastards like Rubus are going to be legendary.'

His eyes narrowed. I raised an enquiring eyebrow. 'Are you imagining them having sex right now? Because I can tell you that if they are, it's definitely Julie who's on top.'

For a brief moment, I thought he was going to take a

swing at me. Instead, he lunged for the champagne bottle. I let him have it. The poor man was clearly in need of a drink.

He gulped it down like water then wiped his mouth with the back of his hand. 'She told him, didn't she? She told him what she is.'

'Yep.' I sniffed. 'Against my advice, I might add. I take it you knew she was considering this action?'

His shoulders slumped. 'She suggested it would be a good idea. She says she's had enough of being weak and defenceless.'

'She's still weak and defenceless,' I pointed out. 'She's just weak and defenceless and now secret-less too.'

'She has nothing to offer Rubus,' Finn reminded me. 'She can't do anything apart from live for a long time and drink blood.'

'She can act.'

He grimaced. 'Yeah. She can certainly do that.'

The large Redcap seemed particularly morose. In the wake of his two dead brothers, he'd transferred his affections to Julie. I suspected that he needed to feel needed by someone. Now that she'd gone out all guns blazing, and revealed her identity to Rubus, she would no longer require his protection. That sucked, whichever way you looked at it.

'Right now he's in awe of her,' I said. 'He's far too smitten to hurt her.'

Finn's large fists bunched up. 'I'd like to see him try.' He tried to take another drink but, finding the bottle empty, tossed the champagne bottle to the side.

'It'll be fine,' I reassured him.

He scowled. 'I don't like it when you're nice. It's not natural. To be honest, it makes me think that the world is about to end.'

I leaned over and gave him a hug. His body stiffened as if he were expecting a wallop instead. 'The last thing I want to do is hurt you, Finn,' I said cheerfully. 'It's still on my to-do list, though.'

'Thank you,' he mumbled. 'I feel better now.'

I pulled back and grinned. 'Any time.' I glanced round. 'Did Morgan have any problems with the car?'

He shook his head. 'Nope. He broke in and got it started easily. He'll dump it somewhere on the outskirts of the city. It'll take Rubus a while to find it.'

I gave a satisfied nod. 'That's what we need.' It wasn't the car that was important, after all; it was the ring that Rubus had popped into the glove box that we wanted.

'When's the meeting with Mendax?' I asked.

'First thing in the morning. He refused to meet us tonight.' Finn's lip curled. 'He's probably busy counting his stupid gold for the umpteenth time.'

I nodded and considered going home to bed. Some sleep would be very welcome but I really wanted to see the look on Rubus's face when he realised someone had boosted his car.

'I've got a good vantage point over there,' Finn said. 'We can make sure Julie is safe and that she leaves the restaurant – and Rubus – without any problems. He'll never know we're here.'

Hmm. I scratched my chin. Keeping her safely out of Rubus's clutches was probably worth staying up for, I supposed.

***

Forty minutes later, I was beyond bored. I mean, there's bored and there's *bored*. Like a blind person in an art gallery bored. Or a eunuch in a brothel on discount

Monday bored.

Finn didn't look bored; his face was constantly alert. If his ears could have pricked up like a dog's, they'd have been standing to attention. His eyes swung up and down the street continuously. I just sighed continuously.

'What course do you think they're on now?' I asked. 'I mean, surely they're having dessert, if not coffee.'

'It looks like they've only just finished their starter,' he said, squinting.

'This is ridiculous. We'll be here all night.' I thought of my bed. It wasn't the most comfortable place in the world but it was better than here. I was getting cramp and it was starting to drizzle. I didn't even have Morgan around to entertain me. Or hug me. 'Do you have a phone on you?'

Finn looked at me suspiciously. 'Why?'

'Well,' I explained, 'I was all set to have dinner with those two before they kicked me out. I've not eaten anything for hours and I'm probably wasting away as we speak. We can order pizza. It'll pass the time and I'll fill my belly.' I patted my stomach fondly. 'I'll let you choose the toppings.'

'Hawaiian,' Finn said instantly.

I recoiled away from him. 'What's wrong with you? Pineapple doesn't belong on pizza!'

'Pizza is the only place where pineapple belongs,' he said serenely.

Yuckity-yuck-yuck. 'Very well. Hand over your phone. I'll call.'

'How do you remember about pineapple on pizza? How do you know you don't like it?'

'It's not that I don't like it,' I told him, taking his phone. 'It's that I instinctively know that pineapple on pizza is rancid. It's a fact of life. I can remember to speak English. I can remember how to walk. And I can remember that pineapple on pizza is only for crazy people.' I glanced down and dialled the number.

Finn's eyes narrowed even further. 'You remember a pizza delivery number?' He leaned over my shoulder. 'What the fuck?'

I shrugged. 'Oops. My finger slipped.'

'999, what's your emergency?' the operator asked.

I dazzled Finn with a broad smile and answered. 'Police, please!' I said breathlessly. 'I'm at La Boheme on South Street. There's a man with a gun. He's…' I broke off into a scream and hung up. Then I stretched my smile even further.

Rather than being impressed, Finn looked furious. 'You know they track mobile phones, right? You know the police have those capabilities?'

'Oh.' I shrugged. 'I guess I have forgotten some things about daily life. Sorry.' I dropped his phone and crunched it under my heel. 'Problem solved.' I clapped him on the arm. 'You can thank me later.'

'You're a bloody idiot.'

I grinned. 'Am I? Do you really want to hang around on this cold, wet street all night while they enjoy themselves inside? We're saving the world, Finny boy. We don't need to be damp and miserable while we're doing it.'

He shook his head. 'I don't get,' he said. 'I just don't get it. What on earth does Morgan see in you?'

'You're just jealous that I don't want to get into your trousers too,' I beamed.

Finn looked faintly disgusted but I was pretty sure I saw a glimmer of happiness too. I suspected it had nothing to do with relief at my declared lack of interest in him and everything to do with the fact that I'd sensibly cut short our stake-out.

'What about my pizza?'

Sirens sounded from a street or two away. ‘I’ll owe you,’ I promised him. ‘Stay down. We need to make sure they don’t spot us.’

He muttered a grumbled curse under his breath but he did as I asked.

I’ll say this for Manchester’s finest: they could certainly move when they wanted to. Five police cars screeched up and, without waiting, the first officers smashed in the glass door to the restaurant. There were dismayed shrieks and squeals from inside. Impressive. Maybe I’d see if I could get myself a police uniform. The colour wouldn’t really suit me but if it garnered that sort of reaction it would be worth it.

All the customers and the staff were directed out onto the street. I watched, satisfied, as Julie and Rubus were included in that number. She looked as calm and relaxed as ever but he looked as if he were about to erupt. From his expression, he didn’t believe for one second that my prank call was a coincidence. I clutched Finn’s arm in ecstatic delight as Rubus whipped round from side to side, an angry light in his green eyes. Any second now…

His gaze fell on the spot where his car had been parked and he appeared to freeze. He marched over, gazing down at the smattering of smashed glass, then he whirled back and started remonstrating with the nearest policeman who was doing his level best to question an older couple about the mysteriously non-existent gun.

‘Someone’s stolen my car!’ Rubus yelled.

‘Sir,’ the policeman said calmly, ‘I’m going to have to ask you to wait. We are investigating a firearms disturbance. I will take your details in a second.’

Julie wandered over. ‘I don’t understand. What’s the problem?’

The copper did a double-take. ‘Julie Chivers!’

She curtsied. Rubus was having none of it, though.

He grabbed the policeman by his collar and yanked him forward. 'My car has been stolen! It was parked right there! This isn't a coincidence. This—' Whatever else he'd been planning to say was muffled by the pavement. Four policemen jumped on him and threw him to the ground, cuffing his wrists with one fluid movement. Rubus continued to yell and struggle.

'This is brilliant!' I whispered to Finn. 'Where's the popcorn? I could watch this all night.' I dusted off my palms. 'Job done. Rubus will be banged up for the night for assaulting a police officer and Julie will be home safe before she can say "Pour me a G and T, darling". Pretty impressive work, if I do say so myself.'

'You've abused police resources. You terrified Julie, not to mention all those humans. The restaurant will need to spend a small fortune repairing both their door and their reputation. And all this because you couldn't be arsed to wait another hour.'

I ticked off my fingers. 'The police were probably bored and they could do with the practice. Julie is getting some extra publicity, which never did an actor any harm. Not to mention the fact that the restaurant will get its name in the papers too. There's no such thing as bad press, you know. Plus they'll have insurance. They'll be fine.' I smiled. 'And we'll be home and dry. Literally.'

'You're mad.' Finn looked a bit ill.

I punched him lightly on the arm. 'I keep telling you. I'm the Madhatter.'

Chapter Eighteen

When I got up the next morning, I was buzzing. I sprang out of bed with far more vim and vigour than I'd felt on previous mornings. I even felt energetic enough to lower myself to the floor and start a series of press-ups. The fact that I only managed half of one was neither here nor there; what was important was that I was on top of the world. No one could stop me. No one would dare.

I pulled on my clothes, pausing every so often to send out an attack jet of magic to the corners of my small room. I had more power than I'd realised. Chunks of plaster broke off from the walls and there were clouds of dust. The minor devastation made me feel even better.

Unwilling to let my good humour go to waste, I abandoned my efforts at magical destruction and skipped out to the corridor in order to find more victims. The very first person I banged into was the faery bouncer who I'd met while he was guarding Rubus's door. I cast a long, slow look across his large frame. I particularly enjoyed his grim, unhappy expression. Amellus, I suddenly remembered. That was what Rubus had called him.

'Morning,' I grinned. I danced round him, making sure that I wiggled my arse just enough to be super annoying.

'Why are you so 'appy?' he growled. 'In't you heard the news?'

I widened my eyes. I was in such a good mood that I didn't even bother to comment on his lack of reasonable pronunciation. 'No,' I said. 'What news?' I clasped my heart with melodramatic zeal. 'Are Kajagoogoo reforming?'

He watched me with a sour look. ‘What in Fey are you on about? Rubus ’as been irrrested.’ He rolled his rs to add extra emphasis to the affront.

In my mind’s eye, I imagined myself being presented with a certificate for Citizen of the Year; it helped me to achieve the perfect look of shock. ‘Oh my goodness!’ I gasped. ‘What happened? What did he do?’

‘He did nuthin’,’ Amellus grunted. ‘Would you believe pigs draggeted him away to jail because his car was nicked?’

I let my brow furrow in confusion. ‘I don’t understand.’

‘Is blatant discrimination.’

Sure it was. I rolled my eyes. ‘Because he’s a faery? The police don’t know that, though.’

Amellus glared at me for daring to contradict him. ‘Dun’t matter. Bastards took him. ’E’s our hero. ’E’s gonna save us all.’ His bottom lip jutted out and trembled. For a brief moment, I wouldn’t have been surprised if he’d started to sob. ‘I wanna go home.’

‘If he’s not done anything wrong, they can’t keep him locked up,’ I said cheerfully. More’s the pity. ‘I’m sure he’ll be back in a jiffy.’

‘S’not fair.’

‘No,’ I agreed. ‘It’s green.’

Amellus merely looked confused. ‘Huh?’

I regarded him thoughtfully. ‘You’re the reason the gene pool needs a lifeguard.’

His bottom lip stopped trembling so he could glower at me with a full-faced sneer. ‘I don’t like you.’

I nodded. ‘I know. I wouldn’t worry about it, though. My brilliance is too dazzling for the likes of you. I’m to be admired, not buddied up with.’

I could see the cogs of his brain whirling for an appropriate come-back. When he was unable to think of one, he wrinkled his nose. 'Gotta go. Guard dooty.'

It was my turn to look puzzled. 'Dooty? What's…' Oh. *Duty*. My face cleared. He really wasn't bright at all. 'If Rubus isn't here, you don't need to guard his rooms.'

He scowled at me. 'Even more reason for dooty. Can't let fookers mess around with his stuff when he in't here.' He spun away and stomped off.

I watched him go, considering. That was interesting. What stuff was Rubus hiding away? It would definitely be worth doing some proper snooping in his rooms when I got the chance. And when this idiot wasn't barricading them.

I reminded myself that Rubus had a mysterious Plan B should his efforts to locate Chen's sphere fail. Perhaps the key to finding out what else he was planning was hidden away under his mattress. I added 'sneaking around' to my to-do list and continued on my way. I seriously doubted that the police would keep Rubus for more than another hour or two; I had to make use of his absence while I had the chance.

Tempting as it was to go poking around for other hapless insult victims whose paths I happened to cross, I managed to exercise some self-restraint and head towards the laboratory instead. Carduus was still something of a mystery to me – and I was making it my mission to discover what he was up to with all his potions, even though the guy thoroughly creeped me out. I had promised I'd show up again that morning but there was no way I was drinking his gloopy potion. I'd accidentally-on-purpose smash the bottle before it passed my lips. Carduus was so self-absorbed, he wouldn't suspect a thing.

When I entered the laboratory, the mad Fey scientist was yet again conspicuously absent. Where on earth did he go to all the time? I walked round the perimeter of the room, examining the shelves to see if there was anything out of place or different. Was he stockpiling anything in particular? Unfortunately my superior powers of deduction weren't giving me any useful information. After several loops, I sighed and ambled over to the papers on his desk. Various incomprehensible bits of formulae were scribbled down. I flicked through but none of them made any sense to me.

I was on the verge of abandoning the lab altogether in favour of somewhere more useful when an odd shuffling sound reached my ears. I glanced up just in time to see a piece of paper wedge itself in the gap underneath the door. A secret note!

Beaming, I hopped over and opened the door. The corridor outside was completely empty. Wrinkling my nose in vexation, I stooped and grabbed the paper. It wasn't a missive to Carduus, though; the name scrawled on the front was mine.

I unfolded the paper and scanned it. Well, well, well.

R is growing suspicious. He's not going to allow you the freedom to

roam around much longer. You have a day or two at most. Act quickly.

It was the same handwriting as the two previous notes but there was still no indication as to who my mysterious friend was.

I ran through various possibilities but came up short. It had to be one of the Fey who had Rubus's ear otherwise they'd have no way knowing what he was up to. Whoever they were, they were certainly adept at keeping a low profile and acting loyal; I hadn't had even an inkling that any of Rubus's inner circle were anything but zealots.

The information that my movements were soon going to be curtailed didn't exactly fill me with joy. Despite occasionally having to deal with Lunaria tagging along, I'd done well to nosy around the city and hold secret assignations with whomever I'd pleased. I'd supposed that it was because I'd done such a fabulous job of getting Rubus to trust me but perhaps what had happened with the car last night – and his subsequent arrest – had been a step too far. I'd just have to hope that Mendax didn't delay our shifty dealings for much longer; the sooner the sphere was out of the way for good, the better.

I was so absorbed in my musings that I almost missed the approaching footsteps. In the nick of time I screwed up the paper and balled it into my palm, a split second before the door opened and Carduus's tight features appeared.

'Oh,' he said with a sour twist to his mouth, 'it's you.'

I stretched my mouth into a grin. 'Cardy, baby! How are you?'

He walked past me, hefting two glass bottles containing purple, swirly liquid onto the nearest table top. 'I'd be a lot better if you didn't keep barging into my workspace,' he muttered. 'But fine. Thank you.' He turned his head towards me. 'What do you want?'

I put my hands into my pockets, hoping my tight trousers wouldn't display the bulge of balled-up paper, and sighed. 'I'm getting really sick of the amnesia. You had that potion you were working on yesterday. I was hoping it was working out and you have a genuine way of curing me by now.'

He tilted his head in a manner that was eerily reminiscent of his niece, Artemesia. The comparison was remarkably unpleasant.

'By which I mean an antidote,' I said, 'which isn't

likely to kill me at the same time. Or make me ill.'

'What I had yesterday won't work. I tested it and it's useless. I'm not a miracle worker. I'm doing my best.' He seemed particularly sulky this morning. 'Rubus got himself arrested last night. I've had other things to do besides run around on your behalf.'

I raised an inquisitive eyebrow. 'Is that what those bottles are for? Is it something to help Rubus?' It seemed a stretch. The arsebadger was always going to be released with a caution, unless he already had a criminal record. That was a thought. I entertained myself briefly with the hope that this was the final strike on a long list of misdemeanours and that Morgan's brother would be put away for a long spell. It would certainly solve a lot of problems.

'Everything I do is to help Rubus,' Carduus snapped.

'Sure,' I drawled. 'And he's lucky to have you.' I arched another grin at him. 'Not as lucky as he is to have *me,* of course.'

The old faery rolled his eyes in irritation. 'If you must know,' he said, tapping his fingernail on the nearest bottle, 'I'm working on a locator spell. In theory it's quite easy to track people using a combination of magic and nature.'

I stiffened. Morgan had used dandelion seeds to track me when he'd needed to. If Carduus was doing the same, I'd never be able to escape. 'In theory?' I asked carefully.

He glowered. 'I've not yet managed it myself. I doubt anyone could.'

I breathed out. That was something, then. Artemesia did a damned good thing when she took all those potion books with her. Without them, this old bastard really was lost.

I didn't relax for long, however. Not when I heard what else he had to say.

'What I have achieved, however,' he said, 'is a potion that will allow us to locate strong magic in objects. Living creatures mess up the equilibrium of the mixture I've created but it's not living creatures that we really want to find – even if that dratted bogle is still on the loose.'

I kept my features slack, not daring to move in case I betrayed the fact that I knew Charrie was already dead. It wasn't that which really worried me, however. 'You're talking about the sphere, aren't you? The one Rubus is so desperate to get hold of.'

'We're all desperate to get hold of it. That sphere contains enough power to return us all to Mag Mell. It's our salvation.'

And this demesne's destruction. I eyed the glass bottles. 'So will that do it?' I enquired casually. 'Will that liquid find the sphere?'

He grimaced. 'It still needs some tweaking but I'm getting close.'

I licked my lips. 'That's … wonderful news.' Gasbudlikins. My stomach twisted. Just how close was close? I edged over to get a closer look at this supposed wonder potion. If I managed to destroy it, how difficult would it be to replace? If only I could destroy Carduus instead. I gritted my teeth. Stupid truce.

A fresh-faced faery popped her head round the door and interrupted us. 'Good news!' she beamed. 'Rubus has been let go.'

Carduus tutted. 'I should think so too.'

I checked my watch. That was good timing. I should get out of here before Rubus returned – and I had a date with a certain slimy dragon to make. Given all that I'd just learned, the faster I made it the better.

***

According to Morgan, Mendax had demanded that we meet him at Castlefield, the location of an old Roman fort as far as the humans were concerned – and the location of a closed border crossing to Mag Mell.

'It's no coincidence that he picked this spot,' I murmured. Thanks to my amnesia, I didn't feel the ache of home as keenly as other Fey did but being here still amplified the homesickness. I could feel the dull pain in my chest blossoming outwards and throbbing through my veins. No wonder so many of us were keen to follow Rubus, with his hard-edged vow to return all faeries to our homeland. It was difficult to know that here we were almost within touching distance of home, even though it was a home I couldn't remember. It was even more difficult to remember that all this was my fault.

Morgan lightly touched my arm. 'Are you alright?'

'I'm fine.'

'Would you like another hug? I rather enjoyed the last one.'

I glanced at him. His eyes were dancing and I could feel my body being pulled towards his as if by some invisible magnet.

Then, from round a row of parked cars, Finn appeared. Darn it. 'I've checked the surrounding area,' he announced. 'No one suspicious is here.'

'Other than us, you mean.'

He snorted. 'Speak for yourself.' He glanced at Morgan. 'Did she tell you what she did last night?'

I smiled smugly. 'I put Rubus in jail. That's more than either of you two geniuses have managed.'

'What did you do? Is he still locked up?' Morgan enquired, looking puzzled.

I waved a hand in the air. 'The police let him go. On a technicality.'

'The technicality being that all he did was grab a police officer,' Finn said. 'It's hardly the crime of the century.'

'Perhaps not,' I said, spotting Mendax across the expanse of grass in front of us. 'But he's planning the crime of the millennium so let's worry about that instead, shall we?'

All three of us straightened our shoulders, watching as Mendax shuffled towards us. He gave a good impression of an old man with arthritis. Given how fast he'd run away from me the first time I'd seen him, I knew better. I wondered what other secrets the old dragon was hiding.

'I don't trust this old bugger,' Finn muttered.

'I'm not sure we have much of a choice,' I said, keeping my voice low to avoid being overheard. 'Carduus is getting close to creating a potion that will trace the sphere. We have to put it out of action for good.'

Morgan threw me a swift, narrow-eyed look. There wasn't time to explain further, however. The dragon was too close.

'Greetings,' Mendax intoned in his high-pitched voice. 'I'm glad to see that you are all here and you are taking our negotiations seriously. This is, after all, a very serious matter.'

Morgan stepped forward, his emerald-green eyes glittering. 'Did you bring the oath breaker?'

Mendax inclined his head. 'I did. Did you bring the ring?'

Morgan dug into his pocket and pulled it out, displaying it for the dragon to see. There was no denying the hungry expression on Mendax's face. Finn was right, I realised: this arsebadger of a dragon was only concerned with gold and riches to hoard for himself. We really couldn't trust him. 'It was not easy to get hold of.'

'No,' Mendax murmured, 'I don't suppose it was. I take it that because of the truce Rubus is still breathing, however.'

'He is.'

The old dragon shrugged. 'Shame.' He reached into his pocket and took out a small box. 'The oath breaker you desire is in here.'

Finn started forward as if to take it but Mendax pulled it just out of reach. 'This exchange is purely to establish trust. You understand that we are here for something far more important.'

'The sphere,' I ground out.

'Indeed.' He turned his coal-black eyes to me. 'Have you … found it?'

Morgan cleared his throat. 'Let's just say we're getting close. It will depend on how effective this oath breaker of yours actually is.'

Mendax bared his teeth in a nasty grin. 'If you follow the instructions, I think you'll find that it's very effective indeed. Why don't we make the exchange and meet again this time tomorrow?'

'That can be arranged.' Morgan didn't move. 'Not here, though.'

The dragon lifted his head and laughed; the sound was particularly grating.

I walked past Morgan and up to Mendax, pausing right in front of him and gazing curiously at his hair. 'I was wondering how you comb that mess of yours so that the horns don't show,' I said.

The laughter ceased abruptly. 'I suppose you think you're funny.'

'No,' I told him. 'I'm just mean.'

'You said it.' Mendax sniffed. 'Well, I'm not the devil and I don't have horns. You know who the real devil is and you have an inkling about what hell will be unleashed if he gets his hands on Chen's sphere. I can stop that. Whether you allow me to is up to you.'

I curled my bottom lip and grabbed the box, twisting away before he could protest. As I walked back, Morgan tossed the ring towards him. 'There,' he said. 'You have the ring and we have the oath breaker. If it works, we'll meet you tomorrow in front of the main library.'

'And you'll bring the sphere?'

'If we can find it.'

'You'd better,' Mendax growled. 'If you don't, all this will cease to exist.' He raised his hand and wiggled his fingers. 'Toodle-oo.' He twisted round and shambled away.

The three of us watched him go. 'Despite his words,' Finn muttered, 'I get the impression that he couldn't give a fuck if this demesne is destroyed. He just wants the sphere.'

'He promised to destroy it.'

Finn gave me a long look. 'Do we believe that?'

I sighed and ran a hand through my hair. 'Do we have a choice?'

Chapter Nineteen

Artemesia examined the box with a critical eye. 'It's very small,' she said. 'Have you opened it?'

I hopped up onto a stool. 'We thought we'd wait and let you do it,' I said with forced cheeriness. 'You know, in case it's actually a bomb or something. That way you'll be the one to get blown up.'

She glared at me. 'You're just charm personified, aren't you?'

Morgan stepped in before matters could escalate. 'Madrona is complicated.'

Finn snorted. 'That's one way of describing her.'

Morgan frowned. 'I can open the damned box, Arty. We just thought it was wise to let you see it first.'

I exhaled loudly. 'Give it to me. I'm the superhero. I'll martyr myself so the rest of you can live. I expect statues and songs and my own public holiday in return, though.'

'You're not getting the public holiday,' Finn declared. 'If anyone's getting the public holiday, it'll be me and my brothers.'

'FinnWinnJinn Day?' I shook my head. 'It'll never catch on.'

'It's a hell of a lot better than Mad Day.'

I put my hands on my hips. 'Mad Day is catchy. Mad Day in Madchester.'

A muscle ticked in Morgan's cheek. 'Both of you are being stupid. Can we please focus on what's important? Besides, we all know it will be Morgan Day.'

Artemesia stared at the three of us. 'Is this condition contagious?' she enquired. 'Because I like my ego where it is, thank you very much.'

'There's nothing wrong with a bit of self-confidence.'

She raised her eyes heavenward. 'There is if this box doesn't work.' Her voice darkened. 'Or if it does indeed blow up in our faces.'

'If you can't engage in some well-placed gallows humour when you're facing the end of the world, when can you?' I asked.

Before anyone could move, I jumped off the stool, snatched the little box from Artemesia's hands and moved to the back of the room. I flipped it open before any of these jokers took my martyrdom away from me. It was almost disappointing when nothing happened.

'Anything interesting inside?' Finn asked. 'Or is the box empty like that dragon's damned soul?'

Morgan strode over to me. 'Don't do anything like that again,' he growled.

'Are you saying that you'd be upset if I got blown to smithereens, Morgan?'

He grabbed my wrist in an iron grip. 'Just don't, Maddy.'

Something about the look in his eye gave me pause and a strange warmth spread through me. 'Okay,' I said quietly. I held the box out to him. 'I can't tell what it is,' I admitted.

Morgan took it from me and stared down. I recognised that look. I wasn't the only one who did, either.

'What is it?' Artemesia asked. 'What's the problem?'

He sighed. 'It's a branch.'

Finn let out a bark of unamused laughter. 'Of course it is. No wonder the old dragon was happy to let it go.'

I gazed at all three of them, thoroughly befuddled. 'He doesn't like trees?'

Morgan reached into the box and, between his thumb and forefinger, gingerly pulled the supposed branch out. It didn't look like a branch to me, it looked like a squidgy sponge-thing. At least it was a pretty colour.

Artemesia drew in a sharp breath. 'It's red.'

'Yep.' Morgan held it up to the light and turned it round. 'You'll need to check it over, Arty. Make sure that it still has enough power left. It's obviously ancient. Goodness only knows where Chen got it from.' He placed it back into the box and passed it over to Artemesia. She took it, albeit rather gingerly.

'Either the lot of you are talking in code,' I said, 'or there's something going on here that I don't understand.'

'Branches in the sense that we mean here,' Morgan explained, 'have nothing to do with trees. They're magically imbued objects. We call them branches because they need to be linked to something else—'

'Or someone else,' Artemesia butted in.

Morgan nodded. 'If they're not linked, they won't work. The fact that this oath-breaking branch is red means that it'll only work if a blood relation uses it on another blood relation. So, in effect it's useful only to either me or Rubus. No other Fey trapped here are blood related.'

'So either you use it to break Rubus from the truce, or he uses it on you.'

'Pretty much.'

'You can't use it on any of his minions?'

'No. It will only work on Rubus and it will only work if I'm the one to wield it.'

I grimaced. That was incredibly disappointing; I'd been looking forward to breaking all of Rubus's hangers-on from the truce so I could ground them into dust.

'This is good news,' Finn said. 'We chop off the head and the rest of the body will fall. It might only stop the truce from working on Rubus but that's a good thing. His idiotic servants won't be able to stop us from hurting him because they'll still be bound by the truce. If the only Fey in this demesne who can be harmed by another Fey is Rubus, then it's win-win. Mendax was right: I could never hurt Rubus on my own because I don't have the strength. My two brothers and I combined couldn't even take down Madrona. But you have enough people on your side, Morgan. We can bring him down without having to worry about what happens to the sphere afterwards.' He shrugged. 'We kill Rubus. Our worries will be over.'

I sneaked a look at Morgan's face. Oh dear. I was beginning to see what the problem was. 'Would you be prepared to commit fratricide?' I asked Finn softly.

'I can't,' he bit back, suddenly stiffening. 'You already did that for me.'

I didn't really have an answer for that – Finn had made a valid point.

'You don't have to kill him, Morganus,' Artemesia said. 'Once you've used the oath breaker, others can take over from you to deal with Rubus. And you knew it might come to this. We just need to be able to hurt him. If he can be hurt, he's vulnerable. You can grab him and lock him up. It'll stop him from doing anything in the future that might cause us problems.'

Morgan drew in a breath. 'I can do it,' he said finally. 'I can even kill him if need be.' He raised his eyes to mine for a second before he glanced away. 'That's what worries me.'

For a long moment we were all silent. I bit my lip then walked over to Morgan and put my arms round him. He didn't resist. 'I'm already a murderer,' I whispered. 'I'll do it, if it comes to that. My shoulders can carry the weight.'

He rested his chin on the top of my head. 'I don't think they can, Maddy.' He sighed. 'Besides, even without the truce in place, it'll take more than one of us to bring down Rubus. He's stronger than you think. And taking down a Fey, whether they're Rubus or someone else, isn't like taking down a human. It won't be easy.'

'There is one other part of this equation that concerns me,' Artemesia said. 'Why would Mendax pass this oath breaker over so easily? Surely he knows that if it works like it's supposed to, the sphere won't matter. We won't need to give it to him to destroy.'

Morgan stepped away from me, his gazing flicking to the oath-breaker box in Artemesia's hands. 'There's always the possibility that if we take out Rubus, someone else will step up and fill his shoes instead.'

'Carduus,' I said.

Both Finn and Morgan looked confused. 'He would never be respected enough to lead.'

'No, but he's working on a locating potion to find out where the sphere is. He told me it wasn't quite ready yet but, from the look on his face, it won't be long before it is.'

Artemesia seemed shocked. 'What? Did you see this potion?'

I grimaced. 'Some sort of liquid with purple swirly bits. Why? Is he talking out of his arse?'

She swallowed. 'I don't know. Such a potion is theoretically possible but it would take considerable skill to make it properly. I never thought my uncle had it in him. Even with all the books and knowledge I've got, I couldn't do it.'

'He works for Rubus,' I said drily. 'And he's a total believer. He has the motivation. That's not all either.' I told them about the note from my mysterious 'friend'.

'You don't have any idea who sent it?'

I shook my head. 'No. I'll work it out sooner or later because obviously I'm a genius and nothing escapes me for long.' I ignored the scoff from both Finn and Artemesia. 'But I have no idea who it's from. Either way, it feels like we're running out of time. We can't dilly-dally and wait for things to happen to us. We have to make them happen if we're going to stay in control.'

Morgan's mouth turned down. 'I agree. And in any case, whether Carduus succeeds or not with his new bespelled potion, the sphere will always be a concern. Rubus or no Rubus, it has to be destroyed.'

'Unless,' Finn added darkly, 'Mendax is looking for an excuse to keep the sphere for himself rather than destroy it. I still don't trust him.'

I shrugged. 'Trust or no trust, Rubus or no Rubus, oath breaker or no oath breaker, I'm still Madrona the Madhatter. We're still going to win.'

Artemesia arched an eyebrow. 'How can you be so sure?'

I pushed myself up onto my tiptoes and spread out my arms, twirling once for effect. I didn't even wobble. 'I don't know how to lose,' I boomed.

'You lost your memory,' Finn said. 'You still don't know where that is.'

'You lost your good sense too,' Artemesia agreed. 'Right around the time you made that teeny-weeny mistake and trapped us all in this demesne.'

Morgan glanced at me. 'You lost me.' His voice was barely audible. 'But I think you might have found me again.' He pointed at the oath breaker. 'Test it, Arty. You've got thirty minutes and then we're going to find Rubus. And we're going to do whatever we can to remove him from this situation for good.'

***

'So,' Morgan said, 'you know what to do?'

I nodded. 'I've got this. It'll be fine.'

Finn waggled his phone. 'Julie's on her way.'

I pointed at him. 'It's your job to keep her safe. It's not that she's weak or anything but she's not like us. Not to mention that the viewers of *St Thomas Close* will come after us with pitchforks if anything happens to her.'

He growled. 'You don't need to tell me to look after her. I've done a great deal more to help her than you have.'

For once I didn't rise to the bait. It was easy because it wasn't true. I'd rescued her in a dark alley. I'd been Tasered for her. I suffered being kicked out of a swanky restaurant because of her. I was super awesome while Finn was … large and hulking. Anyone could be like that if genetics permitted. I didn't say any of this to him, though; I simply stepped over and stretched up so I could kiss him on the cheek. 'You're a fabulous bodyguard,' I told him.

'Get her away from me, Morgan,' Finn said. He looked utterly terrified.

I beamed at him then I cracked my knuckles. 'Let's do this.'

Leaving the boys behind, I strode round the corner and headed towards the main doors of the hide-out. I could feel the buzz of anticipation zipping through my veins. Rubus wouldn't know what had hit him. Being a super spy was all well and good but it was important to slide in some real action. Sneaking around as I'd done so far was producing results at a snail's pace. The next hour was going to prove very different.

It didn't take long to locate the man himself. He was seated in his wannabe throne room, his eyes half-lidded, whilst a pathetic Fey female grovelled in front of him for some dust.

'I'll do whatever you want,' she pleaded. 'I don't even want a lot of pixie dust. I'll just take a bit.'

'There's nothing you can offer me that I need,' Rubus said, not bothering to look at his poor supplicant.

I watched him carefully. It didn't appear that he'd got much sleep during his incarceration; yet again, he was looking both tired and wan.

'I have money!' The Fey reached into her bag and pulled out a scrunched-up wad of notes. 'I've been saving up. Just … please. Give me some.'

Rubus uncrossed his legs and leaned forward, opening his eyes to look at her properly for the first time. 'Hmmm,' he said, tapping his chin as if deep in thought. 'Actually…'

She held her breath, desperate hope springing into her eyes.

'No,' he said. 'You're not getting any.'

Her shoulders sagged.

'It's not my fault,' Rubus said, clearly only pretending to sound reasonable. 'But supplies are low. We have to ration what we have and by my reckoning you took several ounces last week. You also kept them for yourself.' He tutted. 'That simply won't do. I expect my people to share their good fortune with others so that as many as possible can benefit from the healing properties of pixie dust. I don't expect them to keep it all for their own use. That's just selfish.'

I had to hand it to him, he played a far better villain than I did. I was tempted to pull out a pad and pen so I could take notes. Make other people feel bad about their life choices in order to get what you want; that was a neat trick.

I leaned back against the far wall, casting an eye around the others who were waiting. There were even a few humans scattered about although I shouldn't have been surprised by that since Rubus had made use of Dave, the human I'd used to take me to the Metropolitan Bar that first time. All the same, I was impressed by Rubus's gall at using the people he was planning to destroy. Did he care about their futures at all? Then I remembered that all this was my fault in the first place; perhaps I shouldn't think quite so hard about it.

I'd thought that I might have to work to insinuate myself deeper into the room in order to be noticed but I should have realised that Rubus'd know I was there. As soon as he'd dismissed the quivering pixie-dust addict, he crooked his little finger and beckoned me forward.

'I take it you heard what happened last night, Madrona,' he said.

I nodded. 'I did. You should have let me stay in the restaurant with you guys. I'd have quite happily taken the fall for your arrest. You were very brave to attack a police officer.' A bit of ego massage never went amiss.

Unfortunately for me, Rubus's eyes merely narrowed. 'Who told you I attacked a policeman?'

Uh-oh. 'Julie,' I said, without missing a beat. 'She's on her way here now, in fact. I persuaded her to come and cheer you up. She doesn't have much time to spare but I thought you might appreciate seeing her, however briefly. Has your car been recovered?'

'No.'

'That's a shame.' Then, because I couldn't resist, I added, 'And to think that your lovely gold ring was in the glove box too.'

I reckoned that if the truce weren't in place, Rubus would have ordered my execution right there and then. Reminding myself that I needed him to follow my lead, I hastily changed the subject. 'Anyway,' I cooed, 'as I said, Julie is on her way here. Even though she knows you're a faery, it's probably not a good idea to invite her in here. Don't forget she's a vampire. She has no powers at the moment but who knows what latent magic is hiding deep inside her?'

For a brief moment, Rubus looked amused. 'You've hit the nail on the head, Madrona,' he murmured. 'When I use the sphere to re-open the border, the magic that will hit this demesne could have untold effects on the likes of Julie Chivers. She might be impotent now but think about what could happen if the magic took over instead?'

I stared at him. That thought had never occurred to me.

Rubus laughed at my expression. 'It makes you wonder why Chen didn't use the sphere himself. I'm quite certain the after-effects will be extraordinarily beneficial for the dragons too – but they all seem hell-bent on destroying it instead of using it.'

That was because they weren't homicidal, I thought. I smiled weakly. 'What a thought. Dragons that actually breathe fire and vampires that could turn into bats.'

His eyes shone. 'Brilliant, eh?' When no one in the room said anything, he raised his voice. 'I said, that's brilliant, isn't it?'

There was a sudden loud murmur of agreement. If it weren't for the truce, Rubus should really ought to have considered investing in a literal whip as a well as a metaphorical one.

'Anyway,' I said, 'if you're busy here, I'll leave you to it and head out to meet Julie. I'm sure she'll understand that you have other things to do.'

Rubus glanced at me impassively and, for a horrible moment, I thought he was going to agree. It was just as well that I'd been paying attention in Manipulation 101; in the end he stood up, clearly unable to bear the thought that either he was missing out or that I was telling him what to do. 'These people can come back another day. I am excited to see the glamorous Ms Julie Chivers again.'

He'd deliberately name-dropped her so everyone in the room was aware that he was meeting a real-life soap star. It was unfortunate that Lunaria took that moment to enter the room. When she heard his words and saw his leering expression, her face fell half a mile. Man. Maybe I should see if Finn was up for a date or two. She needed something – or rather someone – to distract her from her ridiculous crush.

Rubus swaggered over in my direction with his groin thrust slightly forwards so that none of us were in any doubt that he was indeed a man. I frowned.

'Have you hurt yourself?' I asked, the very picture of solicitous concern. 'Or can faeries get the clap?'

His smile disappeared. 'What?' he snapped.

'You're walking like your balls are swollen.'

He glowered. 'No. They're always this large.' In a muttered undertone, he added, 'Don't push your luck, Madrona. You're still on probation.'

As if I could forget. I offered him a pretty smile and gestured to the door so he could lead the way. If that was what it took to make him feel manly and in charge, I could permit it. He'd learn who was really running this show soon enough.

By the time we made it out onto the street, the sun had disappeared behind an ominous cloud and a steady drizzle was starting to fall. 'This fucking weather,' Rubus complained. 'Another thing to despise about this demesne.'

I shrugged. 'You could always move to the Bahamas.'

He didn't deign to answer. Instead his eyes travelled up and down the length of the road until he finally spied Julie's ostentatious car and strode towards it. She'd obviously only just arrived and opened the door before we reached her, exiting in a manner that suggested either a Swiss finishing school or hours of practice. When I saw the short skirt she was wearing, I understood why – although flashing a bit of inner thigh would probably whet Rubus's appetite further and keep him distracted.

'Darlings!' She clip-clopped towards us, planting an air kiss first near Rubus's cheek and then near mine. As instructed, she didn't pay me much attention; her focus was all on the villain of the hour. 'Are you alright?' she asked. 'I can't believe those terrible policemen treated like you that. You were the victim!'

'They were clearly threatened by me,' Rubus said dismissively. 'They wanted to show who was in charge. It happens to me a lot.'

I blinked. He actually seemed to believe it. And Artemesia had denigrated *my* ego! To match Rubus, I was going to have to try a damn sight harder. I comforted myself with the thought that I couldn't be the best at everything; it wouldn't be fair on the rest of the world.

'Well,' Julie said, 'I'm very glad to see you breathing free air.' She checked her watch. 'I don't have long. I'm supposed to be at the studio in the next hour but perhaps we could arrange to meet for another attempt at dinner in the near future.' She threw me a sly look. 'Sorry, Mads, darling, but perhaps without you joining us.'

I pouted, as if I were crestfallen at not being invited to play gooseberry. I was genuinely surprised that she was suggesting a re-match with Rubus because she had already played her first role for today and lured him out of the building. I'd expected her to let him down gently and say she was too busy to meet him again.

For his part, Rubus was eager to agree to another date. 'Thursday night?' he enquired. 'I know a wonderful little steakhouse. Now I know more about who you really are, I feel it might be more up your alley than Italian. You can order your rib-eye blue and bloody.'

I grimaced but Julie just smiled. 'Excellent. I'll get Mads to give you my address. You can pick me up.'

He raised his eyebrows suggestively. 'It will be my pleasure.'

She turned and went back to her car. Rubus and I watched as she drove off.

'I have to say, Madrona,' Rubus murmured, 'you do have your uses from time to time.'

I curtsied. 'I'm glad to be of service.'

He smiled absently, his mind clearly on other things, then he turned to head back inside. I followed at a slower pace, trying not to look tense. Maybe if I took my time everyone would assume I really enjoyed the rain, especially when it made my hair all frizzy and dripped down my neck.

Fortunately, Morgan stepped up to the plate and chose the perfect moment to appear. Rubus had only just reached the pavement when his voice boomed out.

'Maddy!'

I froze, as if stunned into inaction. Rubus whipped round and glared. Like we were playing out some ancient Western film, Morgan was standing in the middle of the road less than fifty feet away with his hands by his sides. I couldn't prevent a shiver of delight. Planned or not, it really did feel like he was breaching the barricades and risking his life to rescue me from the clutches of the dastardly evil overlord.

I raised my hand to my mouth but made sure that my gasp was still audible. 'Morgan? What are you doing here?'

Even considering how carefully we'd planned this moment, I still half-expected him to pull out a gun from his non-existent holster so that he could defend my honour properly. What he actually did, of course, was simply stride towards me – and what a masterful stride it was. I was genuinely enjoying myself as I watched him approach.

Rubus wasted no time in stamping his way towards me too. He reached me at the same time as Morgan. 'Brother,' he hissed.

Morgan's lip curled. 'You're no brother of mine.' He looked at me as if dismissing Rubus entirely. 'Are you alright?'

I nodded. 'I'm good.'

'Pleased to hear it,' Morgan growled. He took my arm. 'You're coming with me now.'

Rubus narrowed his eyes. 'No, she's not. Madrona is mine. She stays with *me*.'

'Not happening.' Morgan pulled me into him, using his body as a barrier between Rubus and myself. It was a shame this was all just play-acting. I hoped that one of the Fey crowd who'd come out from Rubus's hide-out and were staring at us from the safety of the pavement would take out a phone and record our little show. I'd enjoy watching it back later.

Rubus sneered. 'In case you've forgotten, little brother, she dumped you.'

'The old Madrona dumped me,' Morgan returned. 'The new Madrona is different. She's forgotten how you manipulated her. She's like her old self again.'

'Is she?' Rubus asked. 'Because she's had plenty of opportunity to scurry back to you. She could have left me for you on any number of occasions but she's still here. She's still with me.' He said this last part suggestively, as if there were far more to our relationship than there actually was.

An angry light appeared in Morgan's eyes – and one that I didn't think he was faking. 'You have enough people, Rubus. You don't need her as well.'

Rubus smiled nastily. 'No,' he said. 'I don't need her. But you do. And for that reason alone, she's staying with me.' He looked at me. 'Aren't you?'

I licked my lips. 'Um…'

'Don't forget,' Rubus said, 'there are things I know about you that you don't want little Morganus here to discover.'

Morgan growled. 'What things?'

'Take her,' Rubus said, 'and you'll find out.' He stepped back and folded his arms across his chest. 'Go on, *Maddy*. Let's see just how much my brother really wants you when he discovers the whole truth.'

Even though I was certain that he was referring to the fact that it was my actions that had trapped us here, I felt a genuine tremor of trepidation. Were there other atrocities I'd committed that I didn't yet know about? Truth be told, Rubus could probably say anything and we'd have no way of knowing if he was lying or not. Stupid amnesia.

I looked from Morgan to Rubus and back again. 'I don't know,' I whispered. 'I think I'm better suited to Rubus.'

'I don't care what you've done, Maddy,' Morgan said. 'Whatever it was, it is in the past now. You have nothing to feel guilty about. You have to stop blaming yourself.'

I was no longer sure where the line between acting and reality was. I stared at him and the truth reflected in his eyes. He turned away from Rubus and took my hand, kneeling down in front of me.

'I'll prove it to you,' he said softly. 'I'll prove to you how much you mean to me.' He reached into his pocket and drew out a small box. It wasn't the same one that we'd acquired from Mendax. This version was even smaller. It was also covered in velvet.

'Oh, this is priceless!' Rubus said. 'Are you actually going to propose? You know she'll turn you down. You'll be humiliated in front of everyone again, Morganus.'

Morgan didn't pay his brother any attention. 'I can't imagine a world without you in it,' he said to me. 'You know we can be so good together. I'll help you get past whatever turmoil is going on inside you. I can help you be a better person. We're so much stronger together than we are apart.'

Rubus snorted. 'Madrona doesn't want to be a better person. She knows who she is. She's already a fabulous person, a fabulous person who is loyal to me.'

I stared into Morgan's eyes, melting into their green depths. Then I swallowed. 'Morgan, you're a great guy,' I began.

Rubus crowed. He already knew what was coming.

'But I don't think we belong together.'

Go me. It was a shame Julie wasn't still here. If she were, she'd already be declaring her retirement from acting forever in the face of my Oscar-winning performance.

'It's not you,' I said, gesturing helplessly. 'It's me.'

Morgan's body tensed. To anyone looking, it would have been because he was desperately hurt by my rejection. At least, that's what I hoped.

'We can still be friends,' I continued.

'You can't,' Rubus interrupted.

I ignored him. 'And part of me will always love you, even though I don't remember you.' I sighed. 'The fact is, I'm just not good enough for you.'

'Now you're lying,' Rubus scoffed. 'You know that the opposite is true.' He put a hand on Morgan's shoulder. 'You're making a fool of yourself, bro. Give it up and go home.' He couldn't disguise the glee in his voice.

Morgan's head dropped. I bit my lip. He was overdoing the rejected suitor part, I decided; he wasn't the type to be so publicly devastated. Fortunately, however, it didn't last long. In one swift movement, he thumbed open the box, twisted round and flung the oath breaker into Rubus's face.

The blood-red squidgy gloop attached itself to Rubus's cheek. He yanked himself back, his hand immediately rising upwards. He scrabbled at it, trying desperately to scrape it off. 'What is this? What have you done?'

Morgan stood up and backed away. 'Nothing more than you deserve.'

Several Fey ran over, hands flailing in panic. 'Get this off me!' Rubus roared at them.

Amellus reached up, clawing at the oath breaker in a desperate bid to remove it. The harder he tried, the more it seemed to embed itself. 'Where's Carduus?' he bellowed.

The oath breaker sank deeper and deeper into Rubus's skin. I stepped forward, as if I were trying to help, but Morgan shoved me back. 'What have you done?' I screeched. 'You've hurt Rubus!'

Morgan's eyes glittered. 'Clearly he's all you care about. You can have him.' His lip curled. 'It won't be for long though.' He tossed the box to the ground.

'This was never about me,' I whispered. 'This was always about him. You were expecting me to say no.'

'Because you've not changed at all, Madrona. If anything, you're even worse than you were before. You were a means to an end. That's all.' He cast me a disparaging look. With his back turned to the others – and to the still-yelling Rubus – only I could see the flicker of pain in his eyes. He was losing his grip on his role.

'Fuck off out of here,' I snapped.

'Before I do…' He spun round, curling his fingers into a fist to punch his brother. His hand stopped in mid-air and he emitted a brief, strangled growl of pain. My insides tightened. It wasn't working yet, then; the damned oath breaker still hadn't done what it was supposed to.

'You'll pay for this, Morganus!' Rubus shouted as Carduus finally appeared and started to drag him away to relative safety inside. 'Just you wait and see! You'll pay!'

I glared at Morgan, hoping that the others were watching me. Then, without a backward glance, I sprinted after Rubus. We'd done it. And no one suspected a thing. Stage one complete.

Chapter Twenty

Several Fey barricaded the front doors as if Morgan were about to storm the building. Carduus half carried, half dragged Rubus through the corridor towards the lab. I followed, hot on their heels. Before I could enter with them, however, Amellus jumped in my path and glowered at me.

'Only Carduus and Rubus inside.'

'But he's hurt!' I yelled. 'I want to make sure he's alright, you lumping zounderkite!'

He folded his arms, an implacable statue. I lunged past but he sidestepped in time to stop me. Gasbudlikins. I wanted to make sure the oath breaker was going to start working. I couldn't do that from out here.

'Are you okay, Mads?' Lunaria asked behind me.

I turned to her. Her face was pure white. 'I'm fine,' I said shortly. 'Rubus isn't, though. I want to make sure he's okay. What was that thing that Morgan threw at him?'

She shook her head. 'I have no idea.' Her head dropped. 'Why did you do it?' she mumbled. 'Why did you choose Rubus instead of Morgan?'

I could prevaricate and blurt out reasonable sounding excuses to the others but somehow I didn't think they would work with Lunaria. She was in love with Rubus. I suspected she recognised the same emotion in me, albeit for a different brother. Then I paused. Was I in love with Morgan? What a ridiculous notion. I wanted to shag him senseless, sure. Love was… I shook my head. Nah. I didn't love him. I probably wasn't even capable of such a feeling.

'Maybe the others know what that thing was that Morgan threw,' I said, ignoring her question. 'Let's see.' With a final, evil-eyed stare at Amellus, I grabbed Lunaria's arm and whirled back down the corridor.

We entered the kitchen. Faeries of all shapes and sizes were hovering there, anxious looks on their faces.

'What was Morgan doing?'

'Has he found a way to break the truce?'

'If Rubus dies, we're all lost. We'll be stuck here forever!'

One by one, the mingling Fey fell silent as they saw me. I glared at them. 'What? This isn't my fault!'

I still received several nasty looks. Good grief – what exactly did I have to do to get this lot to trust me? 'You idiots couldn't pour water out of a wellington boot if the instructions were on the side,' I sniped. 'You were there and you didn't do a damned thing to stop Morgan. He forced me back but what was your excuse? When Rubus recovers he's not just going to be disappointed in you. He's going to—'

Amellus appeared in the doorway, interrupting me in mid-flow. 'Boss wants you.'

I stiffened. 'Is he alright then? Has Carduus managed to get that crap off his face?'

'You'll see.' He jerked his head. 'Come with me.'

My heart in my mouth, I trailed after the lumbering faery. I still managed to give the other assembled faeries a sneer of dripping disparagement before I left though. 'Rubus wants me,' I said to them smugly. 'It's obvious who he thinks is worthy of him now.'

Several faces blanched in response, Lunaria's included. I tossed my head and caught up with Amellus. 'I told you I should have been allowed into the lab. I'm one of you guys,' I said. 'I'm not the freaking enemy!'

Amellus didn't say anything. He shuffled down the

corridor and pointed me in. I stuck out my tongue at him as I entered. This was going better than I could have hoped for.

The lab door closed behind me. It took me only a second to realise that there was no sign of either Carduus or Rubus. My eyes narrowed in suspicion. Where exactly had they gone?

'Hello?' I called, in case they'd decided this was an excellent time for a spot of hide-and-seek.

No one answered immediately then I heard a groan. Carduus appeared from behind one of the tables, helping a pale-looking Rubus to his feet. Man, Rubus looked like death. He also had a red stain on his cheek where Morgan had thrown the oath breaker. If I squinted, it looked oddly like the shape of the British Isles. I wondered if it would serve as a permanent reminder of the temporary home that Rubus was effectively seeking to destroy. Talk about poetic justice.

'Are you okay?' I asked.

'Does he look okay?' Carduus snapped.

Rubus raised his head, his bleary green eyes meeting mine. 'I don't feel well,' he admitted.

Blimey. For Rubus to confess to a weakness meant he had to be feeling really off colour. That was good news indeed.

I put on my best sad face. 'I don't know what Morgan thought he was doing. How could he hurt you with the truce in place?'

'For all his selfless posturing, my brother is a selfish bastard,' Rubus croaked. 'I don't know what he's done to me but I have no energy. I don't understand why he's so determined to keep us all trapped here.'

His knees buckled slightly. I rushed to his opposite side to help Carduus keep him upright. It was probably better that way; Rubus wouldn't be able to see me rolling my eyes every time he opened his mouth.

'We have to leave,' Carduus said. 'For all we know, Morganus is on his way back with an army. He'll do anything to keep you down. We can't let him take advantage of you when you're in such a weakened position.'

I was confused. 'But the truce—'

'If he can attack Rubus, he can attack any of us!' the older faery yelled. 'We need to get everyone together and get out of here.'

'Nowhere else is ready,' Rubus said. 'And there's all this stuff to move too.' He waved a weak hand around, indicating the bottles, dried herbs and nonsensical potions.

'We can come back for everything when it's safe.' Carduus raised a bony finger in my direction. 'In fact, she can stay here and guard it. Even if Morgan comes back, he'll leave her in peace.'

'I don't know if you were paying any attention,' I drawled, 'but I'm pretty sure Morgan is over me. He faked a proposal just to get at Rubus.'

'All the same, it's obvious he still has feelings for you.'

Rubus nodded. 'He's right. I know now that I can trust you properly, Madrona, so I'm going to trust you to stay here and look after everything. The rest of us will move back to our last place out at the docks. When I give the all-clear, we'll come back and pick you up, along with our belongings.' His gaze held mine with a surprising amount of intensity for someone who still looked as if he were on the verge of collapse.

I shrugged. 'If that's what you want.' I could hardly argue. Now that I'd finally managed to sneak my way back into the inner circle, I'd have to act like a loyal minion. It wouldn't be for much longer; I reckoned I could cope for another day or two.

‘Good.’ A brief gleam crossed Rubus’s eyes. He jerked his thumb at Carduus. ‘Spread the word. We’re moving out.’ His voice hardened. ‘I’ll deal with my brother when I feel better.’

***

All of Rubus’s faeries left with surprising swiftness. I stood at the door, waving them off. Most of them ignored me but one or two, sensing the winds of change, gave me a smile.

Rather than traipsing out with the others, Lunaria paused by my side. ‘Listen, Mads,’ she said. ‘There’s something you should know.’

Amellus appeared. ‘Move.’

For what was possibly the first time in her life, Lunaria squared her shoulders and stood up for herself. ‘I’m talking to Madrona.’

‘No, you in’t.’ He pointed towards the door.

‘Give her a break,’ I told him. ‘She’s only chatting.’ I watched her curiously. Her expression was taut and I sensed that she had something vitally important to tell me.

Amellus stood his ground but he needn’t have bothered. A second later Rubus appeared, still supported by Carduus. He gestured to Lunaria and, eyes wide, she ran to his side. ‘You look terrible!’ she gasped. ‘What did he do?’

‘I’ll explain everything on the way,’ Rubus said. He offered me a crooked smile that was reminiscent of Morgan. The twinge I felt in my chest prevented me from calling Lunaria back and, all too quickly, all three of them were out of the door and stepping into a sleek black car.

Amellus, who still hadn't moved a muscle, flashed me an ugly smile. 'We'll be seein' you.'

'That sounds like a threat,' I told him.

His smile broadened. Then he left too and I was all alone.

I closed the door, double-checked no one was still hanging around and spying on me, then hastily dug out the shell phone. 'Morgan,' I hissed. 'Are you there?'

There was a crackle and then his reassuringly deep voice spoke. 'I'm here. Are you alright?'

I felt a heart-warming tingle that his first thought was for me and not for whether the oath breaker had worked. 'I'm fine,' I told him. I quickly explained all that had occurred since he'd gone. 'I can't tell whether the oath breaker worked, but Rubus is certainly not looking good. Maybe I should have tried to hit him or something, just to tell.'

'No,' he rumbled. 'You'd have given yourself away. If he trusts you properly now, we still might able to use you. It won't be for much longer, I promise you that.'

'I know.'

There was a pause. 'I'm sorry that I did that to you, Madrona. With the fake proposal.'

'It was what we'd planned. And it worked a treat.'

'Yes, but…' His voice trailed off.

I immediately understood. 'There will be time for that later. What's the next step? Are we going to give Mendax the sphere?'

'We're supposed to meet him in the next hour. I think it's for the best. I'll send a different team to the warehouse to confront Rubus. It's good news that he's backtracking to an old hideout because at least we'll know where to find him. As soon as we have confirmation that the oath breaker has worked – and assuming Mendax doesn't try anything stupid – I'll pass over the sphere. I know you have doubts but we need that thing destroyed. We'll demand to watch him do it so we know for sure that he's done what he's promised. He doesn't seem to have let us down so far.'

I nodded. It was exactly how I would play things. And Morgan was right: it did indeed appear that Mendax was more trustworthy than we'd given him credit for. Whether Rubus was out of action or not, the sphere was too dangerous to leave lying around. 'I'll come and meet you at the library.'

'No.' Morgan's words were growing indistinct. 'Stay where you are. We might still need you there in case someone returns. It'll give you a chance to look through everything properly. You might find details about Rubus's Plan B, whatever the hell it is.'

I grinned. More snooping. Excellent. 'Okay,' I agreed. 'Call me once it's done.'

'I will.'

'The second it's done, Morgan.'

'I will.'

'I mean it,' I warned. 'If you don't, I'll come after you and hurl insults at you for the rest of your natural life.'

'That might not be so bad,' he replied softly. I drew in a breath. 'Take care, Maddy.'

'You too,' I whispered.

You too.

Chapter Twenty-One

It was strange walking through the deserted corridors. Of course, there was only one place that I wanted to rummage through. I didn't pause or allow the pile of forlorn, uneaten cupcakes sitting on a table in the television room sway me from my purpose. That was the sort of focused, unerring super spy I was. Instead, I made a beeline for Rubus's bedroom. Amellus, the anti-grammar bouncer, wouldn't be guarding its entrance now.

I found it curious that the door was locked, as if Rubus had expected to leave it unguarded. I rattled the doorknob and patted my hair in case someone had slipped in a hair pin when I wasn't looking that I could convert to a handy lock pick. Then I shrugged. I was blowing my cover by blowing open the door but, given what was about to happen less than a mile away, I reckoned I could justify it.

Morgan had shown me once that magic could be used to break a lock delicately but I reckoned my method was more fun. I raised my right hand, pointed it at the door and, for only the third time in what was left of my memory, called on a stream of attack magic to blast open the lock.

The first time I'd tried this, I'd flung out magic towards a sniper who'd been some distance away. The second time, in my tiny bedroom, I'd been quite controlled. Those facts probably should have occurred to me now.

This time, with the door less than a metre away from

my outstretched hand, I completely obliterated it in a mini-explosion of flying splinters and wood dust. I shrieked and ducked down, trying to cover my face and eyes. Clearly, I didn't know my own strength. I was forced to pause for several moments and pick out the offending shards of sharp wood from my skin. I could feel beads of warm blood on my cheeks, nose and forehead. No doubt I now looked like I'd been attacked by a vicious swarm of bees. I grimaced. Great.

Blinking away the sting of tears – a physical reaction, not an emotional one – I edged into Rubus's room. The scent of his overpowering aftershave still lingered. I hadn't paid much attention to the actual room when I'd entered it that one time before because Rubus himself had been present. Now that his looming figure was no longer confronting me, I could appreciate its sparse tidiness. The bed was neatly made with a white coverlet and plumped pillows. There was a small cabinet with some papers on top and a wardrobe with an open door and surprisingly few clothes inside. The only untidy part of the room was a corner occupied by a mountain of what I guessed was dirty laundry. A door to the left led into the ensuite bathroom. It was a larger room than mine but it was hardly the Ritz.

For no other reason than to be perverse, I grabbed the corner of the pristine coverlet and wiped the last of the blood off my face. It smeared the white fabric in a particularly pleasing manner. It was Rubus's fault; if he'd not locked the door then I wouldn't have been forced to blow it open. It served him right for being so security conscious.

With my mark on his lair well and truly established, I started to look around. I was hoping for a handy folder marked 'Plan B' but nothing jumped out at me. I flicked through the pile of papers on the bedside cabinet. Some were scrawled with nonsensical notes, some with maps and directions.

Every single page had the same doodle – a little drawing of Chen's magical sphere. I snorted; Rubus was a man obsessed. I crossed my fingers that someone would film the moment that he learned the truth – I wanted to see the expression on his face when he finally found out that we'd had his stupid sphere destroyed. I could feed off his disappointment for years; it would almost make dealing with that slimy wyrm Mendax worth it.

Poor, poor Rubus, I thought fondly, although I also reckoned the loss of the sphere might be the making of him. With no route back to Mag Mell, he'd have to concentrate on life in this demesne instead. If I had the potential to be a semi-good faery and put my past behind me, so did he.

Abandoning the papers, I swivelled and looked slowly round the room. Where next? Afraid to get too close to the pile of unwashed linen in case the lingering scent of Rubus's aftershave rose up and attacked me, I headed into the ensuite bathroom. It was scrupulously clean. There wasn't even a skid mark in the loo.

I opened the mirrored cabinet hanging over the sink. If I'd been expecting several bottles of Viagra then I was disappointed: apart from a slim black case, the cabinet was empty.

Stretching up, I grabbed hold of the case and flipped it open. One half contained a syringe and a small glass bottle; the other half held two small opaque plastic tubes.

I thought of the track marks I'd spotted on Rubus's arm and the occasionally drawn look to his features. I picked up the bottle, fascinated. Heroin, maybe? Or some kind of soluble pixie dust? It seemed incredibly bad practice to inject yourself with your own drugs when you were fully aware of the addiction issues. If Rubus were indeed a dust addict, he'd certainly kept it quiet.

I twisted the bottle in my hands. There was no label on it other than a tiny R etched into the glass. So Carduus marked these drugs separately, then. Perhaps it was a special formula designed just for Rubus. I was rather disappointed that he allowed himself to be so weak.

Returning the bottle to its place, I turned my attention to the plastic tubes. I couldn't work out what they were for. I picked up one, frowned and unscrewed the little lid, peering inside. It was empty apart from an odourless liquid. Even more befuddled, I glanced inside the second tube. There was something in there. I shook out the contents. Two small black discs fell out. Despite their colour, they appeared translucent. Frowning, I gingerly held them up to the light. What…?

My jaw dropped in dismay as an epiphany hit me. Contact lenses – these were coloured contact lenses! I held one up to my eyeball. My vision darkened slightly when I looked through it but it didn't take a genius to realise that these lenses had nothing to do with poor eyesight. They were for cosmetic purposes only.

My fingers scrabbled for the glass bottle, the one with R etched into the side. I threw it down hard onto the tiled floor, smashing the glass and spilling the contents. Then I knelt down and, avoiding the shards, touched the liquid. It seared my skin almost immediately. Hissing in pain, I hastily turned on the tap and washed it off as best as I could.

I was trying to bank down my growing horror but it was next to impossible. The burn of the liquid was familiar. The last time I'd felt a similar sensation was the night when I'd awoken on the golf course when I'd poisoned myself with rowan.

I closed my eyes. I'd told Rubus that one of the side-effects of my poisoning had been a prolonged glamour.

The only part of a Fey that couldn't be affected by a glamour was their eyes – and Rubus had coloured contact lenses hidden in his bathroom cabinet. Black contact lenses. The only person I knew with black irises was Mendax.

Abandoning the mess in the bathroom, I whirled back into the bedroom. I flung off the blood-smeared covers on Rubus's bed and tipped over the mattress. There was nothing. With my heart rate increasing, I stalked over to the wardrobe and threw open the double doors. There was nothing inside apart from a few coat hangers and neatly ironed shirts. Then a thought occurred to me and I slowly turned to the huge pile of dirty laundry.

I wasted no further time. I launched myself at it, hauling the clothes to the side. When I'd pulled off enough of them to see what lay underneath, my body sagged in defeat. The charred edges of a safe greeted me; it could only be Chen's safe, the one Mendax had said was in his possession.

The worst thing was that he hadn't lied. The incontrovertible truth that was punching me in the face over and over again was that Rubus was Mendax. The way both their eyebrows twitched … the strange, high-pitched quality to Mendax's voice … the mysterious illness which had affected Rubus…

Fey could usually only maintain a glamour for about ten minutes. I'd dropped the gift of how to keep one up for a longer period into Rubus's lap. Everything was starting to make sense. Even Rubus's overpowering aftershave fitted; no doubt he'd slathered it on while he was in his own body to mask his pheromones and prevent me from connecting any familiar body scent with Mendax.

I thought of the mysterious jars in the laboratory, the ones that Carduus had been so keen to keep me away from. Now I knew exactly what was inside them. The smell had been familiar because it lingered in the Metropolitan Bar after Morgan and his faery friends cured my own poisoning. It was nux – the only known antidote for rowan poisoning. Carduus had a large supply that was intended for Rubus alone because Rubus was repeatedly injecting himself with rowan to maintain a glamour. And that tracking spell that Carduus had supposedly created to locate the sphere didn't existent; he'd made it all up so we'd be more inclined to pass the sphere over to Mendax for safe-keeping. I was such a freaking idiot.

Every single thing that had happened until this point was because Rubus was playing us. He was truly a master manipulator. I thought I'd been so clever; I thought I'd steered Rubus exactly where I'd wanted him to be and that I was in charge. In reality, he was the puppet master all along. And unless I stopped Morgan from handing the sphere over to him in the next hour, Rubus would have manipulated his way to glory – and to global genocide.

***

I ran as fast as my legs would carry me. There wasn't a single faery left anywhere near the premises. I no longer had any illusions that they'd all gone to the old hideout by the docks; no doubt Rubus had commanded them to wait near the rendezvous point so they could witness his sickening triumph.

As I sprinted out of the building, I fumbled in my pocket for the shell phone. If I could contact Morgan, I might be able to warn him in time.

'Morgan!' I yelled, narrowly avoiding entangling myself with a lethal-looking pram and an even more lethal-looking baby whose mouth was contorted in a petulant scream. I shook the shell. 'Morgan!'

I pelted off the pavement across the road, just as a heavy truck trundled up and slammed on its horn. It wasn't going to brake in time. I didn't want to be squished Madrona at the best of times and I certainly didn't have time for it now. Without making a conscious decision, I flicked out a hand and slowed down the seconds so I could squeeze past in front of it. As soon as I stepped back onto the pavement, I flicked my hand again to disperse the magic. There was a roar of sound as time reasserted itself. I wasn't supposed to do that; the magic used to slow down time wasn't supposed to be good for this demesne. But as the alternative involved a certain apocalypse, I reckoned I'd be forgiven.

Praying that it would be third time lucky, I yelled into the shell again. 'Morgan! I need you to listen!'

I heard only static. Either Morgan didn't have his own shell with him or I'd hit a communication black spot.

I ignored the stares from the other pedestrians. I didn't care if they thought I was crazy – it was their sorry lives I was trying to save. They might never know that was I trying to be their saviour but you didn't need to be recognised as a hero to be one.

At that thought, something odd snapped in the back of my mind and a jolting shudder went through me. I shook it off; I didn't have time for that, either. I had to get to Morgan and I had to get to him now.

I drew on the time-altering magic again. The world around me blurred, the humans virtually freeze-framing like some strange tableau. I'd never maintained this magic for more than a few seconds and I knew there might be consequences for extending it to minutes rather than seconds, but I wasn't sure I had a choice.

I ran. Beads of sweat broke out across my skin, as

much from the exertion of maintaining the time magic as from sprinting. My body trembled and I couldn't tell whether that was because of adrenaline or fear. I cursed to myself. I was a damned faery; surely, the least I should be capable of doing was flying. I was like an idiot savant without the savant part.

All around me the world moved in slow motion. I dashed past faces frozen in comical expressions – the lovesick eyes of two teenagers holding hands, the scowl of a traffic warden approached by the driver of an illegally parked car, the astonished look of delight on a baby's face as it tried to reach for the dancing mobile strung over its pram. Even the birds in the sky flapped their wings with a painful lack of speed and I expected them to start falling out of the sky. But as far as they were concerned, nothing was different. I was the one with the remote control on fast forward; I was the one with the power; I was also the one on whom all their lives depended.

I skidded over the bonnets of the cars at the traffic lights and put on a final spurt as I rounded the corner and the library came into view. They were all standing there – Morgan, Finn, Artemesia. Mendax – or rather Rubus – was there too.

Morgan's hand was outstretched and I knew exactly what he was handing over. I pelted forward, reaching the group just as my grip on time slipped and the seconds and minutes returned to normal.

'Stop!' I shrieked. I barrelled towards Morgan, snatching the small box out of his hand in the nick of time. The ugly scowl that crossed Mendax's face was so similar to one I'd seen Rubus display that I knew I was a fool for not having realised the truth before.

I threw myself up the library steps and twisted to face them all while hugging the box containing the magical sphere to my body.

'The mad bitch has completely lost the plot now,' Finn said. Despite his words, he seemed to have an inkling that the sphere had to be kept away from Mendax and manoeuvred himself between us.

Morgan was also bemused. And wary. 'What's going on, Maddy?' he asked softly.

'He … can't … have … it,' I gasped.

'We've been through this. It's got to be destroyed, not hidden. It's the only way to be sure.'

I shook my head vehemently. 'He's. Not. A. Dragon. It's a glamour. He's been … fooling … us … all along.' I panted. Every word was a struggle. My lungs felt as if they were about to give away and my heart was thumping so hard it was about to burst out of my chest.

All three of them turned and looked at Mendax. 'I can see why she's called the Madhatter,' he remarked. 'She's insane.'

I clutched my chest. If anything, the pain was spreading. I heaved in short, shallow breaths and gulped for air. 'Rubus,' I whispered. 'That's Rubus.'

The man in question let out a high-pitched laugh. 'See? She's nuts! I'm a dragon. I'm not a fucking faery! Do I look like Rubus to any of you?'

'He can't be Rubus, Maddy,' Morgan said. 'We've spent hours in his company. Rubus could never maintain a glamour for this long. None of us can.'

I bent double, using my body to shield the sphere as well as trying to regain my lost breath. 'I did.'

'You were poisoned.'

'So's he!'

'Pah! Why would I poison myself?' Rubus shuffled to the right as if to overtake Finn and get closer to me. Fortunately the Redcap was canny and used his larger frame to keep him back.

'Because I told you,' I said, straightening up. The pain in my chest was easing slightly. At least now I could talk without sounding like a faked sex tape. 'I told you what happened to me. Like a fucking fool, I told you that rowan poisoning enabled me to stay in a glamour for hours. You took that information and used it. Give it up, Rubus. You're not an old dragon any more than I'm a glorious heroine. You've been several steps in front of us the entire time. Well, now you're behind. You're not getting your greasy hands on this sphere. I'll die before that happens.'

His mouth twisted. 'That can be arranged,' he said, in a voice that was all gruff Rubus rather than high-pitched Mendax. He lunged towards me, arms akimbo and hands curled into lethal claws, ready to gouge out my eyes.

Morgan got there first, leaping in front of me and pushing me away. I staggered back and fell to the ground while Rubus laughed nastily. 'She always was your weak spot, brother,' he hissed.

He threw out a punch that connected with Morgan's face. Then he laughed again. 'I knew if I took her back you'd be too distracted to think clearly. She's not as smart as you think she is, you know. I've been sending her little notes and manipulating her all along. She actually believed that one of my faeries was disloyal. Ha! I even made her think that I'd tested her loyalty and she'd passed. Madrona was far better at lying before her amnesia. Now she wouldn't fool a child.'

'Maybe not,' Morgan said evenly. 'But Madrona has more good in her little finger than you have in your entire body.'

Rubus smirked. 'I doubt that. And speaking of little fingers…' He delved into his pocket and pulled out his pinky ring. 'It was fun seeing you steal this from me. It turns out you're not all that clever either, brother.' He twisted the ring onto his finger again and admired it. 'It doesn't quite fit properly when I'm wearing this body. Glamouring myself as a dragon has been fun but I'll be glad to not have to inject myself with rowan again. It's rather unpleasant.'

'You really did poison yourself deliberately, then.'

'I'd cut off my right hand if I thought it would help our kind get home. That's the kind of good faery I am. Fortunately, it won't come to that because it turns out that you're just as foolish as your girlfriend is. You were stupid enough to use the oath breaker. I wasn't sure you would – at every point I thought you'd work out what was really going on. Only my brother could free me from the truce. It was a masterful stroke indeed – and not on your part. Now the truce doesn't affect me. Now I've been truly unleashed.'

He kicked upwards, aiming for Morgan's chest, but fortunately Morgan managed to dodge his foot. Even from my sprawled position, I could see him straining to fight back. His face was twisted in pain. Blood drained from my face as I realised what was wrong. Gasbudlikin bastards. We were fucked.

'You get it now, don't you?' Rubus said, sneeringly. 'The truth has finally penetrated your dim brain. By using the oath breaker, the truce no longer holds for me but it still holds for you. I can hurt you. I can kill you.'

He stretched out his arms and laughed again, the sound echoing round the faery-filled square. 'Chen did well to find that little object. He was quite the master at locating magical items. Not that any of them did him any good in the end because faery objects don't help dragons.' He grinned nastily. 'They've certainly helped me, though. You can't touch me but I can do whatever I want.'

The magnitude of what we'd achieved was almost

too horrifying to accept. We'd handed Rubus the keys to this demesne. By using the oath breaker, we'd granted him the freedom to destroy any faery he wanted to. We'd not thought it through. Rubus would be virtually unstoppable now. All we could do was keep the sphere out of his hands.

Rubus pointed at one of his faeries. 'Give me a gun,' he commanded.

'You don't have to do this.' Morgan's voice rang out loud and clear, without a trace of a tremor. 'You don't have to resort to murder. You don't have to be evil.'

'Evil?' Rubus took the proffered weapon and hefted it in his hands as if he were testing the weight and gleefully anticipating what he would do next. 'You're the one who's evil, Morganus. We have a way home. That sphere can return every single one of us to Mag Mell but you refuse to let us use it. You want to stay here, trapped in this shithole of a demesne.'

'If you use the sphere, the consequences will be disastrous.'

Rubus rolled his eyes. 'Puh-lease. So there will be some proper magic here. So what?'

'That magic will kill the humans.'

There was a squeak from the small crowd of humans who were in the vicinity. They seemed to be frozen to the spot by the drama that was playing out in front of their eyes.

Rubus was oblivious to their presence. 'You don't know that for sure.'

Morgan glared. 'Yes, I do.

'Maybe,' Rubus said softly, 'the risk is worth the reward. We are superior beings. The humans destroyed their homeland in the name of technological advances. Returning them to the Stone Age and introducing real magic will probably do them the world of good.'

'Got that right,' Amellus snorted from the side. I could see other faeries nodding fervently. Surely they couldn't all believe that Rubus was doing the right thing? Or were they so focused on getting home that they were blind to what would happen if Rubus used the sphere?

I glanced round. Only Lunaria looked uncertain, her hands twisting and her expression white and worried. If I could get through to her, there might still be hope.

I heard the blare of sirens in the distance. The police were on their way but they wouldn't understand what was going on. They wouldn't appreciate the danger and their intervention might only make it harder for us to get the sphere away to safety. I had to act.

'I'm a bitch!' I yelled, hauling myself up to my feet. 'But even I'm not such a bitch that I think billions of people should die just so I can get back home. Think about what's happening here!' I yelled. 'Think about what supporting Rubus is really doing! Will you be able to live with yourselves afterwards?'

'You're a murderess, Madrona,' Rubus said calmly. 'You seem to be coping just fine.' He raised his head and glanced round at his assembled minions. 'I should also point out that it's her fault we're here in the first place.'

There was a combined intake of breath and a hundred shocked eyes turned to me.

'If I did that,' I shouted, 'it was a mistake!'

'You know you did it,' Rubus said simply. 'I proved it to you. And I don't think it was a mistake at all. Now hand over the sphere. It's mine. It belongs to me.' He pointed the gun at Morgan then moved it to me. 'Or neither of you will walk out of here. I'll get it in the end so you might as well give it up willingly.'

Finn threw back his head and roared. A moment later, he sprang forward, throwing himself at Rubus and knocking him to the ground. He used his large Redcap body to hold Rubus in place and pin down his hand. Rubus didn't release the gun, though, and several of the hovering faeries lunged for Finn.

'I'll kill him,' Finn screeched. 'I'm not bound by the truce. Come any nearer and I'll destroy Rubus in front of your eyes.'

'A single Redcap is no match for a faery,' Rubus spat.

I shot forward. 'Not under normal circumstances. But you're weakening.' I faced the group, who were virtually slavering at the mouth to get at Finn. 'The truce might not hold for your boss but, until he has some nux and returns to his real body, he's still poisoned. He's probably had so much rowan in his system that much more of this and he'll collapse.' I glanced at Finn, whose eyes met mine. 'You can do it,' I told him. 'You have the power right now.'

'Get this bastard off of me!' Rubus screamed. He writhed and jerked, his hand twisting as he tried to turn the gun back to his advantage.

I was right – he was indeed weakened but unfortunately he wasn't weakened enough.

Amellus rolled up his sleeves and prepared to take the risk and grab Finn.

At that moment, several police vans pulled up. Armed men jumped out of each one. 'Put down the weapons!' a loudspeaker boomed.

A rush of clarity hit me. I knew what to do. 'Give me the sphere,' I hissed at Morgan.

'What?'

'Trust me,' I said through gritted teeth. 'Trust me in this, if nothing else. Otherwise this will become a bloodbath and Rubus will still win.'

Morgan's eyes met mine. There wasn't a trace of doubt in his expression. 'I believe in you,' he said quietly. He dug into his pocket and drew out the sphere. Our fingers brushed as he passed it over. I shivered and then I shoved it into my pocket.

'She's got it!' a faery yelled. 'She's got the sphere!'

Underneath Finn, Rubus jerked. He tried to raise his hand with the gun and let out a shot. The police boomed out another command but, loud as it was, the words seemed indistinct to me.

I threw myself forward towards Finn and Rubus and grabbed the gun, wrestling it out of Rubus's grip and yanking it upwards. I started waving it around.

'I've killed!' I shrieked as loudly as I could. 'I've killed before and I'll kill again.' I pointed the gun upwards and squeezed the trigger. A loud shot cracked through the air and the recoil jerked me downwards. A moment later, there was another shot – but not from me or from one of the armed faeries. It came from behind one of the police vans.

For the briefest moment – and for the last time – I jerked on the magic inside me and caused time to slow. My eyes met Morgan's. He stared at me in stunned confusion and growing horror.

'This is for the best,' I told him. 'This is the way it should be. I deserve it. My belongings will be impounded as evidence. The sphere will be safe, at least for a while. The rest will be up to you. Stop Rubus.'

Comprehension flew across Morgan's face. 'Wait,' he said. 'You…'

I released my hold on time. The first bullet from the police gun had missed but the second, which I hadn't even had time to hear, slammed into me. I deserved this. For one strange second, I didn't feel anything at all then there was a brief searing pain.

Even though I'd engineered this outcome, there was only one thought running through my mind as the world pitched into blackness.

Gasbudlikins.

Thank you so much for reading Quiver of Cobras! The third and final book in the Fractured Faery series, Skulk of Foxes, is available now.

About the author

After teaching English literature in the UK, Japan and Malaysia, Helen Harper left behind the world of education following the worldwide success of her Blood Destiny series of books. She is a professional member of the Alliance of Independent Authors and writes full time, thanking her lucky stars every day that's she lucky enough to do so!

Helen has always been a book lover, devouring science fiction and fantasy tales when she was a child growing up in Scotland.

She currently lives in Devon in the UK with far too many cats – not to mention the dragons, fairies, demons, wizards and vampires that seem to keep appearing from nowhere.

You can find out more by visiting Helen's website: http://helenharper.co.uk

Printed in Great Britain
by Amazon

32954380R00161

About Burning Chair

Burning Chair is an independent publishing company based in the UK, but covering readers and authors around the globe. We are passionate about both writing and reading books and, at our core, we just want to get great books out to the world.

Our aim is to offer something exciting; something innovative; something that puts the author and their book first. From first class editing to cutting edge marketing and promotion, we provide the care and attention that makes sure every book fulfils its potential.

We are:

- Different
- Passionate
- Nimble and cutting edge
- Invested in our authors' success

If you're an author and would like to know more about our submissions requirements and receive our free guide to book publishing, visit:

www.burningchairpublishing.com

If you're a reader and are interested in hearing more about our books, being the first to hear about our new releases or great offers, or becoming a beta reader for us, again please visit:

www.burningchairpublishing.com

Other Books by Burning Chair Publishing

Blue Bird, by Trish Finnegan

The Tom Novak series, by Neil Lancaster
Going Dark
Going Rogue
Going Back

The Other Side of Trust, by Neil Robinson

Burning Bridges, by Matthew Ross

Killer in the Crowd, by P N Johnson

Push Back, by James Marx

The Fall of the House of Thomas Weir, by Andrew Neil Macleod

By Richard Ayre:
Shadow of the Knife
Point of Contact
A Life Eternal

The Brodick Cold War Series, by John Fullerton
Spy Game

Spy Dragon

The Curse of Becton Manor, by Patricia Ayling

Near Death, by Richard Wall

10:59, by N R Baker

Love Is Dead(ly), by Gene Kendall

Haven Wakes, by Fi Phillips

Beyond, by Georgia Springate

Burning, An Anthology of Short Thrillers, edited by Simon Finnie and Peter Oxley

The Infernal Aether series, by Peter Oxley
The Infernal Aether
A Christmas Aether
The Demon Inside
Beyond the Aether
The Old Lady of the Skies: 1: Plague

The Wedding Speech Manual: The Complete Guide to Preparing, Writing and Performing Your Wedding Speech, by Peter Oxley

www.burningchairpublishing.com

Printed in Great Britain
by Amazon

32297452R00172